SOPHIE

powerful r

Dear Reader,

Thank you for choosing a Sophie Lark book! My readers mean everything to me, and I love connecting with you through these stories.

My promise to you:

- **Powerful Escape** from stress. My books are like a movie you can see in your head, complete with illustrations and a soundtrack. You will feel like you're there.
- **Powerful Couples** who trust each other. By the end of the story, my couples are true partners and soulmates who make each other better.
- **Powerful Love** you can believe in. You deserve it in your life—never settle for anything less.

Most of all, I hope to make you laugh along the way...as long as you promise to forgive me if I also make you cry.

Love you all,

Sophie

P.S. Stay rowdy

Illustrator: Line Maria Eriksen

Instagram: @linemeriksen

Cover Design: Emily Wittig

Instagram: @emily_wittig_designs

LOVE CONTRACT

LOVE CONTRACT
BOOK 1

SOPHIE LARK

Here's to taking care of each other 🥂

Xoxo

Sophie Lark

Love Contract Soundtrack

1. Stephen Sanchez - High
2. Marlena Shaw, Diplo - California Soul - Diplo Remix
3. Bazzi - Paradise
4. SEB - seaside_demo
5. Bakar - Hell N Back
6. Peach Tree Rascals - Mango
7. Jungle - All Of The Time
8. MGMT - Electric Feel
9. Hailee Steinfeld, Anderson .Paak - Coast (feat. Anderson .Paak)
10. almost monday - sunburn
11. Ian Hugel - SUMMER GIRL
12. Saint Motel - Sweet Talk
13. Daddy NAT - 1night
14. ROLE MODEL - forever&more
15. Post Malone, Swae Lee - Sunflower - Spider-Man: Into the Spider-Verse
16. Miki Ratsula - Somewhere Only We Know

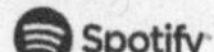

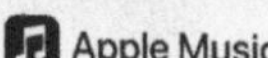

Theo
MAHONEY
CALIFORNIA
LOS ANGELES
CALIFORNIA

1

THEO

The party starts in ten minutes, and it's already a disaster because the centerpieces just arrived and they are bright canary yellow.

That may not sound like a catastrophe of epic proportions, but trust me, in the eyes of my boss, this is a blunder on the scale of the Hindenburg.

Angus *hates* yellow. He hates it with a passion that might make you think he was once married to yellow before yellow cheated on him with his best friend.

Nobody who works for Galactic is allowed to wear yellow. No yellow can be brought into the corporate offices. And most of all, no yellow is allowed at parties.

I have picked yellow Skittles out of candy dishes. I have informed our secretary that she can't park her yellow Beetle in the company lot. I've even thrown a mustard bottle into the lake at a company picnic.

At this point, I might hate yellow almost as much as my boss does.

But none of that is going to help me transform these fluorescent flowers into the nice, calming shade of cream that I ordered.

"How did this happen?" I ask Martinique.

"I don't know!" She gnaws at her thumbnail.

Martinique is my assistant. The assistant to the assistant because after I caught pneumonia over Christmas, Angus finally agreed that my eighty-hour work weeks weren't sustainable.

Since then, she's also become my best friend. And the only person who keeps me sane while my boss slowly tries to drive me mad.

She's been working here long enough to know what a calamity this is. Martinique used to have lovely, manicured nails. She used to weigh twenty pounds more. She used to have a social life.

But she's been chewed up by the meat grinder that is Galactic just as badly as I have.

"Where can we get more flowers?" she moans.

"We can't. There isn't time."

Martinique lets out a wail at the volume of a whisper because she knows that the only thing worse than these yellow flowers is Angus *seeing* these yellow flowers before I can get rid of them.

"What can we *do*?"

A thousand mad ideas whip through my head, including scavenging the planter boxes around the hotel.

Even if I ran out there with a pair of scissors, I don't have time to arrange centerpieces for twenty tables.

I grab Martinique's hands and pull them out of her mouth before she bites her nails to bleeding.

"Can you get me a can of spray paint?"

Exactly eight minutes later, Martinique sprints back to the party with two cans of spray paint in a plastic bag.

I'm waiting out back by the dumpsters, where I spray the centerpieces silver, every leaf and bloom.

When I'm done, they look spiky and inorganic, like they might actually be made of metal. It's weird but also kind of cool. Or at least, I hope that's what my boss will think.

Now I'm sweaty and dusty, and I reek of spray paint. I've also managed to ruin my one and only nice pair of heels—those little silver flecks across the toes are never coming off.

This should work, as long as nobody touches the centerpieces. They're going to take a minute to dry.

The smell will dissipate out on the open rooftop. The party's already filling up with guests, everybody chattering excitedly about Angus' Big Announcement. He's been teasing it for weeks.

I don't even know what it is. Angus loves to hoard his secrets.

All I know is that it's almost certainly going to cause more work and chaos for me.

I'm not cut out to be a personal assistant.

In fact, I was never supposed to be one.

I applied for a completely different job at Galactic, and that's what I was hired for, but Angus gets what he wants, and what he decided he wanted was me jumping at his beck and call, twenty-four hours a day, seven days a week.

A waitress walks by with a tray of beautifully arranged pastry puffs.

I feel a pang of hopeless longing.

Not for the puffs, though they do look delicious.

I'm wishing I could follow that waitress back to the kitchen where I belong. Where I could be wrapped up in a nice cozy chef's jacket instead of this god-awful dress and heels, amid the heat and steam and shimmering scents of butter, saffron, and oregano.

I went to the *Le Cordon Bleu*. I studied pastry and confectionery under the greatest masters in Paris.

Now I pick up dry cleaning.

And I only *wish* that was the worst of my duties...

The crowd starts to heat up, buzzing like bees. They're expecting Angus to arrive any minute.

Angus will be fashionably late—meaning he may show up ten minutes to two hours after we agreed or not at all if something more interesting grabs his attention. It's happened before.

"We're already running low on champagne," Martinique informs me.

"There's five more cases in the walk-in fridge."

"I'll tell the bussers. Did you know you have paint on your nose?"

Could this day get any worse?

"Yes, Martinique—I'm well aware that I have paint on my nose. It's to match the centerpieces."

Martinique stares at me, blinking slowly. "Really?"

"No! Not really. Where's the bathroom?"

Two minutes of scrubbing later, my nose is paint-free but now bright pink.

I hustle out of the bathroom, only to collide face-to-chest with a tall and extremely solid stranger.

Or at least, I think he's a stranger.

Until he grabs my arms to steady me, saying, "Theo! It's been a long time."

That low, rich voice sends an electric current down my spine before I've even looked up into the dark and devilish eyes of Sullivan Rivas.

Somehow, I know it's him and not his brother even though I haven't seen either one in over a decade.

Everybody says they're impossible to tell apart, but I never thought so.

For one thing, Reese Rivas is actually pretty nice. While Sullivan would eat your heart on a platter if he thought it tasted good.

We went to high school together, once upon a time. And let me tell you, there's a reason I don't attend the reunions.

One of those reasons is that I hoped to never lay eyes upon this man again. And definitely not when I'm sweaty, disheveled, and stinking of spray paint.

"That's an...interesting perfume," Sullivan says, the edge of his wickedly beautiful mouth quirking up.

I'll get this out of the way and admit that Sullivan is gorgeous. I'm not talking a normal level of good-looking—that I can handle. I live in Los Angeles. I see good-looking people every day.

Sullivan makes movie stars look dull by comparison. Back in high school, he had a thick head of ink-black hair, the bone structure of a supermodel, luminescent brown skin, and these deep, dark eyes that made you feel like you were swooning every time he looked in your direction. Assuming you were beautiful enough to catch that kind of look.

I was not. But I certainly saw the effect he had on everyone else.

Not much has changed.

In fact, as proof of the utter unfairness of the universe, Sullivan appears to have somehow become even more handsome.

He's dressed in a bespoke suit cut to illustrate that whatever Sullivan has been doing for the last ten years, he has *not* been skipping chest day. His hair is just as thick and lustrous as ever, without a thread of gray. And those full, sensual lips sit above a jawline that has only become more chiseled.

Seriously...fuck this guy.

"What are *you* doing here?" I demand.

Sullivan lays a hand on his chest, pretending to be hurt. Even though I know he's pretending, there's something horribly effective in the way his thick, black brows draw together and the dark eyes beneath gaze at me in soulful reproach. His brother might be the actor, but let it never be forgotten that Sullivan is an identical twin.

"You don't seem that happy to see me, Theo."

My name sounds unspeakably intimate on his lips. The temperature in the bathroom alcove rises several degrees.

I order my cheeks not to blush, no matter what happens. No matter how many times he says "Theo" exactly like that.

"I'd say I'm a little bemused." I cross my arms over my chest. "Since you're not on the guest list."

I should know—I wrote it myself.

Sullivan chuckles.

His laugh is low and wicked, like his voice. It makes me think of melted chocolate, dark and rich, with just a hint of bitterness.

I can feel my skin getting hotter, every bare inch.

He says, "You haven't changed a bit."

That is *not* a compliment. I was a mousy, anxious loser in high school, a lottery student who could barely afford the bus pass to school, while most of my classmates drove Beemers and G-Wagons.

"You have." I lift my chin. "Your hair's really thinning."

This laugh of Sullivan's is a lot more genuine because it's less controlled, like I surprised it out of him.

He runs a hand through his hair, making it spring back like a shampoo commercial. "I think I've got a few good years left."

I bet he does. He'll probably sail into his seventies looking like John Stamos, while I've already found four gray hairs at the ripe old age of twenty-eight.

Angus is responsible for all four of those hairs, not to mention the bags under my eyes and the heartburn that might be turning into an ulcer.

It really *will* be an ulcer if I don't get back to the party.

"What are you doing here?" I repeat.

"I'd like to have a conversation with your boss."

"Not happening."

Angus doesn't meet with anyone unannounced, and he's a germaphobe to boot. He won't even shake hands unless the person attached to that hand has been vetted by his in-house physician.

Plus, I'm not doing Sullivan a favor. Why should I? He already gets to have that hair.

"You can't make an exception for an old friend?"

"We're not friends," I say flatly. "We've never been friends."

I wish I could say we were enemies, but I wasn't even cool enough for that. I was a nobody in high school. A lot like now. I was kind of surprised Sullivan even remembered my name.

He's the one who changed.

I cock my head, trying to figure him out. He looks polished and professional, which is weird enough. The Sullivan I knew skipped more classes than he attended. An effortless athlete who started in three sports but got kicked off all three teams for fighting.

That's why he doesn't look anything like his twin. Reese walks out into the world like he's hunting for rainbows. Sullivan stands with his shoulders hunched, a boxer who never puts down his weapons.

So I'm a little jumpy when he steps closer to touch the outside of my elbow. "I'd like to change that."

His hand is rough and soft, salty-sweet. It makes me leap.

My heart is rabbiting. God, he smells good.

It's unfair. If Sullivan gets to look like that, he should at least smell like moldy socks instead of mahogany. Where's the balance?

I yank back my elbow. "Angus doesn't see anybody without an appointment."

"Even at a party?"

"Especially at a party."

Angus will do his level best to keep at least ten feet between him and his guests at all times, outside of the favored few admitted to his inner circle.

Sullivan gives me the kind of smile you'd give a fellow bank robber. "I'm sure you can get him to make an exception."

"And why would I do that?"

"To stop me telling Angus how you lied at your job interview."

My entire existence grinds to a halt—even my heart, a solid lump in my chest like a seized-up engine.

The air's too thick to breathe. Sweat slides down my spine.

"What did you say?"

Sullivan raises an eyebrow, stone-faced. "I'm guessing you didn't tell him you never actually graduated from culinary school. Or does Galactic hire dropouts?"

My stomach shrivels to the size of a pea while my mouth goes as dry as the Sahara.

Shit.

How does he know that?

"I don't know what you're talking about."

I sound about as convincing as a five-year-old with cookie crumbs all over their face.

Sullivan sighs.

"I'm talking about how Angus' most trusted assistant *lied* to him...I hear he really hates that."

Angus does hate that.

In fact, if he knew the truth, he wouldn't just fire me.

He'd *destroy* me.

He's done it before. Angus Tate's vindictiveness is well-known —especially when he feels betrayed.

"You bastard," I whisper.

Now Sullivan smiles. "I told you, Theo—all I want is for us to be friends. Old friends, the kind you introduce to your boss."

I try to run the calculations in my head—all the ways he could screw me versus all the ways this could blow up in my face.

But really, there's only one thing to calculate: the astronomical rent on my shitty little apartment and how fucked I'll be if I get fired.

"Fine." I hiss. "But that's it, one introduction."

He gestures for me to lead the way.

Sullivan
RIVAS
CALIFORNIA
LOS ANGELES
CALIFORNIA

2

THEO

Sullivan's timing is impeccable—we rejoin the party right as Angus arrives.

Angus descends in his little glass helicopter, which is completely transparent all the way around, so that the three times I've ridden in it, I've had to hyperventilate into my hands while making sure not to look in *any* direction.

Even though he lands on the pad at the other end of the roof, the wind from the blades still manages to send everyone's napkins soaring and ruin a lot of carefully coiffed hair. Not Sullivan's, of course—he just runs a hand through it, and it sweeps back into place.

Mine feels like it has no intention of coming back down to earth. The look on Sullivan's face confirms it—I'm a citizen of Whoville.

"Hold still," he says, smoothing it down.

No, no, no! I am not going to enjoy Sullivan touching my hair and looking into my eyes while he does it. Not while he's in the middle of blackmailing me!

"Come on," I growl. "Let's get this over with."

Sullivan grabs my wrist and pulls me back. "Not yet."

"What are you talking about? You just said—"

"I said...," he pulls me close so his lips brush the rim of my ear, "...not yet."

Angus climbs out of the helicopter. He's wearing a burgundy snakeskin suit and one of those cowboy hats with gator teeth tucked in the band. Subtle, my boss is not. He is also not a patron of PETA.

He's looking fit and tanned from a month at our facility in Cape Canaveral in Florida. That's probably also where he got the gator hat.

He's so full of energy that he immediately bounds up onto the stage and takes his place at the podium, without waiting for all the pomp and circumstance he made us spend three days planning.

"Hello, my friends!" he bellows into the mic.

The crowd cheers back, like they're unbelievably grateful that he just turned the rooftop into a non-consensual blow-dry bar.

"Thank you all for being here! I just got back from our digs down in Florida, and I'm pleased to announce that we have never been closer to commercial space travel! In less than two years, my friends, you could be sipping martinis on the moon!"

Angus is well known for his wild promises and outrageously ambitious plans. Half the things he says never come to pass, but even so, the other half is pretty impressive.

I don't think Sullivan is naive enough to think he'll be sipping a moon martini anytime soon, but he looks pleased by this pronouncement all the same. He's trying to hide it, but I see the smile playing at the edge of his lips.

"In fact," Angus says, "things are going so well that we're going to open a second campus right here in LA!"

The crowd gasps. Even I'm stunned—not to mention terrified.

This is going to be a *huge* undertaking, and I know who'll be right next to Angus, doing all the dirty work.

Strangely, the only person who doesn't seem surprised is Sullivan. As he listens to my boss, his lips twitch enough to show a glint of teeth.

I start to get a very bad feeling.

"*Did you know about this?*" I hiss.

"Shh," Sullivan says.

"As soon as we find the right piece of land, we're going to start building," Angus announces. "And in a year, you'll be seeing those beautiful, bright Galactic rockets racing across the sky!"

The crowd is ecstatic, not at the prospect of moon martinis but at the massive pie Angus is offering up. Be they a journalist, inventor, or investor, everyone here is scheming how to get their slice…including the man standing right next to me.

"Now let's get this party started!" Angus shouts.

"Let's dance." Linking his fingers with mine, Sullivan pulls me into the crowd.

He rests his hand on the small of my back, just high enough not to be vulgar but low enough that his pinky finger rests on the top of my ass.

Of course he's a good dancer. God*damnit.*

This is so extremely weird.

Sullivan smells almost exactly like he used to. But he doesn't look the same—his hair's shorter on the sides now and longer on top. The shadow on his jawline is darker, the jaw itself both wider and heavier.

All of him is heavier. Less boy, more man. His back is thick beneath my fingers.

I step on his foot.

"Was that on purpose?"

"Yes."

No—just clumsy.

I've never danced at one of Angus' parties. It feels transgressive. I'm whipping my head around, trying to monitor the status of the bar and the buffet table while keeping tabs on Angus himself, who must be wondering why I haven't yet appeared at his elbow.

"Relax," Sullivan says. "Everything's going fine."

"How do you know?"

"Because everybody's smiling. Hear that?" He twirls me around, quickly and efficiently, as easy to manipulate as a yoyo. My skirt flares out. *Please tell me that I didn't flash my underwear.* "That's the buzz of a happy party."

He's right—the clink of glasses and chatter of guests and soft music is all in harmony. Even Angus looks pleased, though he casts a curious glance in my direction. He's probably wondering who invited Channing Tatum.

"*I'm not supposed to be dancing,*" I hiss.

"Why not?" Sullivan says. "You're good at it."

I'm not a great dancer, but Sullivan makes it seem like I am. He sweeps me around so it's impossible to do anything but follow, his hand pressed against the small of my back.

He's not looking at Angus. Sullivan gazes into my eyes like he's here to see me and me alone. Like the rest of the party doesn't exist.

It's confusing and unsettling, and I keep ordering myself not to blush. I will *not* be attracted to this man, I don't care how good he smells.

I keep telling myself that as he pulls me closer, our linked fingers cradled against his chest. Even though I know this is all part of some strange charade, the fluttering in my chest feels all too real.

I do not have a crush on Sullivan.

I've never had a crush on Sullivan.

Yes, I used to stare at him a lot in math class. But with pure hatred, I promise you.

He was surly, aggressive, arrogant, demanding…and clearly, nothing has changed.

This fluttering in my stomach, it's just nerves. And confusion. He's being very confusing. That's all it is.

"Why are we dancing?" I mutter. "I thought you wanted to meet Angus?"

"I will," Sullivan says with maddening calm.

At that very moment, my boss appears at *my* elbow.

"Angus!" I squeak.

"Theo…" He glances curiously between Sullivan and me. "You never dance. Who's the lucky guy?"

"Sullivan Rivas." Sullivan holds out his hand.

To my shock, Angus actually shakes it. He must be distracted, trying to puzzle out this mystery of why his assistant is suddenly soft-shoeing like Ginger Rogers on the arm of Fred Astaire.

"He's an old friend," I supply.

"Come on, Theo…" Sullivan wraps his arm around my waist and pulls me tightly against his side. "You can tell him."

"Tell me what?" Angus asks, even more intrigued.

"That we're dating," Sullivan says smoothly.

I turn and stare at him, hoping he can read the silent "*WHAT THE FUCK DO YOU THINK YOU'RE DOING?*" that I'm broadcasting with my eyeballs.

I'm pretty sure he can read it, but he ignores me.

"She didn't want to tell you," Sullivan explains. "She was afraid you'd think her work would suffer. But obviously, it hasn't. I mean, look at this party…"

"I love the flowers…" Angus nods serenely. "Very futuristic."

Then he turns on me, reproachful.

"But, Theo! I can't believe you didn't tell me you had a boyfriend!"

"You know this job means everything to her..." Sullivan gives my hip a squeeze to remind me of exactly that.

"How long has this been going on?" Angus shakes his finger at me like I'm his naughty teenaged daughter.

"Six months," Sullivan supplies. "The best six months of my life."

If I didn't know what a whopper that was, I'd actually believe him. He's scarily convincing.

Angus swallows it, hook, line, and sinker.

"I'm really glad to hear that." He rests a heavy hand on my shoulder. "I worry about you, Theo. She's all alone, you know, ever since—"

"I'm glad you're not mad," I interrupt. "Sorry, I should have told you sooner. You know how it is when it's a new, fresh thing and you're really not sure if it's going to work out."

I shoot a filthy glare at Sullivan.

"Oh, it's gonna work out." He pulls me closer. "Theo's a keeper. I really am a lucky guy."

"She's a treasure," Angus agrees.

My boss has never called me a treasure before.

Once he called me "obnoxiously punctual" and another time he said my handwriting was neat. That's about it.

"Well," Sullivan says, "I won't keep you two—I just dropped by to give Theo a quick kiss."

"Oh," Angus says, a little startled.

Nobody ever ends conversations with Angus first.

Even I'm surprised. I thought the whole point of this was for Sullivan to make some kind of pitch?

But now he's waltzing out of here like the point was that dance.

"See you tonight, sweetie," he says.

And before I can think or react, he hooks his arm around my waist, tugs me close, and plants a kiss on my lips.

His mouth lands on mine, soft, rough, and warm. His scent wraps around me like a blanket.

It's a chaste kiss, no tongue, with my boss watching from a foot away.

And yet, when Sullivan pulls back, my legs are wobbling and the only thing holding me up is his arm around my waist.

What. Is. Happening.

Angus watches with a strange expression on his face.

"You know," he says abruptly, "you should bring him on the yacht next week. What do you think, Sullivan? Want to cruise out to Catalina Island?"

"I'd love to come," Sullivan says before I can so much as blink. "Nice to meet you, Angus."

He gives Angus another firm handshake.

Angus looks almost as dazzled as I am.

That bad feeling is only getting worse.

"I'll walk you out," I croak.

THE MOMENT we're out of my boss' eyesight, I grab Sullivan by the sleeve of his fancy suit and drag him behind a potted plant.

"What the hell was that? That is *not* what we agreed."

"I know." Sullivan shrugs. "But 'old high school friend' doesn't have quite the same cache. Besides, this is going to take more than one conversation. You'll be seeing a lot of me."

"*What's* going to take more than one conversation?" I whisper-shriek. "And no, no I won't be because I'm not doing this! I'm not going to pretend you're my boyfriend! I'm already in this mess for lying to Angus. If he finds out I snuck some scam artist into his circle, he'll cut my throat! Professionally speaking, of course, but honestly, it might be better if he literally cut my throat. Because I won't be able to get a job flipping burgers at McDonald's after this."

Sullivan cocks his head, studying my face. "I don't remember you being this dramatic."

"*Me* dramatic! You were like fucking Daniel Day-Lewis back there, method acting how in love you are... *I'm a lucky guy...* that's creepy, man! How are you so good at that?"

"It's called self-control," Sullivan calmly states. "You should give it a go sometime. And that's not 'love'...just a nice, heady six months' worth of infatuation."

"Have you ever been in love?" My eyebrows must be rising off my face.

"No," Sullivan says, without having to think about it. "But when I am, you won't hear me spouting off nonsense like that. I'll have something real to say because she'll have changed my life."

Okay. That's not what I expected him to say.

I thought Sullivan would snort at even the concept of being in love. I guessed a guy like him would consider it a ball and chain or not believe in it at all.

Instead, that was sort of...thought provoking.

"Why will she have changed your life?"

He smirks. "Because otherwise I'm not in love—I'm just having fun."

Is this man ever not flirting?

I can't believe I let him pull me in again.

"Never mind all that!" I snap. "Stop distracting me."

"You were the one asking personal questions."

"Answer this question: what is your nefarious plan for my boss?"

"What makes you think it's nefarious?"

"The fact that it's *your* plan."

Sullivan gives an offended huff. "I don't know where you developed this villainous opinion of me. I *know* we didn't sleep together in high school, and out of all the people who bullied you, I'm probably not even tenth on the list."

That's so true I could smack him. The first nine were all girls.

I have my reasons for thinking poorly of Sullivan, as he damn well knows, but I'm not about to let him pull me off topic again.

"Never mind high school. I think it's evidence enough that the first thing you did when our paths crossed again was blackmail me."

"It's nothing personal. You're my closest connection to Angus."

There it is. My eyes narrow to slits. "What do you want?"

"I'll tell you—because I expect you to help me. I'm going to broker the deal for the land he needs to build his new campus. And I already have the perfect location."

"Of course you do." I roll my eyes.

"You'll be impressed when you see it."

I snort. "You know I have, like, zero power to get you this deal, right?"

Sullivan laughs, and I'm shocked to feel my lips twitching in return because he really does have a great laugh, the kind you can feel all the way to your bones, wild and energizing.

When he looks into my eyes, I see the old Sullivan is still there, alive and well, dancing like a demon in the darkness.

"Theo, I don't need *you* to get it for me...I'll do it myself. All I need is access."

His confidence is staggering, but also, he's crazy. There's going to be a hundred different brokers vying for this bid. Angus is not going to give it to my 'boyfriend.' He won't even give me a raise.

Besides, there's no way I'm going to play along with this. I get queasy if I even *think* about fudging my tax returns.

Culinary school aside, I really do hate lying. I actually did attend *Le Cordon Bleau*—I just didn't exactly graduate.

I was desperate when I applied for the job at Galactic. Desperate and low and just...

Stupid enough to think that a lie is only for a moment.

It isn't. It follows you and grows, spreading its tentacles everywhere.

It didn't seem to matter before Angus and I really knew each other. But now I've worked for him for four years.

He'll be furious if he finds out that I lied to him all this time.

God *damn* Sullivan for putting me in this position—forcing me to hide my lie with more lies...

My stomach lurches.

"No." I shake my head. "I'm not going to do it."

"Why not?"

"Think of everyone I'll have to lie to! It's not just my boss, it's Martinique and vendors and investors and every single other person we bump into—Angus is probably already telling people."

Sullivan shrugs. "So what. It's a game, Theo—it's all a game of power."

"I don't play games."

Sullivan steps closer, trapping me in the tiny niche of draping vines and potted ferns, his broad frame plugging the exit like a cork in a bottle. The leaves tickle my arms, and so does his breath, swirling across my bare skin as he pins me with his gaze.

"But you already are, Theo...because you're born into this one. All of us are born into the game of power. You can close your eyes, you can refuse to learn the rules, but everyone around you is playing. And they will destroy you."

My heart hammers my ribs. I feel like I'm in a debate with the devil for my soul.

"Think about it, Theo," Sullivan says, and I still can't repress a shiver every time he says my name. "Your boss is a *billionaire.* He makes more money in *three minutes* than your salary *for the entire year*. Think how indispensable you are to him. Why doesn't he pay you two hundred or three hundred thousand? To him, that would be less than pocket change. It'd be thirteen minutes of his earnings. To completely change your life."

My stomach does another slow roll.

"I'll tell you why he doesn't do it..." Sullivan's dark eyes swallow mine. "It's because then you wouldn't need *him.* Let me guess, you get about seventy-two thousand?"

"Sixty-eight," I whisper.

"Just enough for you to survive in LA without ever saving enough to quit."

Sullivan's words are steel chains draping my limbs. Cold, crushing, and inescapable...because they're true.

"He has you right where he wants you." Sullivan won't stop pressing; he keeps me locked in that dark stare. "You weren't even supposed to be an assistant. You applied to be his personal chef. How many meals have you made lately?"

I lick my lips. "How do you know all this?"

"I do my research," he says seriously. "You should, too. Angus is big on promises, short on delivery."

I already know that.

Angus has made me a lot of promises over the years. One in particular that's beginning to feel like a bright, shiny lure continually yanked away.

Before I can stop myself, I admit, "He said he'd help me open a restaurant."

I didn't even ask. Angus just promised it once after I cooked him the most incredible wagyu eggs benedict.

But that was two years ago.

And now, I barely have time to do any cooking at all.

"First business lesson." Sullivan holds up his index finger. "Negotiate the terms up front and get it in writing." He points his finger at my chest like he's shooting me. "That's why Angus hasn't staked your restaurant, and he never will."

His words hit like a bullet.

I don't want to admit how much that dream has been fueling me these last two years. Through all the late nights and the humiliating demands, I kept telling myself, *It'll all be worth it. Angus will help you...*

My voice comes out weak. "You don't know that."

Sullivan's is the opposite. "I know that people do what benefits them. What benefits Angus is to keep you poor and hungry, right by his side."

I stare at him, slowly shaking my head. "You're cynical."

"Realistic."

"Well, I don't trust you. You blackmailed me and you already flipped the script, right in front of my boss."

"Understandable." Sullivan's gaze is steady and unblinking. "But I think you'll find I'm a man of my word. Unlike Angus."

He watches my face.

His is calm and impassive.

I see flares of genuine emotion in him—when he laughed at my dig at his hair. When he's overwhelmingly confident. And strangely, when he talked about love—that was when he seemed most honest.

But the rest of the time, I don't trust him as far as I can throw him.

"I'm not doing it," I say. "Tell Angus whatever you want."

And I walk away from Sullivan.

3

SULLY

I let Theo walk away because she needs time to cool off, and then time to percolate.

This is against her nature, I know.

She's just like she was when I knew her—wearing her emotions all over her face. That's why the mean girls loved to torment her—it was so easy to get those big blue eyes to fill up with tears and those pale cheeks to flush with color.

I'm surprised she managed to lie to Angus at the job interview. He must have been distracted trying to sneak a look down her shirt.

Theo dresses like a nun, but that's only more intriguing to men who are used to women throwing themselves at their feet.

I'll admit, even I was enjoying the curve of her back beneath my palm. I never would have expected to find myself dancing on a rooftop with nerdy little Theo Mahoney, but the universe is endlessly entertaining.

She's grown up since then. Got a little more fire in her.

I was tickled when I did my deep dive into her history and

found that even good-girl Theo has a dirty secret. Granted, hers is relatively tame but exploitable all the same.

She'll come back around. I just need to give her time to marinate.

My phone buzzes on the bar top. I came to the Golden Gopher for a celebratory drink after successfully launching part one of my plan. The number on the screen is some twelve-digit salad that can only be my brother.

I abandon my drink to slip outside and take the call.

"You're alive," I say by way of greeting.

"Unfortunately," Reese replies.

His voice is distant and crackling but so warmly familiar that I might as well be talking to myself. Or at least, the half of myself that's a lovable idiot.

"Filming not going well?"

"You could say that—fourteen sweaty dudes in loincloths, all on a high-protein diet, sharing one bunkhouse...I'm going to suffocate in my sleep. On purpose. To escape the smell."

"I'm sure there's some pretty makeup artist who can console you when she's done spray-painting your abs."

"Nope," Reese says glumly. "The only ones interested in putting their mouths on me are the mosquitoes. And my abs don't need spray-painting, thank you very much—the only thing to do out here is crunches."

My brother is currently filming some swords and sandals show in Sumatra. "Spartacus meets Game of Thrones," according to him.

Reese is continually chasing the One Great Role that will revive his career. He likes to list examples of roles that have done this for other actors, like that means it's only a matter of time for him.

He forgets that none of those actors are best known for their role as a teenaged dreamboat on a Friday-night sitcom. *Rocko*

Rocks! played for only three short seasons, but it became a cult classic among women aged fourteen to way-too-old-to-be-crushing-on-a-teenager-this-hard.

Reese was on the cover of *Seventeen* and *US Weekly*. He was supposed to be the next Leonardo DiCaprio.

Unfortunately, his career ever since has been more like that third Hemsworth brother's.

But he swears this show is his big break.

"Did I tell you it's playing on HBO?"

"Only twelve or thirteen times."

"Well, which one is it? I thought you were the precise brother."

"That made it thirteen. I was being imprecise for comedic effect."

"Thank you. I know that goes against your morals."

"Comedy is the highest law."

If you can't laugh at life, you'll cry. And I'm sure as hell not going to cry.

Reese says, "What have you been up to?"

"I saw Theo Mahoney today."

"Theo...oh, I remember her! She was the one who was always drawing in math class." Reese chuckles. He was also drawing in math class. "What's she up to these days?"

"Grinding away for none other than Angus Tate."

My brother is instantly suspicious. "Sully..."

"Don't worry, I was perfectly polite. Warm and friendly, even..."

Reese groans. "Do I even want to know?"

"Probably not."

Reese really is the nice brother. Softhearted. It's why he gets eaten alive in Hollywood.

"Don't worry," I say. "I'm helping her."

Reese groans. "That's what I'm afraid of."

"If you want to stop me, you better get back here."

"Just a couple more weeks."

"Good."

I miss my brother when he's gone for months at a time.

Not that I'd ever tell him that.

But then, I don't have to tell him. He knows.

"How's Dad?" he asks, like he always does before we end the call.

"Same."

What I mean is, he's no worse. Which at this point is probably the best Reese hoped to hear.

"Good," he says right back to me.

If you played a recording of our two "goods," they'd sound exactly the same.

It's a little eerie, even to me.

We hang up without saying goodbye. It's not goodbye, it's just until the next chat.

Which is two seconds later when Reese texts me:

"Did you know Robert Downey Jr. was uninsurable before Iron Man? Couldn't even get a movie made."

I send back:

"Unsubscribe."

In return, my brother types the pithy and accurate:

"You can't."

Reese is lucky that I love him because I've barely retaken my seat at the bar before the big, beefy guy next to me squints blearily and says, "Hey...you look familiar..."

"I have that kind of a face."

I stare straight forward, hoping that will handle it. But it never does.

"No..." The guy keeps peering at me, tapping his meaty finger impatiently on the bar. "I *know* you..."

I've been getting this for thirteen years. It would be annoying enough if *I* were the one on the TV show. But as an innocent bystander, it's goddamned intolerable.

"You really don't." I grab my drink and stand up from the stool.

"I know!" He seizes my shoulder. "You're that kid from that show!" He points in my face, grinning with glee. "Rocko Rodriguez!"

If I never hear that name again, it'll be too soon.

I've heard it at bars, grocery stores, and job interviews for my entire adult life. It has not lent legitimacy to my career, which is *not* as a pretty-boy actor, thank you very much, Reese.

What was fun for a couple of years in high school has haunted me more than it has him.

"Say it!" The beefy guy orders, like so many have before. "Say the catchphrase!"

What's maddening is that Rocko never actually said the catchphrase—it wasn't a catchphrase at all, just the name of the show. But they always ask for it.

It's so old at this point that I'm not even mad. Just exhausted.

I tell the guy one last time, "I'm not him."

He bellows it anyway, fists in the air: "ROCKO ROCKS!"

If that's the last thing I hear before I die, I'll know I'm going to hell.

He slaps me on the back, and it's the slap that breaks the seal, like a rubber band snapped against my skin. My teeth grit and the old rage rises. Until I swallow it down.

It's a woman who sidles up to me next, flustered and horny.

"Oh my god, it *is* you!" She leans over so her breasts brush against my arm. "I'm sorry, I never do this, but I had to come talk to you...I *loved* your show, it was my absolute favorite..."

From the number of people who have told me this, you'd think *Rocko Rocks!* had a hundred million viewers.

She giggles. "I even had your poster on my wall..."

I bet I know which poster it was: Reese, hair flopping down over his eyes, pouting moodily in a denim jacket with the sleeves ripped off.

"I had such a crush on you...," she breathes, batting her heavily mascaraed lashes.

This woman is actually pretty attractive. She's probably ten years older than me, but that's surprisingly common for the Rocko-loving demographic. She's got that hot-divorcee thing going on, which could mean a night of wonderfully spiteful sex.

But I've never yet sunk to pretending to be my brother to get women. That's a bridge I won't cross.

I remove the divorcee's hand from my arm, gently.

"I hate to tell you this...but I'm not Reese Rivas."

Her expression changes from adoration to annoyance in an instant.

"Liar!" she spits before turning on her heel and wobbling away.

WHEN I GET HOME, the house is completely dark, and the pool house, too, but that doesn't fool me. There's no way my dad's asleep yet.

I knock on the pool house door then walk right in when I don't get an answer.

He's lying on the couch in the dark, TV silent. The vodka

bottle on the coffee table is only a third empty, but who knows if that's the first one of the day.

"Hey, Dad." I sink into the overstuffed chair next to the couch.

"Hey, Sully."

We sit quietly for a time, him thinking his thoughts, me thinking mine.

"I talked to Reese," I say after a while.

"Yeah, he called me, too."

"Says he should be back in a few weeks."

"Yup."

When Reese is in town, he stays in the main house with me. It's big enough that all three of us could live in separate wings without bumping into each other, but our dad won't sleep under that roof. It's too painful for him. But he won't sell the house, either.

"You want to watch a movie?" I say when the silence stretches on.

"Sure," says my dad, though I know he could care less what I put on the screen.

Twenty minutes into *Ghostbusters,* I glance over. He's staring up at the ceiling. He didn't even crack a smile during that first scene with Bill Murray.

"You okay, Dad?"

"Sure." His eyes meet mine, briefly, and then slide over to the TV screen.

But they fix there just as blankly.

No matter what happens in the movie, my dad never laughs.

4

THEO

The next day, I'm a bundle of nerves, wondering if Sullivan really will tell Angus that I'm a filthy, lying dropout.

Angus has bragged about which school I attended about a hundred times—pretty much every time I cook for guests. And while that's barely a part of my job anymore, I know that's the kind of thing that will really piss him off.

He's super paranoid, like all rich people. I mean, I guess it's not really paranoia because everybody around them actually *is* trying to use them. But also, they're using everyone else—that's how they know how it works.

Money warps everything.

Look what a pretzel I'm twisting myself in, all because I can't afford anything, and it feels like constant drowning.

I don't want to be a liar. But I already am. And now I'm trapped...

Right as I'm thinking these thoughts, I pick up the cup in my sink, and the hugest cockroach I've ever seen goes leaping out of the sink and sprinting across my counter. It dives onto my stovetop and somehow wriggles *inside* my range while I'm shrieking and trying to smash it with a spatula.

"*Nooooo,*" I moan, realizing I am never going to be able to find it in the innards of my oven, which means I am going to be forever paranoid that it's living inside there, building some awful cockroach empire with its spawn.

I sink down on the sticky linoleum, spatula still clutched in my fist, fist pressed against my skull. I take tiny, shallow breaths, trying not to scream.

I really can't imagine that Sullivan is just going to let this drop. He's so intense, he makes roller coasters seem chill.

I hate roller coasters.

And I can't stand not knowing when the next drop is going to come.

I'm better off driving over to Angus' place to tell him the truth.

ANGUS LIVES in what looks like a giant concrete saltshaker on the edge of Paradise Cove Bluffs in Malibu. His neighbor is Beyoncé, and no, I haven't met her. If I ever do, I might forgive Angus a few more things.

It's a little risky coming here before 10 a.m. Angus is a night owl, not an early riser, and I've already witnessed my share of women in wrinkled party dresses sneaking out of his place as late as noon.

However, this morning I find him alone and particularly chipper in an open robe and damp swim trunks, blending up an enormous smoothie.

"Theo!" He cries, so pleased to see me that I'm instantly certain that Sullivan hasn't had a chance to rat me out. "Have a smoothie!"

It's an order, not a request.

I take a seat on one of his barstools, gingerly, because I really prefer to be on the opposite side of the kitchen island. Angus is not to be trusted with food. Among other things.

When he pours out the smoothie, it's gray and puffy. He fills two glasses the size of tankards.

"What's in it?" I ask, trying to sniff it without being too obvious.

"Taste it and guess!" Angus beams.

Oh my godddddd....

I give him a watery smile to buy myself time. I can't not drink this smoothie. Not when I'm here to confess my crimes.

Do I have to drink all of it?

Urk...Don't think about that...focus on getting a little bit past your lips...

Angus won't stop watching, his brown eyes wide with way too much anticipation.

I take a careful sip.

Tangy, slippery, with...spicy, chewy bits?

"Mmm..." There is no way I'm making the correct facial expression. "Is that...cloves?"

"Damn!" Angus slaps the countertop with his palm. "You're good."

He picks up his own tankard and chugs so much of it that his formerly flat belly grows a little bulge.

Angus is fit and tan, with a lot of shaggy brown hair. He's pretty good-looking, to the point that at least half the women who date him would still say yes if he was just a millionaire instead of a billionaire. Unless a billionaire happened to walk by.

He can be charming, too, when he's full of energy, beaming like the sun and spewing clever ideas. His plans are grandiose and pretty amazing. When they're not completely bonkers.

He can also be a raging asshole. His tempers are legendary,

and everybody knows to run and hide until it blows over. Except for me, because I can't.

His tankard drained, Angus pats his belly and burps. The bulge disappears.

"I know why you're here," he says, shaking a finger at me.

My throat closes up. "You do?"

"Don't worry, I forgive you."

Warmth spreads in my chest, and my throat relaxes enough that I start babbling. "God, thank you, because I swear, I regretted it *immediately*—"

"But next time," Angus interrupts, "don't keep something like that from me, Theo! I know you're my employee, but we're also friends. I would expect you to share things like that with me, especially a guy you've been dating for *six months!* Who seems extremely committed..."

He lets that sentence hang, eyebrow raised, while I sink all over again, realizing we weren't talking about the same thing.

Sternly, Angus says, "I don't want any secrets between us, Theo. You're one of the only people I can trust."

Oh, god.

He's mad that I didn't tell him about a fake boyfriend.

He'll be so much more pissed about my non-existent diploma.

"I'm sorry," I whisper.

"All is forgiven," Angus says magnanimously. Then, brightly, he adds, "Hey, while you're here, want to whip me up some crepes real quick?"

"Sure," I say, grateful for the reprieve and the chance to use Angus' state-of-the-art kitchen again.

There's nothing "quick" about whipping up crepes, especially ones made the way Angus likes them, with Meyer lemon sauce, hand-beaten cream, and a drizzle of brown-butter caramel.

But that's just fine with me. I'd rather cook than do almost anything else, and right now, I *much* prefer it over trying to fix the mess I made.

Plus, Angus will be much more forgiving after he tastes my crepes.

You can't fire someone who makes these crepes.

Please tell me you can't fire someone who makes these crepes...

While I'm cooking, Angus tries to subtly grill me about Sullivan in a way that isn't subtle at all.

"So, where did you two meet?"

"We went to high school together," I say shortly.

"High school *sweethearts*?" Angus crows.

I can't stand him thinking that, so I snap, "No, not at all. We barely spoke in high school."

I could probably tell you every single time.

The flash of dark eyes in a crowded hallway as we jostled together. That low, taunting voice by my ear: "Careful, Mahoney. That was second base..."

I try to banish Sullivan from my brain. All versions of him.

"Was he popular?" Angus says, like it's obvious I wasn't. "He must have been."

"He and his brother practically ruled the school."

With a guilty squirm, I remember when that stopped. The awful thing that happened...

Reese seemed to handle it okay. But Sullivan changed, from carelessly cruel to a darker kind of anger...

"How did you reconnect?"

Shit. Angus wants details, and I don't have any to give. I don't want to lie, but my bribe isn't ready—this sauce needs ten more minutes at least.

I swallow hard, pulling the caramel off the heat.

"Actually, Angus, we nev—"

He cuts across me, "I forgot to tell you, I need you to work this weekend. I really want to get going on this LA campus!"

Angus is a perpetual interrupter, his brain jumping around like a grasshopper. Never has the timing been worse.

I haven't had a weekend off in two months.

Angus promised me I could see the film festival. I already bought tickets.

But, of course, he doesn't remember that. Or he's pretending not to.

Either way, I don't have a choice. If Angus wants me working this weekend, I'm working.

All of a sudden, the vast, sparkling kitchen feels claustrophobic, and even the sprawling ocean view seems to shrink to the size of a postage stamp.

I. Am. Trapped.

"Thanks, Theo," Angus says, without waiting for my agreement. "What were you saying?"

"I was saying, the food's ready."

I set the crepe in front of him, stuffed with lemon sauce and cream, drizzled with the not-quite-finished caramel.

Angus saws off a bite and places it on his tongue, eyes rolling back.

"*Mmm!*" he groans in orgasmic bliss.

It's my only chance.

I take a deep breath, launching into speech while his mouth is full and he can't interrupt.

"Angus, I really miss cooking. I'd love to get back to doing more of that. Or, you know, start my own restaurant like we talked about. Maybe I could open one on the new campus?"

My heart is racing. The silence in the kitchen is so loud.

The pause that passes seems endless as Angus chews, swallows, and finally says, "Sure! I mean, not right away, of course. That won't be the first priority. But soon enough!"

He's bright and cheery, but there's something plastic in his smile.

Quietly, I say. "Like...when?"

"When it makes sense!" Angus glibly replies. "We're doing incredible things right now, world-changing things! You don't want to miss out on that. Anybody can cook, Theo. You're with *me,* making history! You stick by my side, and you'll have a whole chain of restaurants—on Mars!"

He laughs, expecting me to join in. But nothing has ever seemed less funny.

Angus is talking about restaurants on Mars. While we sit in his nine-figure mansion on the bluffs.

On the drive over here, my engine rattled like it was full of popcorn. I'm still wearing my paint-spattered shoes because I don't own another pair. Cockroaches live in my stove.

In that moment, I almost hate him.

And then I realize, Angus doesn't hate *me.*

He just sees me as weak.

I'm a weak player in a highly lucrative game. All around me are kings, bishops, knights...is it any wonder they use me like a pawn?

Angus said we're friends, but if he fired me, he'd say, *It's just business.*

Sullivan tried to tell me.

All of us are born into the game of power...

He has you right where he wants you...

I see it finally, clear as the daylight pouring in the windows: Angus is never going to help me open a restaurant.

It's a lie, a fantasy. Angus is using me—selling me a dream so I'll help him achieve his.

Sullivan told me the truth.

It's ugly and it hurts, but it's a favor all the same. He yanked me down to reality.

My reality fucking sucks.

Angus is prattling off a list of things he expects me to do this weekend when I should be sitting front row at Greta Gerwig's newest masterpiece.

I can't hear a word coming out of his mouth. I stare at his forehead while my heartbeat thuds in my ears.

You're never getting a restaurant...

You're never getting a restaurant...

You're never getting a restaurant...

YES, I FUCKING WILL.

In that moment, I decide.

I'm tired of being loyal to someone who doesn't keep his promises to me. I'm tired of playing by the rules in a rigged game.

Sullivan isn't trying to hurt Angus—he's just trying to make a deal.

And if all's fair in love and war...then it sure as hell must be in business.

Maybe it's the wrong choice, morally speaking.

But it also feels...fair.

I nod along to Angus while my mind fills with my own plans.

5

SULLY

Theo calls me a whole two days sooner than I expected. Angus must be *really* obnoxious.

I try not to chuckle too much as I pick up the phone.

"Hey, stranger."

"I thought we were *old friends.*"

Theo sounds angry, which puts a low growl in her voice. I kind of like it.

"Let me guess...he offered you a $2,000 raise?"

"He didn't offer me a raise at all," she snarls. "He told me I have to work this weekend but promised me franchise rights to a restaurant on Mars."

I can't help laughing. Angus is making this so easy.

"It's a good thing I would never say the words, *I told you so...*"

"I think you just did."

Theo sounds so salty, I find myself wishing I could see the scowl on her face.

I check my watch. My next meeting isn't for more than an hour.

"Where are you?" I say. "Come meet me for lunch."

THEO ROLLS up to the pizza place in a Camry that belongs in a museum. The thing is so piebald, I'm impressed how neat and chic she looks when she steps out.

The Theo of old was a gentle, anxious person. The Theo of today has a little more sass. She strides toward the restaurant, head up, shoulders determinedly set. In her dark suit, her black hair in a bun, she's almost intimidating.

I never would have said *that* in high school.

But when she slides into the seat across from mine, panting slightly, cheeks tinted pink, those big blue eyes wide and innocent, she hasn't aged a day.

"I'm in," she says. "But I have conditions."

I can tell she was planning this speech the whole drive over.

I sit back to hear it, smiling slightly. "I'd expect nothing less."

"First of all...," she sits upright with that ballerina posture of hers, "I'm not going to help you do anything shady. The one and only thing I'll do is bring you around like you're my boyfriend. If you're trying to like, steal files or something—"

"*Steal files?*" I make a face. "Please, Theo, give me some credit. I told you what I'm going to do."

"Just a perfectly clean land deal?"

"As clean as these things ever are."

She shows me the scowl I was waiting to see. It makes an adorable little line appear between her eyebrows, but otherwise, isn't very scary at all.

"That is not reassuring."

I look her in the eyes and tell her, with complete sincerity, "I promise, I won't do anything illegal."

"Is that a promise to me or a general rule?"

"A general rule—only uncreative people have to break the law. Besides," I grin, "prison wouldn't suit me."

"Not enough salon-quality hair mousse?"

"You really have it out for my hair, don't you?"

Theo's eyes flick up to the offending part of my head, then down to the tabletop as she blushes furiously. "I don't want to go to jail, that's all."

"Do you want to touch it?" I tease her.

"Oh, shut up," she hisses. "You're so full of yourself."

It's just another of Theo's flimsy insults, but my smile slips. "You'd be surprised."

Her eyes meet mine. She flinches, puzzled.

"Sorry," she mutters.

"Nothing to be sorry for." I brush it aside.

Her hands twist in her lap. She says, apologetically, "I'm stressed. I'm not cut out to be a spy, and I'm definitely not an actor."

"You could be a mime...they're expressive."

Her cheeks glow like a sunset as she glares at me. "I *hate* how easily I blush and cry. Half the reason I love working in kitchens is that everybody's flushed and teary-eyed in all the onions and steam."

"What's the other half?"

She blinks, soot-black lashes like fans sweeping the freckles that dust her cheeks. "I guess...I love the feeling of cooking. There's a rhythm to it...," her hands describe invisible shapes in the air, "...balance and timing. It's delicate, like a dance. All the noise and chaos are waves in the ocean, and I sail right through."

"That makes sense."

"It does?" She sounds surprised.

"Sure. I love working with my hands."

"In what way?" She's half-disbelieving, half-curious.

"Woodworking, mostly."

"Oh...," she breathes. "I was right!"

"About what?"

Now her blush looks terminal. "When we danced, I thought you smelled like mahogany."

That makes me laugh. "What are you, one of those super smellers?"

"Maybe." She wrinkles her nose. "And it's not all it's cracked up to be. Especially in *my* neighborhood."

Unexpectedly, she grabs my hand and turns it over. She runs her fingers over my palm, finding the callouses.

"Huh! Not such a pretty boy after all."

"Oh, I'm still pretty," I growl, closing my hand over hers. "But I also know how to use a lathe."

Theo laughs, a sound like raindrops down my spine. She takes her hand back. Mine feels cooler and emptier without hers inside of it.

"Plus, I like feeding people," she says. "Maybe it's not feminist or whatever, but I like taking care of people."

"You have to be heartless to be feminist?" It's almost impossible not to tease Theo.

"You know what I mean." She shrugs. "I know I'm supposed to be ambitious and take over the world, but really I just want a restaurant small enough that I can peek out and see people's faces when they try the food."

An image pops into my head of a tiny brick space, cozy and warm, live plants all around. Theo in a black apron, knife in hand, her dark hair piled on her head, cheeks pink with steam.

"Anyway." I push that aside. "What are your other conditions?"

She sits up a little straighter, remembering her speech. "Second, no funny business."

"I would never. I take business very seriously—it's never funny."

"I mean it," Theo fixes me with those big, clear eyes. "No flirting with me, and no fucking with my head. I know you're not actually interested in me, and I'm not ever going to trust you. Which brings me to my last point..."

"Hold on," I interrupt. "What makes you think you won't ever trust me?"

"We've been over this." Theo crosses her arms.

"I'm not the same person I was in high school." *Not even fucking close.* "You don't look like you are, either."

"No," she says, with a firm shake of her head. "I'm not."

"So let the past be the past—including me twisting your arm the other day. I put the pressure on, but I'm not going to fuck you. In any sense of the word."

Theo lets slip a small smile. Then tucks it away. "I'm going to make sure of that—I want it in writing."

I nod soberly. "Very wise."

"Yeah, an *old friend* gave me some business advice..." She points a stern finger. "This is what I want, written out and signed by you—when you make the deal with Angus, I want ten percent of the cut."

"Ahh..." The whole room gets a little brighter, a little sharper. "Now the tiger comes out."

"Don't think you're going to bullshit me," she says flatly. "This is a seven-figure deal. I want ten percent, not a penny less. And that's generous—I could ask for half."

"You could ask," I say, low and dangerous.

Theo shivers, her pale hand twitching on the tabletop. I feel an impulse to lay my hand over hers again, to calm her.

Maybe it's because I keep remembering the softness of her skin, on the backs of her hands and the side of her arm, the few places I've touched, so silky it surprises me each time. It makes me want to let my fingers linger...

No. Touching her now would send the wrong message. I

shouldn't be thinking about that at all.

Right now, we're making a deal.

The exact deal I wanted—with a ten percent haircut. That's okay, I respect the hustle. In fact, I like her better for asking.

"Done," I say, without argument.

Theo narrows her eyes suspiciously. "In writing," she insists.

"Notarized by a lawyer," I agree. "Now, let's get to work."

"Right now?" Her eyebrows rise like question marks.

"No time like the present." Theo has no idea how true that is—this deal is a ticking time bomb, in more ways than one. "What can you tell me about the yacht party?"

"Practically everything. I'm the one who organized it."

Our pizza arrives. I ordered pepperoni and jalapeño. Theo asked for mushroom. Not mushroom and something else—just a whole pile of fungi.

"Did you become a vegetarian?"

"Nope." She takes a huge bite. "I just love mushrooms."

I have to admit, it looks pretty good.

"Give me a piece."

"Only if you give me one of yours."

"Same time trade..." I swap a slice of my pepperoni for her mushroom, Indiana Jones style.

Theo laughs. The food has relaxed her a little. Eating with your hands helps; it's why I picked pizza.

I spend the rest of lunch grilling her about the guest list, the activities, and Angus' favorite haunts. Some of this, I already know. Like I said, I do my research. But Theo has an eye for detail and an excellent memory. She's filling in all kinds of information that I bet Angus doesn't even know she knows.

She's not telling me anything proprietary—just the psychology and habits of the major players.

I need to know what to look for.

Because when you know what to look for...you can see everything.

It's Theo who's become the real puzzle.

She's changed. I can't put my finger on it, but she seems... sadder now. But harder, too, bits of flint in her. Before, she was so shy, you could have gotten her to jump out of a window just by barking at her.

I was impressed that she stood up to me at the party. And even more impressed that she changed her mind once she took a good, hard look at the facts.

Angus doesn't give a fuck about her. If he did, he'd never let her drive around in that death trap of a Camry. He wouldn't run her ragged until the dark circles under her eyes are deep as thumbprints.

I remember the way he talked to her at the party, condescending as fuck.

Yeah, I really don't like this guy.

In fact, I'm going to enjoy taking his money.

But not just yet. Angus is no fool; people try to put their hands in his pockets every single day. This will require a delicate touch.

Which is why I'm not annoyed at Theo. In fact, I'm *glad* to see she's grown a spine. I've already put months of work into this deal, not to mention every fucking penny I own. I can't risk it all falling apart at the first sign of pressure.

"Are you sure you're up for all this?" I watch her across the table. "I don't want you cracking under the pressure halfway through..."

Theo sets down her half-eaten slice, frowning.

"I want this just as badly as you do. Probably even more."

I doubt that very much.

"Sucks working for Angus?" I say, smiling.

"You can't imagine."

"Are you sure? I've got a pretty good imagination..."

I let my eyes drop just for a moment, satisfying myself that, yes, Theo still looks like some sort of stern business ballerina, and it's still hot as hell. When I return to her face, that pretty pink flush is back in her cheeks, which makes me want to do it more.

She says, "One time I peed myself because he made me take notes on his dreams for four hours."

That's awful, but I can't help laughing. Thank god Theo smiles, too, eventually.

"I can't decide what's worse...peeing your pants or listening to someone's dream?"

"Not just listening...taking notes. *Pages* of notes..." Theo pouts adorably, her lower lip sticking out. "Oh well. The chair I peed on was his favorite, so I got the last laugh in the end."

I'm snorting. Theo looks startled for a moment, and then pleased at how hard she made me laugh. A little piece of hair has slipped out of her bun, trailing across the edge of her eyebrow.

I do *not* reach across the table and smooth it back with my hand—I'll save that shit for when Angus is watching. But the urge keeps nagging at me all the same.

"Angus is already looking at land," Theo warns me.

"I'll handle all of that—don't tell him what I do and definitely don't mention the land."

Theo frowns at me, her adorable version of a scowl, about as frightening as an angry kitten. "Is this how you always do business?"

I shrug. "Every deal's different. It's a fucking jungle out there; the only constant is you have to improvise. Winners are the people who can react to shit going wrong because it always does. It'll be the same for you when you open your restaurant—you know, eighty percent of them fail in the first five years."

Theo lifts her chin. "Not mine."

There's that fire again, so fragile it seems like a puff could blow it out, but it always surges back again.

I lift my water to toast her. "To beating the odds."

A genuine grin creeps across Theo's face. I haven't gotten many of those out of her yet. It starts slowly but gradually brightens, revealing a row of pretty teeth and a tiny dimple on the right side.

Theo raises her glass and touches it against mine.

"To beating the odds."

6

THEO

The morning of the yacht party, I find a grubby envelope stuffed under my door that informs me that the building managers have heard the many complaints about the humongous roaches and will finally be fumigating.

This seems like good news until I realize they expect us to vacate the premises for an entire week.

Shit.

Getting a hotel will be pricey. I could ask Martinique if I could stay at her place, but she lives in a studio even tinier than mine. Her kitchen, bedroom, and bathroom are all one room, with a plastic curtain and about two feet of space dividing the shower and bed.

I feel that sinking feeling I get when I remember that outside of Martinique, I really don't have anybody. Nobody I can call for a big favor in a pinch. Nobody I could rely on if I was sick or injured. Even if I had a really good piece of news...there's no particular person I'd be dying to tell.

How did I get so isolated?

This job sure hasn't helped. I haven't been on a date in months.

That's probably why my hormones have been a little overactive where Sullivan is concerned.

He's probably not even that good-looking, all surly and brutish. If I'd had sex recently, he'd only be a...*sigh*. 12/10.

He's picking me up this morning so we can drive to the dock together. You know, like a boyfriend and girlfriend would do.

I'm wearing what I usually wear to go on the yacht, which is longish denim shorts and a top that looks nautical. I mean, it's a T-shirt with red stripes on it, so maybe I look more like a gondolier, but it still works.

Or at least, that's what I think until Sullivan knocks on my door twenty minutes early.

I'm surprised to see he's got two coffees in hand, plus a grease-spotted paper bag with something heavenly smelling inside.

I can't remember the last time somebody brought *me* coffee. It feels, somehow, even fancier than the fact that I'm about to get on a yacht.

"Thanks." I take a sip. "*Whoa,* that's good."

"Wait until you try the sandwich." Sullivan thrusts the paper bag into my free hand. "It's just a hole-in-the-wall place, but they make the best bacon egg croissant in the whole damn city."

"The whole city?" I'm laughing until I take a bite. Then I'm instantly converted. "Oh my *god!*"

"Told you." Sullivan grins. "Pretty sure I've tried them all, running around to early-morning appointments."

"Are you with an agency or something?"

"I was." Sullivan scowls. "Now I'm out on my own."

"Sounds like it didn't end well."

"No," he says shortly. "It didn't. And it didn't start well, either —my boss would *not* stop calling me Rocko the whole interview."

I chortle, spitting a tiny amount of croissant out of my mouth onto Sullivan's sleeve.

"Oh, god." I brush it off. "I'm sorry. But that's really funny."

"It is around the first twenty times," Sullivan says wearily.

"I'm surprised anybody even remembers that show."

"I really wish they didn't."

I smile, thinking it's nice to know that not everything in Sullivan's life is absolutely perfect. Makes him seem just a little more human.

"What's Reese up to these days?"

"Filming some HBO show in Sumatra."

"Oh, wow! So he's still acting?"

"For anyone who'll let him—and I mean literally anyone. His last pilot was filmed up in Northern Canada. *Mounties and Moose,* I think it was called. Or *Mounties Getting Mounted?* I can't remember. Obviously, it got cancelled. They all get cancelled."

"Poor Reese."

"Don't feel bad for him. He's doing what he loves. And he's got a pretty good role on this next one, or so he tells me."

"Did you want some of this?" Guiltily, I hold out the last remaining scrap of sandwich to Sullivan.

"I already ate mine." He eyes the tiny bite remaining. "Luckily."

"Sorry," I pop it in my mouth. "It's just so good."

He gazes around at my dingy apartment. "Nice place, by the way."

"You really are a liar."

"I'm not lying—you've done a lot with it." He nods toward the gauzy curtains I made for the windows to disguise the fact that said windows look out onto nothing more interesting than the brick wall of the building opposite, and to the vintage glassware I scavenged from thrift shops, lined up on the open shelves so the sun shines through and makes colored patches on the opposite wall. "That's pretty."

I think about mentioning the cockroaches, but they're disgusting, and I already spit croissant on Sullivan's sleeve.

His eyes fix on my outfit instead. "Do you need to get dressed?"

"No." I frown. "This is what I'm wearing."

"I was afraid you were going to say that."

He hands me the last bag he was carrying, which looks like a shopping bag but the kind that's so thick and heavy, with so much scented tissue inside, that I know it didn't come from anywhere as pedestrian as Forever 21.

"What's this?" I take possession of the bag gingerly, like he's handing me a bomb.

"Better clothes," Sullivan bluntly informs me. "Time to level up your game—if you want to swim with the sharks, you can't dress like a minnow."

"You don't even know my size!"

His dark eyes rest on my body. "I'm pretty sure I do."

I hustle out of the room, clutching the shopping bag to my chest. God*damn* these pink, pink cheeks making me look like a virgin in a Victorian novel.

I'm not a virgin. Unless half a year without sex resets the factory settings.

And I'm not a prudish Victorian, either—just really easily embarrassed. I've never liked attention. Which is why I prefer the back of the kitchen to a front of house position.

In fact, if I'd known more about Angus, I never would have applied for the job at Galactic. If I'd realized how famous he was, and how much time I'd spend next to him, surrounded by cameras, I probably would have run for the hills.

I'll admit, it's been kind of fun traveling around with him, getting a peek at this world I never knew existed. But it's a lot like pressing my nose against a bakery window—a feast for the eyes, while my stomach's still growling.

I'm tired of looking. I want to eat.

I slip into my bedroom, which is about two feet away from the kitchen. I can still hear Sullivan moving around, looking at my stuff. I hope he doesn't pick anything up and find a cockroach underneath.

The scent of expensive perfume hits me as I open the bag. I tear the tissue and find not one but several outfits neatly folded inside.

One of those "outfits" is a one-piece bathing suit with a plunging neckline and a matching flowing robe in the same jungle-ish print.

I march back out to the kitchen, holding up the bathing suit.

"Is this supposed to be for today?"

"I think so," Sullivan says. "Unless you have a different yacht party planned for later in the week."

"I'm not going to wear this around my *boss*."

"Why not?"

"Because it's not appropriate!"

"Trust me, Theo," Sullivan shakes his head. "That T-shirt's not appropriate—for life. You should burn it."

"Well, I'm not going to wear this around Angus. He'll think I'm trying to—seduce him or something."

"First of all," Sullivan says, "that's more clothes than most of the women around Angus will be wearing. And second, you shouldn't be so afraid to stir things up. You need to take your power back with him. You've been too predictable, too amenable. Right now, you're his little mouse. You need to show him that he's dealing with a tiger."

That's the second time Sullivan has called me a tiger.

Nothing could seem less fitting.

I've never been a tiger. In fact, I don't even say anything when someone budges me in line.

"He's going to be suspicious," I say as one last-ditch attempt to avoid attracting attention.

"No, he won't." Sullivan contradicts. "He'll be stunned."

AN HOUR LATER, we're aboard the *Kraken,* Angus' glossy black yacht that looks like something a supervillain would use to deposit nuclear warheads in Antarctica.

Angus is dressed on theme, in black silk swim trunks and a pair of shiny wrap-around shades, silver chains draped around his neck and just as many rings on his fingers.

For the second time, Sullivan makes no move to approach Angus. Instead, he slips into the crowd and starts talking to Angus' friends. In minutes, he's cozied up to several key players.

I watch him, confused and unnerved.

People always gravitated to the Rivas twins, but Reese was the charmer, the one everybody loved. Sullivan was moody and intimidating.

Now he's plastered on a smile that looks almost exactly like Reese's, and he's chatting away like he's running for mayor of the ocean. You'd never guess in a million years that this was the guy who got suspended six times his senior year.

I guess he really has changed. Or gotten better at hiding it.

Watching him work is impressive. He fits in better than I do, and I've been on this yacht a dozen times.

At least Martinique always makes me feel cool.

"Oh my god! You look amazing!" She fingers the material of the robe, which feels like it was sewn from angel's wings.

"Thanks," I say without thinking. "Sullivan bought it for me."

Martinique lets out an excited squeal. "Angus said you got a boyfriend! Why didn't you tell me?"

Of course he did, that gossip.

"We haven't been dating that long." I try to lie without lying too much—which, of course, is impossible.

It feels like shit fibbing to Martinique, especially when she's so excited for me.

"Where is he?" She spins around in a circle, scanning the crowd.

"Right there." I point.

Sullivan is standing with a group of venture capitalists. He must have made some joke because the other men laugh.

"*Him*?" Martinique says with unflattering disbelief.

Sullivan takes that moment to strip off his shirt so he can join the others in their swim trunks. It's a slow-motion slap to the face —the flex and roll of muscle, the reveal of his sun-burnished skin, finished with a flick of his head as he pulls the shirt free, his thick, black mane sweeping back in the wind...

"Sweet Holy Jesus," Martinique whispers.

All I can say is, "Yeah."

The body that looked good under a suit should be illegal topless. In fact, it must be illegal because it's currently killing me.

Sullivan looks like Captain America if Captain America were a lot more olive toned. Call him Captain Italy. Or Captain Spain. Where's the name Rivas from, anyway?

"Is he, like, a model or something?" Martinique murmurs.

"He's in real estate."

"Then I need to buy a house..." She gazes at Sullivan in awe. "Where did you two meet? Are there more of him there?"

"We went to high school together. And actually..." I laugh. "He has a twin brother. So there's another just like him."

"Shut your mouth!" Martinique slaps a hand to her chest. "Why didn't you bring the other one to the party?"

"Apparently he's filming a pilot in Sumatra."

She drops her hand, pouting. "The other one's an actor? You know my rule about actors."

I quote, "'*The only thing worse than dating an actor is dating a stand-up comedian.*'"

"That's right." Martinique nods firmly. "No actors, no musicians, and *definitely* no comedians."

"You know that's, like, half the single guys in LA, right?"

"The broke-ass half."

I laugh. "You're broke, too!"

"Not as broke as them. At least I pay my bills before I run out of money."

"Sullivan's brother was on that show, you know the old one with all the kids in high school?"

"*Degrassi High*?" Martinique guesses. "*Saved By the Bell*?"

"No, the other one."

"Oh, *Rocko Rocks!*"

"Shh!"

Too late—his bat ears tuned to those three syllables, Sullivan fixes Martinique with a dark stare.

She claps her hands over her mouth. "He looked at me!"

"And now he's coming over."

"*Eek*!" Martinique literally says 'eek' out loud, hands plastered to her cheeks like the Home Alone kid.

"Are you spilling my secrets?" Sullivan says in his low, outrageously sexy voice. He slips his arm around my waist, his fingers resting on my hip.

I don't know how he does these things so naturally.

I can't help reacting. My whole body turns to him like a flower to the sun. All of a sudden, my palms are on his bare chest and I'm looking up into his face.

"Hey, gorgeous." He plants a light kiss on my mouth. "I was missing you."

The warmth and softness of Sullivan's lips are an instant lobotomy. The only response I can come up with is a dazed and drunken, "Hi."

Martinique watches with her mouth hanging open.

I really wish she would act less surprised, like this is the kind of guy I pull on the regular.

Except, there aren't any other guys who look like this. Other than Reese, I suppose.

"I'm Martinique," she interjects when the kiss is over. "The assistant to the assistant."

Sullivan laughs. "Is that like the assistant to the regional manager?"

"Yes," Martinique breathes, staring into his eyes like she didn't hear a word out of his mouth.

"Theo told me all about you—she's so lucky to be working with such a good friend."

Funnily enough, of all the details I spilled to Sullivan over our lunch, I didn't tell him that Martinique has become my closest friend. He figured that out for himself.

"Theo's the best!" Martinique gives me a conspiratorial look. "If we didn't have each other, we'd murder Angus."

"Take out a life insurance policy first," Sullivan advises. "But then...wait a while."

Martinique stares at him a moment, then laughs way too hard. "Oh my god! You didn't tell me he was funny."

"Well, I only just told you he existed."

"What's up with that?" Sullivan teases. "Are you embarrassed of me?"

"No way!" Martinique rushes to my defense. Unfortunately, by blurting, "She was probably just worried you'd dump her, like Trent."

"*Martinique...*," I hiss.

"Oops!" She claps her hand over her mouth again.

"Leave it there," I instruct. "For the rest of the party."

"No, I'm going to put you on the payroll..." Sullivan smiles at her. "Tell me more about this Trent."

Martinique glances back and forth between us, weighing her loyalties. Sullivan's charm trounces a year of friendship in less than two seconds.

"He was such a dick! He dumped Theo the week before Christmas."

When I had pneumonia.

I spent Christmas Day in the hospital, alone.

I fucking hate hospitals. I hate the lowered voices and quiet shuffling, broken by that very specific beep from the monitoring machines. I hate the smell, bland food and antiseptic. And most of all...I hate the memories.

Martinique came to visit me the day after, bringing a whole basket of her mama's sweet potato pie and rolls and leftover turkey. We used the rolls to make pie-and-turkey sandwiches.

But other than that, it was about the worst week of my life.

Well...second worst.

Martinique was just the receptionist, then. We were barely more than acquaintances. Still, she was the only one who came to see me. Angus was scuba-diving in the Maldives.

"It wasn't going anywhere," I say. "It was good we broke up."

"Good for *me.*" Sullivan links his fingers with mine.

I know he means that in the most selfish way possible, but even so, his hand feels nice wrapped around mine.

And the look he gives me is surprisingly sympathetic.

"His loss," he says, too low for Martinique to hear, spoken just for me.

Uh, oh.

A Sullivan bearing gifts is a dangerous creature. First the coffee and sandwich, then the clothes, and now he's being nice to me?

No, way, sister. I'm not falling for this.

We are not dating, and Sullivan is not a kind person.

I pull my hand free.

"Anyway," I say. "I better check in with Angus."

"I'll come with you," Martinique sighs, as glumly as if she were accompanying me to the firing squad. I don't think she's nervous to see Angus—she just doesn't want to leave Sullivan behind.

We find Angus at the back of the boat, arguing about the tensile strength of stainless steel. Angus is highly involved in the design of his rockets, and he's about as controlling there as he is everywhere else, constantly squabbling with his engineers.

Of course, there are no engineers on this boat—just rich people trying to get richer.

The person Angus is arguing with is an investor named Corgus Brent.

"Theo!" Angus cries, motioning for me to get closer. "You come tell Corgus what a load of shit this is that we can't get the casing three millimeters thicker. I told him...," he breaks off, staring at me. "Wow. You look...nice."

The way he's staring at my body in this swimsuit isn't "nice" at all. Actually, it's making me extremely uncomfortable.

But then, he says, "Let me get you a drink," and a cool flute of champagne slips into my palm.

Angus has never gotten me a drink before.

Corgus is also looking at my body, but not like he thinks it's "nice"—more like he wants to throw it overboard so it stops getting in the way of his conversation.

"Can we get back to—"

"Later," Angus interrupts. "I need to chat with Theo."

Angus waves him aside. Literally waves his hand like a French prince.

Corgus is dismissed.

In favor of me.

This has also never happened before.

I really wish it wasn't happening now because of a swimsuit.

Martinique gives me a wide-eyed look while Corgus stomps off.

"Holy shit!" she whispers.

My face burns. Did Sullivan do this on purpose? Just to show me how differently Angus would treat me? Or is this somehow playing into his game...

Angus gives me another slow up-and-down, and my stomach churns.

If Sullivan thinks he's going to pimp me off to my boss, he's more than just crazy—he's going to get his teeth knocked out.

But Sullivan appears at my elbow before Angus can pull me into a cozy corner for our "chat."

"Theo," he says. "I brought you a drink."

He takes Angus' champagne out of my hand and sets it aside.

My new drink is a Dirty Shirley, which is happens to be my favorite. Though I don't know how in the *hell* Sullivan knew that.

I wouldn't want him to know that. It's not the coolest drink of choice. But goddamn, is it delicious.

I take a huge sip, and the whole day turns a little brighter. The sea air is brisk. The material of my glorious new robe slides like butter against my thighs.

And Sullivan—well, he might as well be dipped in gold.

The breeze tosses his luscious dark hair. He grins at me, a flash of white in his lean, tanned face.

Even Angus is staring.

Not at me anymore, let me make that perfectly clear—at my *boyfriend,* who looks like this whole entire party was assembled so someone could take a picture of him to sell this yacht.

He is so fucking gorgeous, his swim trunks low on his hips,

his skin that clear, glowing brown that glimmers from the inside out.

Angus is a *billionaire.* He could buy a sports team for fun. He could eradicate a disease. Yet, right now, he's intimidated. And probably a little bit jealous.

Sullivan, despite all his handsomeness, does not look happy. Actually, he seems just a tiny bit annoyed.

That's because Angus just laid his hand on my arm in a possessive kind of way. I don't even know if he realizes he's doing it.

"Theo was about to fill me in on how the party's going so far," Angus says.

It's a kiss-off. A subtle, "*Let me talk to my employee now*," to put Sullivan back in his place.

Sullivan ignores it completely.

Instead, he gazes around appreciatively at the dazzling sunshine, the glittering water, the mounds of shrimp on ice, and says, "You're not going to have anything like this on Mars."

The hair on the back of my neck stands up. Martinique gives a strangled squeak.

If there was one single rule in dealing with Angus, it's Never Doubt The Mission To Mars.

It's his one driving ambition. The goal that shines above any other: a colony on Mars. Man's great insurance policy. Against woman. Who should kill him.

That's what I'm thinking as I carefully step on Sullivan's foot.

"Of course we will," Angus says, his hand dropping off my arm.

Calm and assured, Sullivan says, "Not like this."

His confidence makes Angus instantly agitated. "Anything you have on Earth, you could have up there."

"Nah." Sullivan puts his arm around my waist and pulls me close. "I don't think so."

I'm a little bit hyperventilating.

Why is he picking a fight with Angus? About the one thing Angus cares about most?

This has to be a sales technique I've never heard of called Offend The Client As Quickly As You Can.

But Angus doesn't look offended. Not really. More roused, in the sense of rising to battle. He musters all his best arguments to explain to Sullivan how, over time and with terraforming, Mars could be a habitable home.

This goes on for over an hour.

The other party guests are ignored while Sullivan and Angus debate actual quality of life on a second planet.

Martinique and I cuddle up on the couch getting increasingly tipsy on Dirty Shirleys. I'm ignoring all the guests and all the things I'm supposed to be doing. It doesn't matter—Angus is completely distracted.

I get the most incredible tan. I eat an ungodly amount of shrimp. And finally, closer to two hours later, Sullivan winds the argument to a close.

He never let it get heated. But he also never quite gave in.

In the end, he says to Angus, "You might almost convince me. But there's one thing Mars will never have."

"What's that?" Angus says, jovial and half-drunk on Dirty Shirleys.

Sullivan looks right at me and winks.

"It'll never have Theo."

7

SULLY

When we anchor at Catalina Island, there's a flurry of activity. Theo helps to corral the guests, though probably not with her usual efficiency, since she's about four Dirty Shirleys deep. Angus doesn't seem to notice because he's had at least six.

I've been nursing a single drink so I can stay sharp.

There's plenty to observe in the many dramas unfolding on Angus' yacht.

First, I'm checking out my competition. At least six other people here are trying to snag this land deal with Angus, whether they'll admit it or not. The biggest threat at this point appears to be Corgus. He owns a minority stake in Galactic, and it's pretty clear that he's trying to wriggle his way deeper into the project.

He's a large, bald-headed man with hands the size of baseball mitts and a deep, booming voice. There's some sort of antipathy between him and Theo though I haven't quite figured out why—I'm guessing he resents her closeness to Angus.

Like all circles of power, the people surrounding Angus Tate resemble nobles in a royal court. Everyone is angling to increase their wealth and influence.

Angus sits at the center like Louis the Sun King, the players revolving around him.

And just like a king, the image of invulnerability is an illusion.

Angus has his weaknesses like everyone else. I just need to find them.

I already put my finger on one: Little Miss Theo.

It didn't take much digging to realize how heavily Angus relies on her. Now that I'm here, I can see it for myself. He asks for Theo's opinion constantly though he doesn't take her advice any more than he does Corgus'.

His attachment to her goes far beyond her usefulness. She's more like his security blanket.

If Theo leaves his eyesight for more than ten minutes, Angus is sure to look for her, and if twenty minutes pass, he starts asking where she went. Even if he just sent her to accomplish some task that would obviously take more than twenty minutes.

Martinique does her best to fill the gaps, but Angus mostly uses her to relay instructions for Theo that Martinique could easily handle herself.

"Tell Theo to get the snorkel equipment ready," he orders Martinique as the anchor plunges down.

I find Theo at the back of the boat, looking slightly green.

"What's wrong?" I ask, assuming seasickness.

"Angus will make me go swimming," she mutters.

"What's wrong with that?"

She looks down at the dark water, her face paler than ever.

"There's sharks down there...among other things."

I resist the urge to tease Theo about what could possibly be swimming around in the ocean that scares her more than sharks.

Theo is still an anxious person, even if she's made strides as an adult. This situation I've concocted isn't helping—she's been on edge from the moment I picked her up from her tiny apartment.

She was right when she said she's no actor—she's painfully transparent in her nervousness, her stress, and her desire to please. Luckily for me, it all feeds into the "awkward girl in a new relationship" role I'm forcing her to play.

Maybe if Theo had brought her old boyfriend around, Angus would notice the difference, but I've already wormed it out of Martinique that despite Theo dating this "Trent" person for almost a year, Angus never met him.

Martinique met him twice and wasn't impressed.

"Theo gets used by people," she murmured to me after several Dirty Shirleys. "She doesn't stand up for herself."

She squinted at me, hiccupping softly.

"You won't hurt her, will you? I don't think she could stand another broken heart."

I gave Martinique my most reassuring smile. "Theo's heart is safe with me."

Whatever happens between us, there won't be any hearts involved.

And if all goes according to plan, I'll leave Theo both richer and happier than when I found her.

It's a win, win, win, even for Angus—what could possibly go wrong?

I glance over at Theo, who's still peering down at the water with a highly anxious look on her face.

Meanwhile, Angus sneaks up behind her, his expression comically villainous.

Before I can say or do anything, he shoves her hard in the back, pushing her off the dive ramp so she drops the significant distance to the water, screaming the whole way down.

Angus bellows laughter, hands on his knees.

My reaction is a little different: blinding fucking rage.

I leap in after Theo, diving down headfirst and coming up beneath her in the churning chaos of her bare legs. She's struggling and sputtering, hyperventilating and splashing around in a way that absolutely would draw sharks if there were any present.

"Shh," I say into her ear, wrapping my arms around her to calm her down and laying her back against my chest, keeping her afloat by treading water with my legs. "Relax, I'm right here."

She's shaking in my arms, adrenaline zipping through her blood, covered in goosebumps from the shock of the cold.

"That f-f-f-fucker!" she stammers, her lips blue.

"Don't be mad, Theo!" Angus calls from the pack of laughing sycophants up on the deck. "You were getting a sunburn!"

Theo glares up at him, blinking seawater out of her lashes. The trembling of her lips becomes trembling of her chin.

"He's s-s-s-such an ass!" she stutters, and I realize she's about to cry.

"Oh, come on you big baby, it was only a joke!" Angus shouts.

He takes a step off the ramp, toes pointed and arms flattened at his sides so he plunges down like a spear.

I don't know what comes over me.

I spent the last decade of my life working my body in the gym and training my mind just as relentlessly. It's been ten years of grueling effort, fighting daily to mold myself into the man I want to be.

Now, I don't make a move unless it's planned out three days ahead. Before I ever approached Theo at that party, I spent weeks strategizing exactly what I'd say to her, and to Angus.

But as Theo gazes up at me with those big blue eyes, blinking tears and seawater out of her lashes, she looks just like her old self, and suddenly, I'm the old Sullivan.

When Angus jumps into that water, I act without thinking.

I swim over, and right as he's about to emerge to suck in a big breath, I dunk him under again. HARD.

I shove him under the surface and hold him there while he struggles for air. Once, twice, three times he tries to come up, and I push him back under.

It's only when he really begins to panic, when his arms and legs are thrashing like Theo's, that I finally let him up.

He sucks in a huge gulp of air, hacking and choking.

"What the *fuck*?" he spits when he can breathe again.

"Just helping out," I say, with the fakest of smiles spread across my face. I let the smile drop, intentionally, so my face goes blank. "You were getting a sunburn."

Angus stares at me, scarlet with shock and anger, not from the sun.

Several more people jump in the water, wearing an array of fins, spouts, and goggles. Corgus paddles over with an extra set for Angus.

I swim back to Theo.

"What was *that*?" she whispers, still blue lipped and breathing hard. "Were you trying to drown him?"

"He's fine," I say dismissively.

Theo stares at me. "I really don't get your strategy."

"Don't worry about it—I know what I'm doing."

Complete and utter bullshit.

I don't know what I'm doing—I don't know what I just *did*.

What the fuck, Sully?

That wasn't part of the plan. That was the exact opposite of the plan, actually, for those wondering.

Theo's sky-high eyebrows don't show much confidence. "I guess I'll just have to trust you."

"Thanks," I say, with about the same level of confidence.

It's not Theo who's got me concerned—for the first time in years, I'm worried about myself.

I don't act impulsively anymore. *Ever.* Especially not when it'll fuck up my carefully laid plans.

When Angus forms his little snorkeling party, he grabs Corgus and three other dudes and heads out to the reef. He doesn't even glance at Theo and me.

"He's pissed," Theo observes as they swim away.

"Looks like it," I agree.

"Why did you do that?" She's swimming with a little space between us, head tilted as she examines me.

I don't want to admit the truth, which is that I was overcome by a single, powerful emotion that pulsed through me, taking control of my body and my brain.

So all I say is, "I don't like bullies."

Theo makes a soft sound. "Huh..."

That little line has reappeared between her eyebrows.

"What is it?"

"Nothing," she says, embarrassed, dropping her gaze.

I tread water, my heart still beating hard.

Even in the frigid water, my body burns with anger. At myself, not at Angus.

I was out of control. And I can guess what Theo was thinking:

You're worse than he is.

Theo sighs, gazing toward the half-submerged reef where her boss just vanished.

"Well, at least that means I don't have to go snorkeling."

"Guess not. Though...you're already in the water. Might as well see some fish."

Martinique plops in beside us, opting for a slow descent down the ladder instead of the faster but more alarming way down. She brought two extra pairs of masks and fins.

"Aren't you coming?" she says to Theo, fitting her own mask into place.

"I wasn't planning on it..." Theo reaches up to grasp the bottom of the ladder.

She gazes up at the remaining guests on deck, her nose scrunching. She's probably remembering that if she climbs up there, she's going to have to entertain whoever remained on board, while if she stays in the water, she's got no one to please except me and Martinique.

"Stick with us," I urge. "I'll fight off any sharks."

Theo gives me a small smile that shows a hint of those pretty teeth. "You scared them off, fucking up Angus."

"What did he do to Angus?" Martinique perks up. She was busy with the snorkel gear.

"Tried to drown him," Theo says nonchalantly.

"Wish you'd tried harder," Martinique mutters.

She finally gets her mask as tight as she likes and sets the snorkel spout in place.

"*Cmomom!*" she trumpets through the tube, diving down into the water with a flick of her fins.

"Ready?" I say to Theo, holding out my hand.

She gives the dark water one more nervous look, then links her wet fingers with mine.

"Don't let go of me."

THEO and I float just beneath the surface, hand in hand. At first, I hold onto her to keep us together so I can match her glacial swimming pace. Martinique is part dolphin and has already left us far behind.

Soon, Theo loses her death grip on my hand, and I can tell she isn't nervous anymore. I keep our fingers linked because floating like this, in the sun-warmed upper layers of the ocean, is surprisingly...nice.

We gaze down into a diorama of fish, coral, urchins, and crabs, long ribbons of seaweed trailing against our legs.

With Angus occupied and no one else around, there's nothing to worry about, no schemes and no strategies. It's one of the rare instances where I can just relax.

Theo's dark hair floats around her face in a storm cloud. Her limbs flash silver as she passes through bars of sunlight, the low-cut swimsuit clinging to every curve.

I've tried not to look at her body in that suit, but I have to admit, Theo was hiding a whole lot more than I expected...the shape of her breasts is so natural and beautiful that I've already imagined them naked ten times at least while sternly reminding myself that it's a mystery that will never be answered.

There's no talking down here. My communication with Theo becomes a pantomime where she touches my shoulder to show me the brightest fish and I tug her hand to gently take her where I want to go.

Dunking our faces beneath the water reveals this whole other world, full of life and movement, invisible from the surface.

Every person is an ocean, with unknown depths. In the hearts of some lie hidden treasures, while deep in others, monsters dwell...

What will I find in Theo?

She was a mystery to me, back in high school. A lottery student, obvious despite the uniforms because of the cheapness of her backpack and shoes. Her grades were mediocre, and I never saw her raise her hand in class. In fact, Theo did just about everything she could to avoid attention, but I noticed her anyway.

There was something secret about her, even then. I'd watch her reading or drawing or writing in her little notebook. I'd catch the hint of a smile that was only for herself, and I'd wonder what she found so interesting in another tedious school day.

She glances over now, wide-eyed behind her mask as she

points to a bat ray cutting through the water like a dark angel, wings flapping, tail extended behind.

Theo takes chase, following the ray at a cautious distance as it floats sedately over the sand.

We stay together, her hand in mine.

There's something ethereal about the ink-dark ray. This world beneath the water might as well be an alien planet. I've been snorkeling before but never like this, slow and quiet, with someone else by my side.

Seeing this world through Theo's eyes is different, punctuated by the soft and steady rush of her breath through the snorkeling tube. She looks like a sea creature herself, her long hair trailing behind her like a mermaid.

We don't have to talk. We can't talk.

In the strangest way, it reminds me of spending time with Reese. It's comfortable, natural...requiring nothing but peace.

We've swum far from where the boat was anchored, out into open water, away from the island and the reef.

The sand below drops away as the ray swims out over a canyon. The dark water spirals down into nothingness, and Theo pauses like she could fall over the edge, though of course we're still floating near the surface.

The sense of depth is dizzying, like looking up into the sky and realizing there's no end to how far you could fall.

Theo clings to me, her hands on my shoulders, her feet treading over empty space.

I gently tow her back until we're floating over bright gold sand once more.

"Thanks!" she gasps when we pop our heads above the water. "Jesus, that's creepy!"

"Do you want to head back?" I nod toward the anchored boat, tiny as a toy from this distance.

"We'd better," Theo says, her teeth beginning to chatter. "Before I get too cold."

"Come here." Once more, I sweep her into my arms and hold her pressed against my chest, sharing a little of that perpetual furnace inside me that only burns hotter from swimming. And a little bit from how that swimsuit hugs her curves...

"How are you so warm?" Theo says, looking into my face.

Hers is stamped with red marks in the shape of her snorkeling mask, now pushed up on her forehead.

Theo might be the only person on the planet who looks good in goggles. Even inch-thick plastic can't dull those bright blue eyes or hide those outrageous lashes.

She looks cuter than ever, mask pushed back like a crown, wet hair plastered to her cheeks, her pearly teeth bared in a grin, her heart pounding against mine.

I remember what Theo said, the reason she likes cooking so much...

I like taking care of people...

I get it.

It feels good to take care of Theo, to protect her, to keep her safe...

But I already have two people I have to take care of.

And neither of them is Theo.

So I gently push her away even though she hasn't had enough time to get warm.

"Come on," I say gruffly. "Let's get back to the boat."

8

THEO

Several hours later as I'm steaming clams down on the beach, I can't stop thinking about snorkeling with Sullivan.

I've never been able to relax and enjoy myself in the ocean. The soundtrack to *Jaws* runs constantly in my head, and each strand of seaweed that touches my foot feels like the teeth of a Great White taking a nibble in advance of the Big Bite.

But with Sullivan beside me, it felt like nothing could hurt me.

That's ironic considering Sullivan used to scare me more than any shark. In high school, his temper was legendary. And apparently, it's still right there under the surface. He may have learned how to charm everyone else on the boat, but when he shoved Angus under the water, he looked exactly like the guy I knew before—fucking scary.

Angus is still pissed at him for the aggressive dunking. I can tell because he's barely speaking to me, either, other than snarking that I forgot to bring "one of those pigs on a stick." Never mind that Angus specifically asked for clams.

Honestly, it's an improvement when he ignores me. It means less obnoxious requests. Angus seems to delight in demanding impossible things then watching while I scramble to obey.

I'm sure it makes him feel powerful.

It makes *me* feel like a court jester.

God, I can't wait to be my own boss. Then when things go wrong, at least it'll be *my* shit going wrong. And when I fix it, I'll be fixing it for myself.

I am happy that I get to do some cooking tonight. I've got the clams steaming nicely on a bed of coals, and now I'm dicing up fresh papaya for the green papaya salad.

Martinique is helping me. She likes cooking almost as much as I do. We've gotten so good at working together, it's like a sixth sense.

"Pass me the sea salt," I call, right as she tosses it to me behind her back.

"Already on it!"

Unfortunately, Martinique's throwing arm is not on par with her knife skills. The salt goes flying over my head.

Sullivan snatches it out of the air.

He catches it one-handed, a neat little underhand snag that makes my stomach fold in on itself.

"Here you go, gorgeous," he growls, pressing the saltshaker into my palm. His low voice tickles the hair by my ear. His fingers brush against mine.

I become aware that I'm extremely sweaty and probably smell like clams.

"Thanks," I gulp.

"My pleasure."

Sullivan takes a seat by the fire, striking up a conversation with Corgus. Every once in a while, he glances back at me and smiles. Every single time he does, my stomach performs a backflip.

"God, he's dreamy," Martinique sighs.

"I know."

It's not a good thing.

Actually, Sullivan's sexiness is a major problem because it's only making this more difficult.

He is *not* my boyfriend, no matter how well he plays the role.

And every time he looks at me or calls me some sweet pet name or, worst of all, puts his arm around me and makes my whole body burst into butterflies, he's only feeding a craving that's already spiraling out of control.

Especially when he defends me against Angus.

What was that about?

Sullivan says he doesn't like bullies.

That's ironic considering the way he behaved back in school.

This new version of him confuses me. Charming, deliberate, controlled—until he isn't.

I've seen Sullivan lose control once before. It was fucking terrifying.

Prom night. The last time I saw him for about eleven years...

Sullivan's lucky he didn't end up in jail.

He sent my date to the ER with a broken nose, three broken ribs, and a dislocated shoulder.

It came out of nowhere. At the start of the night, Sullivan and Davis were sharing sips out of Sullivan's pocket flask. Two hours later, he attacked without warning, beating the ever-loving shit out of my date behind the school gym.

I asked Davis what happened during our six-hour wait in the emergency room. He said, *That's just how Sullivan is; he's got a temper—especially when he's been drinking.*

I notice Sullivan doesn't drink much anymore—he nursed the same Dirty Shirley for hours while the rest of us were getting tipsy.

Yet he still lost his shit on Angus when Angus shoved me off the boat.

Maybe people change. Or maybe they just get better at hiding it.

I glance at Sullivan once more. As if he can sense it, he turns and catches my eye and smiles.

I don't smile back.

"Martinique..." I draw closer to her so Sullivan won't hear. "Is there any way I could stay at your place next week? My apartment's being fumigated."

"Sure!" How quickly she answers makes me want to hug her. "But you know I only have one bed."

"No problem—I'll bring an air mattress."

"Why are they fumigating? You don't have bed bugs, do you?" She inches away from me by several degrees. "My mom had bed bugs once, and I still get nightmares of creepy-crawlies climbing my legs..."

"No bed bugs," I assure her. "Just the world's most disgusting cockroaches."

"Never thought I'd be relieved to hear that," Martinique snickers. "How come you don't stay at Sullivan's place?"

How come, indeed?

"He...snores." I squirm at even that pathetic lie.

Martinique doesn't seem to notice. "Glad to hear he's not completely perfect."

"What are you two girls whispering about?" Angus interrupts.

He grabs a stick and starts poking at the clams, which really annoys me because he's letting out all the steam.

"Nothing," I say, snatching back the stick.

"Theo and I are planning a week-long sleepover," Martinique informs him, ever the blabbermouth. "Her apartment is being fumigated."

Angus pretends to wrinkle his nose at me. "Well, that explains the smell..."

"They don't start until next week," I say with as much dignity as possible considering I'm holding a filthy, sand-covered stick and probably do smell like smoke, sweat, clams, and fish guts.

"Don't you live in a studio?" Angus asks Martinique. His eyes dart over to Sullivan then back to me. "Just stay at my place, Theo —I've got four spare rooms."

I stare at Angus while Martinique stares at me.

I've never stayed the night at Angus' house. And I don't think he'd be inviting me right now except to get back at Sullivan in some sideways fashion.

As if summoned, Sullivan appears at my elbow.

"No need," he says smoothly. "She'll be staying with me."

His face shows no anger, but his chin is lowered, his dark eyes flickering with firelight.

"You don't have room..." I squeak.

I have no idea if that's true, but the idea of me and Sullivan alone at his place is immediately horrifying. What if *I* snore? What if I fart in my sleep? What if he comes in while I'm wearing my mouthguard?

No, this can't happen.

But Sullivan brushes me aside.

"Of course I have room, don't be silly. Can't have my girl staying at her *boss's* house..." His eyes narrow ever so slightly in Angus' direction. "Or even with her best friend. Not when I could have you wrapped up in my arms all night long."

Even though I know I'll most likely be sleeping on the couch, the image that sneaks into my brain makes me flush all the way down to my toes.

What would it be like to sleep in Sullivan's arms?

Fucking heavenly...

Like being rocked in a hammock made of muscles and the world's most tantalizing cologne...

Honestly, even his couch is probably pretty nice if it's anything like the cushy leather seats in his BMW.

At least Sullivan *has* a couch. Martinique only has two rickety folding chairs.

"Okay," I say hesitantly, "...thanks."

Angus doesn't look pleased.

"Where do you live?" he snaps at Sullivan. "I don't want Theo coming into work late again."

That makes me flush for a completely different reason. I've only been late twice the entire time I've worked for Angus, both times because my car broke down. In fact, if he would recall, I'm actually *obnoxiously punctual...*

Sullivan says, "I live on Mermaid Lane."

"*Mermaid Lane*?" Angus snorts. "Where the hell is that?"

Sullivan refuses to take the bait. "Ten minutes from your office. And I'll be driving Theo to work in the morning, so you don't have to worry about a thing."

I'm pretty sure he said that last part just to annoy Angus. After all, I have my own car and I'm perfectly capable of driving myself. On the days that it runs.

"Great," Angus says through gritted teeth.

Martinique's eyes pinball back and forth between the two men glaring at each other, with me in the middle in a shimmering haze of clam-scented steam.

"...Okay...," she says slowly. "Then I guess it's just me in my shoebox."

"Don't worry," Sullivan winks at her. "You can come visit me and Theo."

He does not extend the same invitation to Angus.

9

THEO

That's how I find myself, late in the evening, driving to someplace called "Mermaid Lane" after a brief stop at my own cockroach-infested apartment. Those cockroaches better enjoy their last day on earth. Their kingdom inside my oven is coming to an end.

"You really don't have to do this," I tell Sullivan, probably for the twentieth time.

"I told you, it's no big deal. I live alone in a huge house. Well, pretty much alone—Reese lives there, too, when he's in town. But he won't be back for weeks."

"Okay..."

The idea of staying in Sullivan's mansion doesn't exactly thrill me. His wealth already makes me uncomfortable. The beautiful wooden dashboard of his car looks like the inside of an old-timey airplane, and the clothes he bought me so casually probably cost more than I make in a month.

I guess I should be used to it from hanging around Angus, but really that's only made me more conscious of the difference between me and the ultrarich.

I already got a pretty hefty taste of all that back in high school. My mom was so excited when I won the lottery slot at Piedmont Prep, there was no way she'd let me turn it down. But I never fit in at that place, and struggling to exist among the uber-wealthy really fucked with a sense of self-esteem that wasn't that robust to begin with.

Maybe it was something subconscious when I applied for the job with Angus—maybe, deep down, I like torturing myself. Standing next to the money and success I'll never actually achieve...

But no, I'm not going to think like that.

I'm done being a second-rate loser, the nice girl who always finishes last.

I *will* achieve wealth and success. I'm going to get my restaurant. And Sullivan's going to help me do it.

So what if I have to stay a week at his ultrabougie man-mansion; how bad can it be? At least he won't have a cockroach infes—

My mouth gapes as we pull onto Mermaid Lane.

Sullivan's mansion is *not* bougie.

Actually, it's completely falling apart.

If Sullivan's house were a ship, it would be an old freighter that was lost in a storm for fifty years and then came back as a ghost.

The roof is sagging, the paint is patchy and peeling, and the yard is overgrown like a jungle, with waist-high weeds, moss-draped trees, and ivy clambering up the walls. The porch is so shaggy with wisteria, I doubt you could even see out most of the windows on the main level.

The rest of the street doesn't look much better.

Mermaid Lane is a mishmash of moldering mansions that have clearly seen better days. Those that have been renovated show a level of taste that could be charitably described as "eccentric," standing next to shambling estates that are full-on batshit crazy. The house next to Sullivan's is painted electric purple, while the one two doors down sits amidst a forest of glittering windchimes, lawn gnomes, and plastic pink flamingos.

"Wow...," I say, 'cause I'm fast on my feet like that.

"Not what you were expecting?" Sullivan gives me a sideways smirk.

He climbs out of the car, retrieving my bag from the trunk and carrying it up the front steps. It's a duffle bag, mostly stuffed with the clothes Sullivan just bought me.

Now I'm feeling like he probably should have invested in a new porch light instead. Or some paint for this door...

Sullivan walks inside without bothering with a key.

"You don't lock your front door?"

"There's not much to steal."

That's true. The palatial space has a strange sense of emptiness. It's dark and echoing inside, most of the walls bare, no rugs on the floor.

"Here's the living room..." Sullivan flicks on a light.

The living room contains a single battered leather sofa in front of a television and literally nothing else.

"And there's the kitchen..."

Sullivan's kitchen is extremely clean but, again, almost empty. Not a single appliance sits on the countertops, and the fruit bowl contains one lone orange.

A coffee cup sits in the sink, half full of water. When I open the fridge, the milk, eggs, butter, and yogurt look like they've never met each other, satellites in the barren, fluorescent-lighted space.

"I'll get some more groceries tomorrow." Sullivan eyes the sparse contents of the fridge.

"I take it you don't cook much..."

"I do sometimes...." He's a little defensive. "When my dad's sob—I mean, home."

Sullivan jerks his chin toward the kitchen window that looks out over a backyard even more overgrown than the front. Distantly, beyond a cracked and empty, weed-choked swimming pool, I spy a pool house almost buried in wisteria.

"Don't worry," Sullivan says. "He never comes in the main house, so you won't see him."

"I don't mind meeting your dad."

"You won't," Sullivan repeats.

"Okay."

I can't quite read the expression on Sullivan's face—he looks unhappy and maybe even a little embarrassed, which doesn't make sense to me because even if his house is shabby and sort of lonely, it's still massive and ten times nicer than my garbage apartment.

I could spin around in circles with my arms out and not touch anything in this place. I could run up and down the hallways bellowing, and you wouldn't even hear me from one of the distant wings.

I could live in this place for a week without bumping into Sullivan *or* his dad.

"Wishing you stayed with Martinique?" Sullivan asks.

"No! Why would you say that?"

His dark hair falls down over his eyes. He shoves it back, defiant, bluntly noting, "It's not as nice as you expected."

"Noooo...." I can't even make the word come out right. It sounds like, "*Newwww...*"

Sullivan shakes his head at me. "You're a terrible liar. One of the worst I've ever seen. If I'd known that ahead of time, I would have had serious concerns about our plan."

"*Your* plan," I remind him. "And I did warn you that I can't act."

"Yes, you did," Sullivan says fairly.

"And I'm sorry I was...um...surprised. I was under the distinct impression that you were loaded."

Sullivan snorts. "Sorry to disappoint. Now you know the dirty truth—I'm not rich."

He was, though. Back in high school. I'm not wrong about that.

His parents must have been rich when they bought this house. But that was twenty years ago, at least.

And I'm afraid I have a pretty good idea of exactly when the decline started...

My stomach gives a slow, unhappy roll. I glance out the back window at that dark and distant pool house.

"Every penny I have is sunk into that land," Sullivan says. "I'm all in on this deal with Angus, sink or swim."

I guess that's a good thing. It means he needs this as badly as I do.

"Well..." I tilt my head, unconvinced. "You're still sort of rich. You've got this house. And that car. And all your fancy suits..."

Sullivan shrugs. "Appearances matter. The first thing I did with my very first paycheck was buy a proper suit. Nobody takes you seriously otherwise."

"Is that why you bought me all those clothes?"

"That's exactly why. And look how differently Angus treated you."

I bite at the edge of my thumbnail. "I hated how he was acting today."

"You never like how he acts. At least today, you had the upper hand."

I frown, crossing my arms over my chest, leaning back against Sullivan's kitchen counter. "I'm not sure if I agree with that assessment."

He reminds me, "You did get half the day off work..."

I did. And I was grateful for it, but it was hardly free of strings. Or future complications...

"Yeah, but now Angus is acting all mad and jealous. What if he starts hitting on me?"

"He won't." Sullivan grins. "Remember, he thinks you have a boyfriend."

God, that smile does incredible things to his face. It lights him up and creates the burning impulse inside me to tell a joke or cook or do jumping jacks or something—whatever I can to impress him.

Instead, I shake my head, forcing myself to focus.

"Isn't that going to complicate your scheme?"

"Not at all. It's a key part of my scheme."

My face flushes and I stand up a little straighter, fixing Sullivan with a stern glare. "I'm not going to flirt with Angus to get you what you want."

"What *we* want," Sullivan reminds me. "This is your ticket out of your bullshit job, too, remember."

"I don't care. I'm not going to flirt with him to get it. Or anything worse..."

"You won't have to," Sullivan assures me. "Fucking Angus is not part of the plan—for either of us."

That tugs a snort out of me. "You sure? The chemistry was undeniable..."

"I mean, I'll do what I have to do," he deadpans, "but let's stick with Plan A for now."

"Glad to hear you're committed."

"I am," Sullivan says, all jokes falling away. "But I won't make you do anything you don't want to do. Do you trust me?"

He waits, face open, eyes clear.

Sullivan looks sincere.

He *sounds* sincere.

But I've already witnessed how convincing he can be.

"I don't know if I can trust you," I say at last. "This whole thing is a lie."

I expect him to be offended by that statement, but he takes my words calmly, nodding his head slowly like he's considering what I've said.

"Understandable—it's disorienting, playing this game. Especially since I *am* the better actor." He smiles slightly. "So how about this, Theo...no matter what I have to say or do to anyone else, I promise never to lie to you."

"Never?"

There's a flicker of hesitation as he considers the full weight of the promise. Then, firmly, he says, "*Never*. I'll answer anything you ask me, fully and honestly."

The idea imbues me with a strange sense of power. I can ask Sullivan anything...and he has to answer?

It creates a bond between us, thin and shimmering like chain-link steel.

"But..." Sullivan's eyes darken as he takes a step closer. "I expect the same from you. It wouldn't be fair if I were honest with you, but you were holding back from me."

My heart pitter-patters in my chest. This sprawling kitchen suddenly seems very small and very warm as Sullivan invades my space. He backs me up until my ass meets the countertop and there's nowhere else to retreat.

"Well?" His thighs brush my knees. I have to tilt up my chin to look at him. "Do we have a deal?"

"I'm an open book."

Sullivan gives a low chuckle. "I doubt that very much. I want to hear you say it...do you swear to tell me the truth, Theo? No matter what?"

His eyes bore into mine, deeply dark and penetrating. It's like he can see all the way down to the bottom of my soul.

"Sure," I promise recklessly. "The whole truth and nothing but the truth, so help me god."

I hold up my hand while I say it, like I'm swearing an oath in court.

I meant it flippantly, but there's something solemn in Sullivan's dark eyes. The mood in the kitchen is hushed and serious.

"Good," he says softly. "When it's just you and me, we'll have perfect honesty between us."

It feels like I just made a vow...one that will have consequences.

10

SULLY

I asked Theo to stay at my place because I had to. I obviously wasn't going to let her stay with Angus, and it was too risky to send her home with Martinique. Theo is sure to crack and spill everything if she spends too much time alone with her best friend, and especially if she sleeps at her house.

Now that she's here, I remember why I never invite anyone over.

This house feels like a ghost town. It always has.

Or at least, it has for the last ten years.

I debate over whether I should put her in the east or the west wing. The east wing is empty right now—that's where Reese sleeps when he happens to be in town. But it seems weird to put Theo so far away from me. What if she needs more towels? Or she can't get the A/C to work?

I lead her to the west wing instead.

"That's my room..." I point to the one at the end of the hall. "You can take any of these."

Three doorways stand open to nearly identical bedrooms. My

parents thought they'd fill this wing of the house with kids. The first two came so easily, they thought there'd be many more.

But that's how life fucks you. It gives you what you never wanted and holds back everything you thought you'd get.

Life is a cruel and tricky bitch who delights in torturing us. That's why the concept of irony exists—so we can pretend to laugh at all the creative fuck-yous.

But I'm determined to come out on top this time. The moment I realized that Angus Tate's right-hand woman was none other than Theo Mahoney, I knew it had to be destiny.

It *has to* be my turn for something to go right.

So I swallow the embarrassment of Theo seeing how run down and shabby this place has gotten even though I'm observing it fresh through her eyes.

Jesus. Why I haven't I hung up some pictures? Or painted...anything?

I know why.

Because then my dad would think I'm moving on.

It might make him angry. Or send him into a spiral.

Or, or, or...

When you're scared and you have no idea what to do, it seems safest to do nothing. Even while your whole life is falling apart around you, somehow even *that* feels safe. Because at least you're used to it.

"I guess...I'll take this one." Theo selects the smallest bedroom, farthest from mine.

"Do you need shampoo or anything?"

She shakes her head. "I brought all that."

"Okay."

We stand there a moment in awkward silence. It's pretty late at night—we spent all day on the yacht with Angus and most of the evening on the beach, chowing down on Theo's clams.

Through it all, there was a sense of connection between us—

the secret we share. Our relationship is fake, but it's a cord tying us together all the same, so that when I'm pretending to be her boyfriend, I'm thinking about Theo, watching her everywhere she goes, behaving like I would if I were in love. Making sure she's protected and happy.

I guess the afterglow is what's making me linger in the hallway, wondering if I should offer her a drink or something before bed. I feel like I'm still supposed to be taking care of her.

But I don't want to give her the wrong impression—like I'm trying to get her drunk to take advantage of her or something. She's probably suspicious of me inviting her to stay here in the first place.

"You want...some water or something?"

"I'm okay." Theo digs her bare toes into the carpet, sneaking a quick glance up at me. "Thanks, though. And... thank you for distracting Angus today. And for taking me snorkeling. And for the bathing suit...it was gorgeous, even if I felt like a fool in it."

"You didn't look like a fool."

That pretty, soft pink spreads through her pale cheeks like watercolor.

Theo's skin truly is the softest thing I've ever touched. I find myself inventing reasons to touch her again when other people are around, when I have an excuse.

But right now, there's no excuse.

I'm not supposed to do it.

I'm not even supposed to think about it.

Because if I were to kiss her for real or touch her for real, here at my house...that would be crossing a serious line.

I blackmailed this woman to be here. I dug up her most painful secret and threatened to tell her vindictive boss for the express purpose of getting her fired.

Now, would I ever actually do that?

Not a chance. If Theo would have told me to fuck off, I never would have ratted her out to Angus—I'd find another angle.

But she doesn't know that, and that's the whole, entire point. As long as I'm dangling that threat over her head, it would be super fucked up for me to kiss her or even make her worry that I might while she's staying at my house.

There are things I'll blackmail somebody to do and things I won't. I have standards.

Besides, I knew Theo wouldn't tell me to fuck off, and that's also why this isn't fair.

I knew what Angus would do, which is be a selfish ass, the most predictable of human behaviors. I knew the position that would put Theo in. And I took advantage, I applied pressure. And I'm going to keep doing it until I get what I want.

So I cannot also touch Theo's silky soft skin right now, no matter how much it's tempting me to do so.

This is strictly business. I have a plan, and dunking Angus aside, I'm going to damn well stick to it.

Now, the only problem is...Theo herself.

She hasn't yet gone into her bedroom. Actually, she's lingering in the hallway, leaning one shoulder against the doorframe.

And Theo in this moment...looks extra goddamn cute. She's been out in the sun all day, so she's burned across her nose and shoulders, just enough to turn her pink. Her lips are plump and heart shaped, and her face is heart shaped, too, with those big blue eyes gazing up at me, vulnerable and soft...

That same errant strand of hair has slipped out of the messier-than-usual beachy bun on her head. It's like it's daring me to tuck it behind her ear.

Theo's hair is sleek and dark, but this little piece has gone curly and wild from the salty sea air.

It dances in the breeze from the open windows throughout the house.

It's like we're back on that boat, in the sun, when I had all the excuses in the world to touch her...

But we're not.

We're here. All alone in this big empty house.

So I shove both hands in my pockets and bite down on my lip.

"Sleep tight."

Theo blinks and sucks in a breath, her face closing up.

"Right," she says, shrinking back into her room. "You, too."

I stand there in the hallway, looking at her closed door.

It feels like Theo hasn't moved inside the bedroom. Like she's standing on the other side, doing the same thing as I am.

Jesus, I'm losing it.

I hustle off down the hall.

AT AROUND 2:00 A.M., I hear scuffling in the kitchen.

It isn't noisy enough to wake me up, but I never actually fell asleep. I've just been lying here, tossing and turning in the dark.

I know it's Theo, and the fact that she's awake is cheering. Usually when I'm sleepless and alone, I stay that way until morning.

I pull on a pair of sweatpants and shuffle out to the kitchen, flattening my hair on the way.

Theo is just turning around, arms full of everything she's pillaged from my fridge. She shrieks and the food goes flying. She manages to save the carton of eggs with a pretty impressive catch at knee level, but the block of cheese bounces off her toe.

"*Ow*!" she howls, hopping around on one foot, still clutching the eggs.

I hold up my hands. "It's just me, not a burglar."

"There's not going to be any burglars," Theo says. "I locked your door."

"That's a shame. I was hoping somebody would take that shitty couch."

Theo sets the eggs down on the counter and retrieves the cheese.

"I was going to make scrambled eggs," she says apologetically. "When I drink, I get hungry again later."

"Me too."

She brightens. "You want some?"

"If you're cooking."

I loathe cooking. I try to do it at least twice a week so I can make sure my dad's eating something that doesn't come out of a box, but more often than not, I fuck it up. And then it's an hour wasted on something that both of us can barely choke down.

Theo moves around the kitchen with easy grace, like she already knows her way around the place better than I do. I noticed the same thing when she was making the clams and the papaya salad—Theo is practically a ballerina when she's cooking. All her anxiety melts away, and she could almost be dancing.

She cracks the eggs one-handed into the bowl, neatly tossing the shells into the trash, and then she whips them up with a whisk, the yellow liquid whirling up to the edge of the bowl without splashing a single drop.

She throws a generous pat of butter into the pan and waits for it to sizzle before pouring in the eggs. I watch while she pushes them into peaks, removing the pan from the heat while the eggs are still wet.

"Kind of...gooey, aren't they?" I say apprehensively.

Theo laughs. "Everybody overcooks their eggs. I take them off the heat to add the cheese."

She sprinkles the top of the scrambled eggs with a generous portion of grated cheese, as well as salt and pepper.

"Now watch...," she says.

She flips over the entire pile so the cheese is on the bottom, then sets it back on the heat to melt.

"The eggs will finish cooking," she explains. "But the cheese will keep them from burning."

Right on time, our toast pops.

Theo snatches the slices out of the toaster and slathers on more butter.

"Here you go..." With a neat little flick of the pan, she flips a portion of eggs so the melted cheese is back on top, the eggs sailing through the air to land on my plate right next to the toast.

When Theo's cooking...she's kind of fucking cool. It's a whole other level of confidence.

I dig into the eggs and toast.

"Holy shit..." I say, mouth stuffed full. "This is incredible!"

Theo laughs. "It's just scrambled eggs."

"Yeah, but these are the best eggs I've ever tasted. How'd you get them so buttery?"

She snorts. "I think it was all the butter I used."

"And how are they so fluffy?" I've demolished the whole pile in four bites.

Theo is pink cheeked and pleased. I'm learning to differentiate between her many blushes—when she's upset, her whole face goes red and her eyes get watery, but when she's happy or only a little embarrassed, the color stays in her cheeks.

"Scrambled eggs were the first thing I learned to make," she says. "I used to cook them for my mom when she worked the night shift."

"What night shift?"

"She was a nurse," Theo clarifies.

"Oh yeah? Where is she now?"

I'm expecting her to say Boca or wherever nurses go to retire. But I should have read the slight sag in her shoulders and the drop in her voice.

Too late, I realize my mistake.

"She died," Theo says softly. "Four years ago."

Four years that haven't seemed long, at least not to her.

You can hear it...a weight in the voice. Real grief.

I blundered into it, and I don't know how the fuck I could have done that. You'd think I'd pay attention to *that*, of all things.

But then I realize something much, much worse...

Four years ago is when Theo dropped out of *Le Cordon Bleu*. To come back here, suddenly. Right before graduation. From the prestigious school she loved.

It hits me like a hammer:

I. AM. AN. ASSHOLE.

And she doesn't even tell me. She doesn't connect the dots for me at all, her mother dying and her dropping out of school. I don't even know which one happened first—did she come home to take care of her mom? Or did she lose her first and then fall into a depression and flunk out?

Either way, I used her mother's death against her. 'Cause I didn't fucking do my research.

I can't just let this pass—as much as I'd like to as I burn with embarrassment.

"Is that why you never graduated?"

Theo's eyes flick up to meet mine, and she bites down hard on the center of her lip.

"Well...yeah," she admits. "She didn't want me to drop out, she said she'd be fine, I could finish the last few months. She was supposed to have another two years. But...cancer's a bitch."

Theo looks down at her hands. Two quick, hot tears slip down her cheeks.

"She died a month later." Fiercely swiping at her cheeks, she says, "I don't regret dropping out. That month is what I hold on to —I wouldn't trade it for anything."

I swallow hard. "I didn't know any of that. And either way...I was an asshole for blackmailing you. I know you probably don't believe me, but I wouldn't really have gotten you fired. I still won't, if you don't want to do this. I never should have forced you. I'm sorry."

Theo sits up a little straighter, pulling back her shoulders, taking a deep breath. Her eyes are wet and red, but she looks calm and resolute.

"We're in the middle of it now. And anyway, you were right about Angus—he's using me and stringing me along. I was blind to it because I wanted to believe that he'd help me. That all my hard work would pay off."

"It will," I say. "But not with him. It'll pay off when you're working for yourself."

"Working for you, you mean," Theo says with a small smile.

"No, I don't mean that." I shake my head, speaking seriously. "We're partners. You don't work for me any more than I work for you. We'll close this deal together, and you'll get your cut and open your restaurant. I have your contract right here."

I pull it out of the kitchen drawer and bring it to her, notarized by a lawyer just like I promised, with her ten percent cut of the commission spelled out in clean black ink.

Theo reads it over carefully before signing.

Her name in pretty cursive pleases me—another link between us, binding us to this pact.

I like being connected to Theo. I like working with her. She's resourceful and determined. She's brave even when she's scared.

And she's doing this alone. Theo doesn't have any siblings, and I remember from high school there's no dad in the picture. When she lost her mom, she lost everything.

I can relate.

I still have Reese and my father, but when my mom died, it ripped the heart out of all of us. We've never been the same.

As Theo can see for herself.

Her eyes drift out the kitchen window to the unlit pool house, strangled in vines.

Quietly, she says, "I know you lost your mom, too."

She knows because we were still in school together when it happened. Everyone knew. It was splashed across every newspaper and magazine, everywhere I went:

Starlet Slain by Stalker...

Actress Gunned Down in Her Own Home...

My mother died on our front porch. The man shot her the moment she opened the door.

I was there. I found her.

My stomach clenches, and all the blood seems to drain from my head. The kitchen floor feels like it's tilting beneath my feet.

"Yup," I say. "It fucking sucks."

Theo lays her cool, soft hand over mine. "It really does."

Her hand is like an anchor, holding me in place.

The kitchen straightens and everything is back in place, steady and still.

I turn my hand over and link my fingers with hers, squeezing once.

It feels good, this moment of connection, of shared pain, shared comfort.

It feels so good, in fact, that the pulse of warmth is immediately followed by waves of guilt and fear. Fear that I better not get used to this, and guilt because I don't deserve it.

I push back from the table, my chair scraping beneath me.

Avoiding Theo's clear blue eyes, I say, "Thanks again for the eggs—I better get to bed."

11

THEO

The next day is Sunday, so I expect Sullivan to sleep in, but he's in the kitchen in one of his sleek, dark suits by 8:00 a.m.

"Where are you going?" I ask him, rubbing sleep out of my eyes.

"Hustling isn't nine-to-five," he says, gulping down his coffee and adding a second empty mug to the one already sitting in the sink. "I've got other deals to make."

"I thought you said you were all in on this one?"

"I am...but I still need to pay the bills in the meantime."

I'm guessing one of those bills is the mortgage on this big, empty mansion—or at least the property taxes, which would be ruinous all on their own. I get the impression that Sullivan lives here out of obligation, not because he actually likes the place.

He gives me a wave that looks a bit like a salute as he hurries out the door. "Make yourself comfortable...eat whatever you want, do whatever you want. There's a grocery order coming at ten."

When he's gone, the house settles into a stillness that's almost unbearable.

All this empty space is eerie. There's probably twenty rooms in this place, rooms that were meant for friends and family, for parties that never came to pass…

I start exploring because I don't want to feel like I'm lost. I want to know where everything is and where I am inside of it.

Soon I see that the house is essentially shaped like a giant bird, with two long wings extending to the east and west and the body of the bird being the large, central space encompassing the entryway, kitchen, living room, and formal dining room.

I check out the east wing first, finding Reese's bedroom, which is messy and chaotic, stuffed with the most belongings of any of the spaces I've seen so far, even though, apparently, he only lives here part-time.

Next door sits a music room full of all sorts of instruments, including an entire wall of electric guitars. Some are signed, but all look battered and well-used, especially the drum set in the corner. There's a piano, a saxophone, and even an Autoharp, which my mom taught me to play once upon a time.

There's a gym, also well used, I would assume, from the scent of sweat and all the smudges on the mirrors.

But then, farther down…the main suite.

I noticed that Sullivan doesn't stay in the main suite himself. His bedroom is a normal-sized room like mine.

The suite is probably three times as large as the other rooms, palatial and beautiful with its big bay windows looking out over what must have been a spectacular rose garden, once upon a time.

But almost as soon as I open the double doors, I close them again, without even venturing into the marble-clad bathroom or the walk-in closet larger than my entire apartment.

The reason I don't enter is because I can see several sparkling gowns still hanging in the closet. And next to that, a huge portrait of a woman in a wedding dress, her graceful face so achingly familiar that I let out a little gasp when my eyes meet hers, closing the doors quickly in embarrassment.

Sullivan's mother, Stella Rivas. I've seen pictures of her before, like everyone has. She was very famous twenty years ago. Dark haired and dark eyed like her sons, elegant like Audrey Hepburn, but with a dash of slapstick charm like Emma Stone.

This was her room. And the other person who should be living in this suite...apparently stays in the pool house and won't even come inside.

An image flashes in my head, glimpsed in some long-ago magazine: Sullivan's mother standing on a red carpet, dressed in a dazzling, gem-draped gown....

I try to remember the man next to her, tall, broad shouldered, sandy haired, smiling with his arm around her waist...

I can't recall his face, but I remember how perfectly they complemented each other, young and healthy and happy and shining like stars.

I knew Sullivan when his family was at their peak, famous, successful, streaking through the sky...

And I heard when they were struck with tragedy...

But I never saw the aftermath of their fall.

Now here it is, all around me...the dark and silent house. The extreme neglect of the property. The isolation of the remaining members of the family...

They're not okay and they haven't been okay.

I saw Sullivan last night in the kitchen when we talked about our mothers. His face was the mirror image of how I feel every time I think of my mom.

Sullivan's so gorgeous and intimidating, it's like I didn't really believe he could feel pain or sorrow or hopelessness like a normal person. He seemed so untouchable.

But now I'm realizing he's just as vulnerable as me.

The thought is somewhat dizzying.

Sullivan seemed safer when I thought he was just an asshole taking advantage of me. It left me free to resent him, resist him, or scheme against him.

This is a whole lot messier.

I'm creeping down the west wing now, toward his bedroom at the end of the hall.

I hesitate, my hand outstretched toward the doorknob.

Looking in Sullivan's room seems a lot more invasive than peeking around the rest of the house. He said I could do whatever I wanted, but I'm not sure this is what he had in mind...

On the other hand, the pull to peer inside his secret space is almost irresistible. I get glimpses of the real Sullivan, but he's careful and guarded. I have to know who he really is if I'm going to trust him...don't I?

With that justification firmly in place, I crack open his bedroom door and peek inside.

Sullivan's scent rushes out. It's like uncorking a bottle of cologne, but this is the smell of his skin, his sweat, his breath, his sheets...I've caught it before, when we danced, when we kissed, when I got in his car, but now I step all the way inside his room and I'm swimming in it, taking full, deep breaths that make my head whirl.

Unlike his brother's, Sullivan's bedroom is tidy. His bed is made, the pillows fluffed and covers folded back. The only things on his nightstand are several stacked books. I'm going to have to do more than just glance around if I want to learn anything.

I cross over to the bed to examine the spines of the books. *Black Swan Events*, Steve Jobs' biography, and *Atomic Habits*...

I flip through that last one, noting that Sullivan has highlighted passages on almost every page, in multi-colored pens.

"Nerd...," I whisper, smiling to myself as I close the book, setting it back exactly where I found it.

I would not have pegged Sullivan as a dedicated highlighter. But then, he did get pretty good grades for someone who pretended not to give a shit.

Standing this close to the bed is like standing right next to Sullivan himself. I can tell which pillow he uses most often because it's flatter.

Impulsively, I pull back the covers and slide between his sheets. I put my head down on his most-used pillow and pull the blankets partway over my head.

Holy hell, it's intoxicating in here.

My head spins like I'm huffing paint.

Sullivan's scent is feral, warm, and delicious. It conjures up a flickering carousel of images: those deep, dark eyes, the slow fall of his hair before he swipes it back with his hand, the look of his forearms when he turns back his sleeves, the wicked glint of his teeth when he smiles at me...

My thighs clench together beneath the sheets.

I'm wearing an oversized T-shirt and a baggy pair of shorts.

It's easy to slip my hand beneath the waistband of those shorts and let it find its way down to where I'm warm and throbbing...

This is wrong on many levels, I'm aware of that.

I shouldn't have come into Sullivan's room. I shouldn't be lying in his bed.

But now that I am, his scent on the pillow is pure euphoria. I can breathe it in over and over without anyone knowing.

And who does it hurt, if I touch myself just a little bit?

I'm not naked, I'm not dirtying his sheets...

I'm just lightly pressing my fingers in the place that feels the best while my thighs squeeze together and my hips gently rock...

I'm barely moving at all, mostly just lying here.

And after all, Sullivan said I could do whatever I want...

I breathe in and out, eyes closed, remembering the feel of his lips against my hair, his breath tickling my ear...

Here you go, gorgeous...

He was just passing me the salt, but it set my whole body alight.

It's been a long time since someone called me a pet name or touched my hand or asked me to dance...

Is it so bad if I pretend it was real, just for a moment?

My lips part as I remember the two times we've kissed. The first time, I barely had a chance to register the warmth and softness of his mouth before it was over. The second time, as he ducked his head toward me, I braced myself, helplessly giddy with anticipation. And even then, it surprised me all over again, how a pair of lips could brush against mine for less than a second and steal all my breath.

It was a chaste kiss.

I imagine what never actually happened, his lips parting, his tongue sliding against mine...and I groan as I touch myself, my fingers wet and slippery...

I think of the way his gaze rested on my body when I said he didn't know my size.

I'm pretty sure I do...

And then I remember his flash of annoyance at Angus' hand resting on my arm...

The climax surprises me, blooming like a flower in my belly, my lungs full of the scent of Sullivan's pillow and Sullivan's sheets.

I didn't mean to go that far, but I tipped over so easily.

Once it starts, it's impossible to stop. Pleasure drenches my body. I soak it in, every last drop, until it saturates my cells and ebbs away...

Embarrassed, I slip out from under the sheets and hurriedly remake the bed, my body still flushed, head light and floating.

Wow. Haven't felt that in a while...

Well, that's good. I cleared my head. Now I can calm down and stop acting like a kid with a crush.

I have a contract with Sullivan, signed in ink.

And if the parameters of this agreement are a little unorthodox...that's all the more reason that I have to remember that *this isn't real.*

No matter how good certain things feel or what moments might arise of unexpected intimacy, Sullivan wants one thing and one thing only from me: access to Angus.

I can't let myself forget that.

Sullivan doesn't.

Any time we get too close to each other, like in the hallway or the kitchen, he breaks it off abruptly.

I need to do the same. I need to guard my boundaries like levees or the flood of Sullivan's uncanny ability to pretend to adore me will wash me away, and when this whole thing is over, I'll be left high and dry, longing for something that never existed in the first place.

Right while I'm making that commitment to myself, I'm sneaking into Sullivan's bathroom to examine his toiletries and even the medicine cabinet behind his mirror.

When I find a mouthguard inside a plastic case, I feel the funniest little zing. More evidence that the gorgeous Sullivan truly is a human being.

It really is comforting.

Lastly, I peek inside his closet, finding a small selection of high-end clothes. He owns three suits, including the one he was wearing today, and two pairs of dress shoes. That's one more than me, but still...

It seemed like Sullivan had everything in high school, like he led a charmed existence. When I met him again, he seemed to radiate confidence and success.

Now I see how fragile his life really is. His BMW is actually pretty old, even though he keeps it in such good condition. Last night, I noticed that his phone screen is cracked.

I bet he's scrambling to cover his expenses in the cutthroat LA real estate market of feast or famine. Especially if he's paying bills for his brother and his dad...

In the strangest way, it makes me more determined than ever that Sullivan is going to get this deal with Angus.

He's working hard, I can see that. And he's not as lucky as I thought.

In fact, I could almost feel bad for him.

Which is something I never thought I'd say about Sullivan Rivas.

12

THEO

The groceries arrive promptly at ten, just like Sullivan promised. It takes me twenty minutes to bring in all the bags and unload them into the fridge and pantry—he bought enough food to feed a small army.

These are not your normal groceries. This is gourmet food, the kinds of ingredients I drool over at the grocery store but can never actually afford.

I get a thrill at the sight of all those crisp, shining peppers and apples, all the bright and bloody packs of meat, loaves of uncut bread, and packs of fragrant, fancy cheeses.

I could make so many delicious things...

Sullivan's kitchen may be slightly out of date, steeped in the styles of the early 2000s, like everything in this house, but it's still large and well designed. The only problem is the shit quality of his pots and knives, clearly bought by someone who has no idea how to cook.

Those gorgeous loaves of bread and a pack of butcher's bacon help me decide what to make. I pluck tomatoes off the vine that holds them together like a six pack of soda and get started on a truly epic BLT.

With nothing to do and nowhere to go, I spend a full two hours whipping up my own homemade chipotle mayonnaise, carefully braising the bacon in brown sugar, and grilling thick slices of the multigrain bread.

I even boil a pot of oil and shoestring two massive tubers so I can make my own sweet potato fries.

When I'm finished, I've got two plates that look like they belong on the counter of an upscale diner, the sandwiches cut into triangles and speared with the type of toothpicks that has flags on the ends.

Come to think of it, a gourmet diner would be pretty cool...

My brain starts spinning with all the dishes I could make.

Fried chicken and waffles with homemade pickles, pork chops with pear sauce, and maybe some of those crazy milkshakes with outrageous garnishes like sparklers or an entire piece of cake speared on the rim...

I used to come up with restaurant ideas all the time. I'd spend my entire weekend creating pretend menus in the notebook stuffed under my bed.

But I haven't done much of that lately. I guess deep down I knew there was no point.

Now I'm feeling excited again. My brain is full of ideas, charged up and fizzing like my blood is carbonated.

I made two plates because I sort of hoped Sullivan would come home while I was cooking. But now I've got this stunning sandwich and no company in sight.

Except...

My eyes drift over to the kitchen window that looks out at the pool house.

The tiny building is still dark and motionless, covered in vines.

I keep thinking about Sullivan's dad out there.

The way Sullivan talked about us meeting, (*You won't...*), was not inviting.

But on the other hand...we live thirty feet away from each other. For this week, at least. It seems like I should introduce myself...

And who could say no to a free sandwich?

I cover the plate with an upside-down mixing bowl and carry it out into the backyard.

The jungle swallows me. This must have been an incredible garden, once—now half the trees are browning, choked in weeds, and the rose bushes look like they might be concealing Sleeping Beauty's castle.

The swimming pool is especially sad, with entire bushes growing up through cracked cement that might once have been painted blue but has chipped away to speckled gray.

The neglect of this place is almost willful.

Considering how neat Sullivan's bedroom is, I bet it bothers him.

Yet, he doesn't fix it.

Is that because he's stretched too thin, working long hours? Or because his dad won't let him?

My nervousness increases as I approach the pool house door. The house is tiny, its door Hobbit-like with a round little window and a large brass knob.

I knock softly then louder when I doubt he could have heard me.

After the second knock, the door wrenches open. I'm met with a man who looks nothing like that long-ago picture in a glossy movie magazine.

This man is a wild animal.

His sandy hair sticks up in every direction, his eyes bloodshot and his face flushed. The liquor leeching from his pores is eye watering, not to mention the smell of somebody who hasn't taken a shower yet today. Or yesterday, either, probably.

"Who the hell are you?"

The level of aggression in that question ranks somewhere between "confronting a Jehovah's Witness on your porch" and "threatening a burglar."

Meanwhile, my level of bravery is rapidly shrinking from "curious adventurer" to "grandma who got caught at Coachella." I'm regretting my decisions and I want to retreat.

"I'm Theo," I squeak. "I'm a friend of Sullivan's."

"Sullivan lives over there." He jerks his head toward the main house while he tries to close the door in my face.

I should let him. But my foot has a mind of its own—it darts out and wedges itself in the doorway.

His eyes flick down to my sneaker then back up to my face.

Sullivan's father has blue eyes, remarkably bright, like the Pacific on a sunny summer day. But if you're imagining them in any way to be gentler than his son's, think again—at this moment, with their current level of bloodshot, those eyes could belong to Cujo. And their owner looks about as pleased by my presence on his property as an actual rabid Saint Bernard.

"I'm staying with Sullivan," I babble, "because my apartment's being fumigated. I was cooking lunch. I'm a chef—I mean, usually I'm a chef, not exactly right now... But anyway, I made extra, so I thought..."

I trail off, feeling stupid.

He runs a hand back through his hair in almost exactly the same way that Sullivan does. But that's where the comparison ends because while Sullivan is impeccably groomed and wickedly charming, his father is half-dressed, unshaven, swaying slightly on his feet, and seems incapable of smiling.

In fact, judging by the deep lines carved in his forehead and etched at the edges of his mouth, I'm not sure this man has ever cracked a smile.

"So let me get this straight...," he says in a gravelly voice that sounds like he hasn't cleared his throat in about a hundred years. "You're a chef *sometimes*...but not right now...and since you made yourself lunch, you found it imperative to walk over here, bang on my door, and wake me up to tell me about it."

"Well...not just to tell you about it." I hold out the plate with its mixing-bowl dome. "I brought you some."

He regards the plate and, after a moment, allows me to place it in his hand. He kind of has to because of the way I shove it at him.

Now the mixing bowl lid looks ridiculous. I'm wishing I'd used plastic wrap instead.

So I pull it off with a flourish, trying to salvage this whole thing by saying, "Ta-da!" as I reveal the sandwich and sweet potato fries.

Sullivan's dad stares down at the plate. His face goes pale—I watch it happen, the color draining away until his eyes look almost as dark as his son's.

"Why did you make this?"

"W-what?" I stammer.

He glares at me as color floods back into his face, red as brick now and furious.

"*Who told you to make this?*"

The hand not holding the plate has clenched into a fist. He's so angry, I think he's about to fling the whole meal in my face.

"I...I'm sorry..." I stutter, stumbling back. "I didn't mean to—"

"Get out."

He doesn't have to tell me twice.

I turn tail and sprint back to the house, leaving the plate and sandwich behind because there's no way I'm going to risk taking them out of his hands.

An hour later, I'm sitting in Sullivan's kitchen, sniffling after a good, solid cry.

I do not like confrontation. Or making people upset. Especially when I'm not sure what I did wrong.

Why was Sullivan's dad suddenly so furious?

Was it just because I woke him up?

Granted, it was noon, but he wasn't expecting anybody... maybe he works nights and that was like midnight to him. I haven't even asked Sullivan what his dad does.

Maybe I should ask him right now? Maybe I should tell him what happened...it's probably better if he hears it from me before he finds out from his dad...

Usually, I'd call Martinique in this sort of situation, but I'm worried about awkward questions. She's going to wonder why Sullivan didn't introduce me to his dad in the first place, and even more, why said father wasn't informed that I exist.

Plus, it's unsatisfying asking Martinique for advice when I can't tell her what's really going on. Even the smallest fibs to my best friend make me feel like shit.

I glance at my phone, imagining Sullivan saying hello in the way he does, like we're already in the middle of a conversation, like he was just waiting for me to call...

On impulse, I snatch up the phone and press his number.

He answers on the second ring.

"Hey," he says, slightly breathless, "is everything okay?"

"Yeah," I answer automatically, though it isn't at all, "everything's great."

"Did the groceries arrive?"

"Yup—I put them in the fridge."

"Not the ice cream, I hope..."

"Ice cream's in the freezer—I learned that much at school before I dropped out."

Sullivan laughs, and it feels like someone set a heating pad on the center of my chest.

Distantly, an angry voice snarls, "*Take your time, Sullivan...*"

My shoulders stiffen, and I clutch the phone to my ear. "Do you need to go?"

"Nah," Sullivan says. "I can talk."

"*I don't have all fucking day...*"

"Are you sure?"

"Trust me," he says, and I hear shoes against pavement as he walks a little farther away, "it's better if he has a minute to cool off. We're not quite seeing eye to eye on this deal."

"Sounds like your job's about as fun as mine."

Sullivan's chuckle is a fingertip stroking down my spine.

"You're not the only one trying to climb out of the shit, Theo."

I've never particularly loved my name—it's boyish, and the only famous Theodore is that chubby little chipmunk. Plus, Teddy Roosevelt, I guess.

The point is, only one person has ever made my name sound sexy.

Sullivan says *Theo* with an intoxicating intimacy, like he knows everything about me, like we've always been friends.

Even though that isn't true at all.

We've never been friends. We're still not—this is a business arrangement.

But if we were to become friends...that might not be so bad.

Sullivan may be arrogant and demanding, with morals that are cinderblock gray, but he's also funny and surprisingly considerate.

It's the little things, like the way he picked up as soon as I called and how he's talking to me right now while that asshole in the background taps his toe...

He brought me breakfast and the prettiest swimsuit I've ever worn. He offered me a place to stay without hesitation and ordered gourmet groceries for my amusement...

Sullivan treats me like a friend.

I value that highly because I haven't had many.

I like the way he says my name. And I feel better now that I've called him even though I haven't told him what happened yet.

In fact, I'm wondering if I should mention it at all. If Sullivan's already having a bad day, he doesn't need any more drama from me. I can tell him what happened later, when he gets home.

"I didn't know you were in the shit," I admit. "I thought your life was perfect."

Sullivan's laugh carries a slight edge. "Is that why you never liked me?"

I'm glad he can't see my face right now—I guarantee it's flaming red.

"Who said I didn't like you?"

"Theo..." His voice is low and stern. "I can tell."

"Don't be ridiculous. We hardly knew each other."

That's technically true but false in every way that matters. My brain floods with a hundred times I saw Sullivan in hallways and classrooms and across a crowded gym. Our circles rarely overlapped because his was everyone who mattered and mine was me and a few other misfits.

But there was hardly a day when I didn't think about Sullivan Rivas.

There's always been a thread between us, invisible, but tugging at me all the same—eye contact that lasted a little too long. A few words in passing that made my heart beat harder for days...

I was watching him.

And it sounds like sometimes...he was watching me.

"I always wondered what was going on inside that head of

yours," Sullivan says. "You were so quiet. But you were always reading, writing, drawing something..."

"You intimidated me," I admit. "I was afraid of you."

My stomach twists as I remember prom night—when I saw the ugliest side of Sullivan.

"I was an asshole," he says baldly.

"Maybe a little..." *Or a whole hell of a lot...* "But you're not so bad now."

"You think so?" I can hear his smile, and that makes me see it in my mind, that flash of wicked white in his deeply tanned face. "Well, you can be the first member of my fan club. I get jealous of Reese."

In the background, I hear Sullivan's irritable companion shouting something. It sounds like, *Get your fucking ass over here or I'm leaving...*

"I don't think *he's* going to join."

Sullivan laughs. "Not a chance—especially not after I tell him the final offer from my client."

"I should let you go..."

"Probably," he says, never questioning why I called in the first place. "But know this, Theo—I'm not spending all my Sundays like this. We're getting out of the shit. You and me, together."

Now that heat in my chest is like a head-to-toe blanket, fresh out of the dryer. I'm wrapped in the warmth of his words.

Sullivan is better than a friend.

He's a partner.

And I haven't had one of those...pretty much ever.

When I hang up the phone, I look around the kitchen. I haven't cleaned up the dirty dishes from lunch, so I can still see the greasy bacon pan and scattered toothpicks—remnants of the offensive BLT.

But instead of viewing it as evidence of my failure, another example of how I always manage to fuck things up, I hear Sullivan's voice in my head:

We're getting out of the shit...You and me, together...

I shove my mistake to the back of my mind, replacing it with images of exactly what that future might look like.

I imagine retro vinyl booths, an old-fashioned jukebox, maybe some pin-up posters on the walls...

The ingredients spread across the countertops become vibrant and alive once more, like they're calling to me, like they're begging me to take them in my hands and shape them into something new...

Instead of failure, I see opportunity.

And I retie my apron and get to work.

RIVAS
CALIFORNIA
LOS ANGELES

13

SULLY

It takes several more hours to close out one of the most obnoxious deals of my life. The way this guy's going back and forth on every last tedious detail makes me want to take him up to the top floor of the building to show him the view then give him a good, hard shove.

When he finally puts pen to paper to sign the lease, I text Theo to let her know I'll be home soon, but it's 8:00 p.m. before I actually pull into the driveway.

Since it's Sunday night, I expect to find her kicking back in sweatpants with a glass of wine, watching TV or enjoying a good book, if she's even home at all.

Instead, I walk into what looks like an epic ten-course dinner in progress. Theo has dozens of pots and pans and bowls spread across the stove and countertops, several still boiling and bubbling away, the air full of the mingled scents of sweet and savory.

Theo herself is whirling like a windstorm. She's got an apron cinched around her waist and her hair twisted up in a knot on her head, with a streak of something dark across her cheek. Her face is flushed and dewy, her eyes bright and manic.

"Oh, good, you're here!" she cries. "Try this!"

She pops a spoon in my mouth.

Usually, I'm opposed to being fed, stemming back to the time when Reese offered me a spoonful of peanut butter that turned out to be Vegemite. However, whatever Theo just put in my mouth is a revelation.

"What is *that*?" I ask when I can speak again.

"My country brunch skillet," Theo says proudly. "What do you think?"

"I think pour it into a bowl and then pour that bowl into my mouth."

Theo laughs delightedly. "Oh, I've got way more than that for you to try!"

She takes me on a tour of my own kitchen, showing off the fruits of her labors.

"So here we've got a brisket grilled cheese, and those are quail egg sliders...try this, they're jalapeño poppers with Mexican chorizo...and that's smoked caramel apple pie with homemade ice cream..."

It might be the best homecoming of my life. I'm ravenous after a day on my feet where I only had time to grab a single greasy slice of pizza from a street vendor eight hours ago. My stomach is howling just from the smell, and as soon as Theo starts feeding me samples of her creations, I'm completely undone, stuffing my face with both hands.

"Oh my god! What did you say was in this?"

"Brisket!" she says gleefully. "Do you like it?"

"Theo," I say with utmost sincerity, "it's like I was on prison rations my whole life. Until I met you, I don't think I even knew what food was."

She laughs, even while she shakes her head. "You're just being nice."

I toss one of the jalapeño poppers in my mouth, crunching down on the fiesta of spice. "I'm many things, but none of them are nice."

"Tell me your favorites!" she demands as I sample each dish.

"How am I supposed to pick favorites?" I take a massive bite off a wedge of apple pie then demolish two of the sliders. "That's like trying to pick between the Mona Lisa and the Last Supper."

Theo bounces with pleasure. "You really like them?"

"Can't you see how much I'm eating?"

I'm going to gain ten pounds if Theo stays with me for a week.

Not to mention, I haven't come home to a lit-up house and a warm meal in...too goddamn long. I better not get used to this.

"What's all this for?" I ask, setting down my fork.

"It was an idea I had this afternoon," Theo explains. "For an upscale diner. I was experimenting with the kinds of dishes I could make..."

She shows me the menu she's written out in her adorable curly script on a spare sheet of paper. I can see she's already tweaked a few of the dishes based off her efforts today, scratching out ingredients and making notes in the margins.

"What made you think of a diner?"

"There was this place my mom and I used to visit in Old Hollywood. It was a 50s style restaurant, only the owner was Cantonese, so there were all these cool twists on the menu—warm pineapple buns and congee with bacon and eggs...that sort of thing. When I was making BLTs for lunch, I started thinking what twists I could put on diner food if I wanted to make it fancy..."

"I love BLTs." I pick up my fork once more so I can steal another bite of that country skillet. One bite turns to six as I shovel potatoes directly from the cast-iron skillet into my mouth.

"I don't think your dad does," Theo says ruefully.

I lower the pan, my stomach sinking. "What do you mean?"

"Well..." Theo grimaces. "I brought a plate over for your dad. But he got really upset."

"Oh, shit..."

"I'm sorry—I shouldn't have woken him up."

"It's not that." I set the skillet gently back on the stove.

"What is it?" Theo bites at her lip. "What did I do wrong?"

"Nothing." I shake my head. "It's just bad luck. BLTs were the only thing my mom knew how to make."

"Oh..." Theo's hands drop to her sides and her shoulders slump.

"She was a great actress but a terrible cook. She'd even burn the shit out of the bacon, but my dad didn't care." My throat tightens so the words come out slightly squeezed. "He thought everything she did was...absolutely perfect."

"Oh my god. He must have thought I made it on purpose... here you go, your wife's favorite meal." Theo covers her face with her hands.

"I'll talk to him." I take a step toward the back kitchen door, but Theo blocks my way, both palms on my chest.

I look down at her hands and she drops them hastily. "Please don't do that—I really don't want you to say anything; it wasn't that big a deal."

"Was he rude to you?"

"No!" she cries, obviously lying. "No, no, he just..." She's backing toward the door, making sure I can't get past her. "I must have surprised him."

I shift in place, wondering how much I should say.

"It's my fault. I told him you were staying here, but he was—" *(drunk)* "—tired at the time."

"Right, yes, totally get it...," Theo says, her back pressed against the door, her body a barricade, "but I shouldn't have gone over there and woken him up."

We face off, all the words unspoken swirling in the air. Theo isn't stupid, she knows what's going on.

"It's probably best if you don't visit him," I say at last. "He's not doing very well."

That's the understatement of the decade.

But Theo gets it.

"Of course. I'll just let him have his space."

"Thank you." I let out a breath that releases the pressure in my chest. "Thanks for understanding."

Theo nods. After a moment, she says quietly, "My dad used to drink. Before he left us."

I give a quick jerk of my chin, acknowledging reality, even while my heart rejects that my dad could be anything like hers.

"My dad wouldn't leave us. And I'm not leaving him."

Theo gazes at me steadily, unblinking, unjudging. "Is that why you're doing all this?"

The gesture of her small hands seems to encompass my expensive suit and worn shoes, the clock on the wall revealing the lateness of the hour, and Theo herself, living in my house as part of this elaborate plan.

"Yes," I say simply and firmly. "I'm going to pay off what's left on the house so my dad always has it, even if he's drowning at the bottom of a bottle. I'm going to keep floating Reese when he's between paychecks, even if he's down to singing telegrams. I'm going to make enough money that I won't give a shit the next time someone calls me Rocko Rocks because I'll be laughing all the way to the bank. And I'm going to get you your restaurant, Theo, whether it's a diner or a fancy French chateau, because I may not be nice, but what I am is relentless. I don't give up. I don't quit. And I don't go back on my word."

"I believe you," Theo says softly. "And you can believe in me. We're in this together."

It's not hard to believe in Theo with the evidence of her genius all around me. Not to mention, sitting in my stomach.

And even though I know she's repeating back what I said to her, it feels good to hear it.

I'm not alone. Not right now.

"Good," I say. "Then give me another piece of that pie 'cause it's the best thing that happened to me all day."

The warm, buttery pie truly is exceptional.

But as Theo heaps another slice on my plate, I can't help thinking that the real best part of my day, the moment that shone brightest, was when Theo opened the door, face flushed with steam, that dark streak under one eye.

"What are you smiling about?" she says.

"You look like a baseball player."

Theo peeks in the closest mirror and squawks with annoyance.

"Why didn't you tell me I have grease on my face?"

I didn't tell her because I didn't want her to wash it off, which is exactly what she does, scrubbing with a cloth until she's clean again.

14

THEO

Sullivan insists on driving me to work Monday morning, despite the fact that my car is running just fine.

"It's not that I'm complaining," I say, sinking into his plush leather passenger seat. "God knows I've always wanted my own chauffeur. But I don't quite understand how this will help us?"

Sullivan starts the engine and pulls smoothly onto the road.

"Let me ask you something, Theo...what do you think Angus wants?"

"To go to Mars," I say at once.

Everybody knows that.

"But what else?" Sullivan says.

I shrug, guessing, "I don't know—maybe a girlfriend who's not just using him for his money? Or a family member who hasn't sued him...or electrolysis on his back? He's got everything else."

"Exactly," Sullivan says with strange satisfaction. "And that's why he's fucking miserable."

"Miserable!" I scoff. "It's me who's miserable. Angus is living the dream."

"Dreams don't satisfy," Sullivan says. "It's pursuit that drives us. Angus is so goddamned bored that he's looking for a whole other planet to entertain him."

"Angus has always been obsessed with Mars."

"Maybe," Sullivan says, changing lanes. "Or maybe it's the one thing he can't buy with a swipe of his credit card. People want what they can't have...The best way to make Angus desperately want my land is to make him think he can't have it."

"And how are you going to do that?"

Sullivan takes his eyes off the road to give me a maddening smile. "You'll see."

HE DROPS me off at work without even attempting to manufacture a meeting with Angus. At this rate, Sullivan should close his deal in about two hundred years.

Unfortunately for us, Angus isn't going to wait that long.

I've hardly stepped inside before he shouts, "Theo! Hope you brought comfy shoes—we've got properties to walk."

I did not bring comfy shoes—why would I? Everyone but Angus dresses in standard office wear. However, I *do* have a pair of sneakers stashed under my desk because isn't the first time Angus has sprung an outdoor adventure on me.

While I'm swapping out my paint-spattered stilettos, Martinique pokes her head into my phonebooth-sized office.

"Did Sullivan drop you off at work?"

"Yes," I say carefully.

"What's wrong?" She gives me a sneaky side-eye. "Couldn't drive yourself after your all-night fuck fest?"

"Martinique!" I pull her inside and close the door. "Don't say fuck fest at the office; you've already gotten two warnings from HR."

"*Pfft.*" She flaps her hand dismissively. "Only one of those was valid."

"It wasn't valid when you slapped our accountant on the ass?"

Martinique shrugs. "I thought she was you—that was the day she dyed her hair. Well, actually, probably the day after...I'm assuming she didn't dye it in the morning. Anyway, quit changing the subject—why are we talking about uptight Leanne-from-accounting when we could be discussing *Sullivan*?"

She says his name like it has eight syllables and several different tones.

I can tell I'm already blushing, though not for the reason Martinique thinks.

"It's really not like that," I say, wondering how I'm going to make it through even one day of this. "We haven't been dating that long."

"Wait..." Martinique tilts her head to the side so her glossy dark bob almost touches one shoulder. "Are you saying you haven't slept with him yet?"

"Uh..." *Why in the hell didn't I practice answering these questions before I came into work?* "Not exactly."

"*WHAT?*" Martinique shrieks.

I press my finger into my ear.

"How is that possible?" she demands. "I wouldn't have made it past the first date. Like, if he swiped right on me on Tinder, I'd show up to dinner in lingerie and heels."

"That's because you've had more boyfriends than Taylor Swift." I chew the edge of my lip. "Sullivan intimidates me."

"Even though he's obviously crazy about you?" Martinique nudges her elbow into my ribs. "Come on...I saw the way he was looking at you on the yacht."

I know Sullivan was faking, but a hot little coal ignites in my chest all the same. Martinique is as sharp-eyed as a hawk. She notices things.

"And he tried to drown Angus for you," she reminds me. "I would have fucked his brains out for that alone."

"I was tempted."

"Then what are you waiting for?"

Martinique smiles at me, her dark eyes bright and expectant.

I wish, I wish, I wish I could just tell her the truth. Then I could get her real advice. But Sullivan made me promise that, above all, I wouldn't spill the beans to Martinique.

For good reason—she's about as contained as a sieve. Martinique is speak first, think later

So all I say is, "I want everything to be right."

"Take your time, then, but remember...," she raises a warning finger, "a guy like that isn't used to waiting."

"Theo!" Angus pounds on my office door. "Shake a leg! I've got the car pulled up out front!"

I stuff my shoes into my purse.

"Gotta go," I say to Martinique.

But when I open the door, instead of Angus' impatient face, I'm met with a delivery driver holding a double armful of lavender roses.

"Theo Mahoney?" he says.

The scent of fresh blooms fills my office. The bouquet takes up almost my entire desk as he sets the vase down next to my computer.

The card is a scrap of folded paper, nestled in the stems—

Missing you already
—S

"See?" Martinique says triumphantly. "Completely obsessed."

I don't think these flowers have anything to do with me. But as I look across the office, I can see they're having a hell of an effect on Angus. He's pacing near the exit, agitated, glancing back at the outrageously oversized bouquet at least three times.

Why does it bother him?

He never cared when I was dating Trent.

But then, Trent never sent me a hundred purple roses.

Clearly, I don't understand male psychology.

Sullivan does. He's burrowing under Angus' skin like a tick. Eating away at him.

As soon as we climb in the car together, Angus says, "You two must have had quite the weekend."

I'm sure I look guilty, though not for the reason Angus thinks. I mutter, "Sullivan's very thoughtful."

Angus is driving too fast, taking the turns hard enough that my shoulder presses against the passenger-side door. He always drives that way, so it has nothing to do with the flowers. But there's an edge to his voice when he says, "I saw he dropped you off this morning."

"Yup."

Angus jerks across two lanes without using his blinker.

"You're not moving in with him permanently, are you? Six months isn't very long to make that kind of decision."

That's rich coming from Angus, who's already been married and divorced three times, none of those nuptials lasting longer than a year.

His hypocrisy irritates me enough to say, "I don't know—Sullivan's got a huge place, and you know what a shithole my apartment is." Then, to really turn the screws, I add, "Plus, it's closer to the office. I know how much you hate when I'm late."

Angus' knuckles tighten on the wheel. "So, it's getting serious?"

He really won't let this drop.

I sneak a glance at him, heat creeping up my neck. Usually, on a drive like this, Angus would be nattering away about work shit, all the things he expects me to do, and all his brilliant plans he wants complimented.

Instead, he's edgy and agitated, picking at this boyfriend thing like a scab.

Is Sullivan right? Could this actually work?

Recklessly, I say, "Yeah, it's pretty serious. Sullivan's incredible —so considerate and attentive. He's really smart, too. Like the smartest person I've ever met."

I knew that one would hurt. Angus likes to believe he's the smartest person *anybody's* ever met.

His jaw tightens, and he takes a turn that makes the wheels screech. "Is that right?"

"Oh, yeah..." I'm really laying it on thick. "He could be on Jeopardy. Every time we watch it, he knows all the answers first."

Angus loves Jeopardy. He cried when Alex Trebek died.

A dull, brick-colored flush blooms beneath his tan. He looks so angry, I'm wondering if I crossed the line.

But then he says, "Well, if it's that serious, I better get to know him. Why don't we all go for dinner this weekend?"

"Sure." I turn to look out the window so Angus won't catch my smile.

ANGUS and I visit a property out in Irvine that includes some fifty acres of undeveloped land. It has most of the things Angus needs in terms of square footage and access to utilities, but he seems distracted and irritated throughout the tour.

He's snappy with Corgus, who keeps trying to sing the praises of the developer without noticing that Angus isn't listening to a word he says.

"What do you think, Theo?" Corgus says to me at last, out of pure desperation.

I glance over at Angus, trying to imagine what Sullivan would say.

If I talk shit on this place, it will be too obvious, and it will make Corgus mad. This one is his pick—that's why he trotted it out first.

But if I agree that it's perfect, Angus might buy it on the spot, and then Sullivan won't get the chance to make his pitch.

Thinking fast, I say, "I love it! I'm surprised Jeff Bezos passed."

"He did?" Angus is instantly engaged. He has a love-hate fixation with the one man on the planet whose net worth eclipses his own.

Awkwardly, Corgus says, "He looked at it briefly for an Amazon facility, but I don't think there was any serious consideration..."

He shoots me a filthy look, but I already plastered a sweetly innocent expression across my face.

"Well, he was a fool to let it go!" I say cheerfully. "One man's trash is another man's treasure."

"Hm," Angus says, lips pursed.

I think if he turned his back right now, Corgus would strangle me.

Luckily, Angus doesn't turn his back.

"Come on, Theo," he says. "We'll keep this one on the list."

As we stroll away from Corgus, I'm practically bouncing.

Turns out, I can be sneaky, too.

15

THEO

By the time Angus and I are done with our real estate safari, it's well past six o'clock.

"I'll drop you off at your place," he says with smug satisfaction.

"Sullivan's place," I remind him.

"Right, that's what I meant."

When we pull up in front of the house, I get to see my own surprise and confusion of a few days before repeated on Angus' face.

Except now, somehow, I find it offensive.

"What the hell happened to this place?" Angus snorts.

I know that's exactly what *I* thought, but when he says it, he sounds like a judgmental asshole.

Angus has no idea what happened here.

And I'm not going to tell him.

"I think Sullivan's flipping it."

The lie comes out easier than ever. In fact, it's a little disturbing how quickly I'm getting good at this.

It's not that I'm embarrassed of Sullivan's house—not at all.

Actually, the longer I stay here, the more I'm coming to like it. But I can't stand that look on Angus' face—like he's so goddamned superior.

Sullivan's only here because he cares about his dad. That, I know for certain.

I see it burning in his face, his defense of the people he loves.

I used to feel exactly the same, when I had somebody to love.

I'm not going to let anyone look down their nose at Sullivan and what he's managed to protect.

"See you tomorrow," I tell Angus, closing the car door in his face.

I already texted Sullivan to let him know I wouldn't need him to pick me up.

As soon as I walk inside, I can tell that I beat him home. The house has a stale silence that can only mean I'm alone.

Starved from missing lunch, I head straight to the kitchen and start pulling things out of the fridge. I go full werewolf when I see the steaks, stomach growling and mouth instantly drooling.

I fire up the grill on the back porch, chopping up veggies and skewering them on bamboo sticks, brushing pineapple wedges in butter and brown sugar.

Cooking in Sullivan's kitchen is a blast—so much more fun than in my tiny apartment. It's a pleasure to spread everything out on the countertops, to use his matching set of bowls, practically untouched.

I play some music on the speaker, "High" by Stephen Sanchez because that's how I'm feeling right now.

The stress of the day falls away. I spin around in all that space, sashaying across the aisleways of that big, bright kitchen.

I can take all the time in the world with these lovely ingredients at my fingertips...

If paradise is having everything you desire, exactly the way you want it, then for the next hour, I'm in paradise.

I get the neat little hibachi smoking. Soon the scent of grilled meat and caramelized pineapple drifts across the yard.

Sullivan comes out the back door, sniffing the air like one of those cartoon characters carried along by a delicious smell.

I light up when I see him. I'm like a kid, proud of what I have to show and tell—all this food and good news as well.

He flashes his bright white smile at me. "Theo, if you keep this up, I'm never going to let you go..."

Promises, promises.

"I'm not going anywhere." I pop a piece of pineapple in my mouth. "I'm moving into your fridge."

It would be a crime to leave before I sample those mission figs. Or that espresso cheese...

I hold out the last cube of pineapple to Sullivan. This is the most perfect piece. You can tell when I hold it up to the sun—every cell is saturated with golden juice.

His mouth shocks me, swooping in to snatch it off my fingers. I gasp at the sudden warmth of his lips around my fingertips.

All my insides go liquid and my thighs press together, sudden and hot. Why does that happen, where one thing feels like another? My face burns.

Sullivan crushes the pineapple against the roof of his mouth with his tongue. His whole face lights up, and heat bursts in my chest like a firework.

"Well, if that's not the best goddamned pineapple I ever ate..."

"You bought it."

"I'm great at buying food." He winks at me. "What I need is someone to make sure I don't ruin it."

Why does he flirt with me at home?

Maybe he can't turn it off.

It's like asking a bird not to fly or a bee not to sting. Sullivan is sexy.

I am not.

I'm too awkward. And too honest.

"It's pretty hard to ruin a rib eye." I lift the lid to give them a flip, taking several swift, smoky breaths while I have the chance.

How does it feel cooler over here by the grill?

"And yet, somehow I manage." Sullivan shoots me a mischievous look. "That being said…would you like some help?"

I can't help but laugh. It's his delivery—the way he knows he's outrageous. "After that endorsement? How could I say no?"

"I think I can be trusted…under the supervision of a professional."

I am a professional. A goddamned professional.

I will channel my inner Gordon Ramsay. He wouldn't put up with Sullivan's shit.

"Wash your hands, then, and grab an apron."

Leaving the grill, I follow Sullivan into the kitchen.

Sullivan did not own any aprons before my arrival, so he grabs one of the two I brought with me. Unfortunately for him, it's the apron my mom sewed for me when I first started cooking, so it's pink and frilly. Give me a break, I was only eight at the time.

"Pink's your color," I tease.

"Is it?" He turns to shake his booty at me. "I was afraid it was a bit revealing."

His butt is, of course, covered by his trousers, but with the apron tied around his waist, it's framed in a way that makes it impossible to ignore the fact that Sullivan Rivas has a fantastic ass.

When he turns around again, my eyes are still staring down. It's incredibly obvious as I drag them back up again. Sullivan laughs at me.

This is outrageous. I'm supposed to be the chef here.

"Quit flashing that thing around and get to work. Can you chop a tomato?"

"Sure." Sullivan grins. "If you don't mind bits of finger in it."

I slide the knife out of the block. "You're making me nervous..."

He comes close to take it from my hand.

"Am I?" he growls right by my ear.

His hand rests heavy over mine. His breath slips down the neck of my shirt. All the little hairs stand up on my arm, and I know he can see it.

Sullivan never plays fair.

I watch him cut through the tomato, which takes more effort than it should because his knives are dull.

His technique is awful. I have to fix it, it's painful to watch.

"Like this..." I put my hand over his, on top of the handle. "With a chef's knife, you want to rock the blade..."

Sullivan already took off his suit jacket and tossed it over the back of a chair. His body heat pumps through his thin dress shirt like it's tissue, like it's not even there.

His scent mixes with the smell of grilled meat and sweet pineapple. I must still be in werewolf mode because my mouth is watering...

I think of his bed, of the exact feel of his sheets.

I remember how it felt, to be wrapped in his scent...

If Sullivan keeps driving me to work, when can I sneak back in there?

God, I'm such a fucking pervert.

He wouldn't sneak into my room. He's a gentleman.

Or is he?

His ass presses against my hips. Somehow our bodies have aligned all the way down, my arm curved around his back.

It feels like when we were dancing, like the sensation doesn't stop in my body but extends all the way through his hand. Two moving like one. The feeling is addictive—birds crave it. Butterflies, too. The invisible line between two living things...

My chin rests on his shoulder, his thick, black hair soft against my cheek.

All I can smell is his scent. If he turned his head, our mouths would meet...

I let go and take a step back, drawing in breath. It's too hot in the kitchen; I'm getting dizzy.

Sullivan gazes at me with those deep, dark eyes.

I stepped back but not very far. I'm still close enough to see his black and tangled lashes and the bits of gold dancing in all that darkness. His face swoops closer while the rest of the kitchen blurs with steam. *What steam? I don't even have a pot boiling!*

"You're a good teacher." His voice is low and husky. It has a texture, it rasps across my skin...

My heart is beating so hard, there's no way he can't hear it in the quiet kitchen, in the long silence stretching between us.

I say, "What are you doing?"

Sullivan tilts his head, smiling. "I'm not doing anything."

"Yes, you are."

He raises his eyebrows in a way that's supposed to look innocent but doesn't fool me for a second...I know he's only amused.

"What am I doing?"

"You're..." *How can I say this without sounding stupid?* "...cutting the tomatoes sexy."

Yup. There it is.

Sullivan repeats it so I can hear from his lips just how stupid I sound:

"I'm...*cutting the tomatoes sexy?*"

I cross my arms over my chest.

"Yes."

His lips twitch but he smothers the smile. "Why would I do that?"

"Because you like messing with me. You like knowing..." *Say it, you pussy...* "...that I'm attracted to you."

Sullivan steps a little closer, dropping his chin slightly so we stare eye-to-eye.

"Well, that's a problem, Theo. What are we going to do about this? Because I have to tell you...I'm attracted to you, too."

What?

I suck in tiny, baby breaths.

I thought, maybe, sometimes...he might be. A little bit. To parts of me.

But right now, Sullivan is not looking like he's attracted to parts of me. He's looking like he wants to eat me up like a whole, entire meal. Like he's starving to do it.

And that feels extremely dangerous.

Because what I want...and what's actually good for me...are two opposite things.

Each beat of my heart feels like the squeeze of a fist.

"We're not going to do anything...that would be a disaster."

"Really?" Sullivan says mildly. "How come?"

"Because this isn't real. We're not dating. And if we have sex—"

"What?" He's standing very close again, our bodies almost touching. His large hand reaches out, fingertips grazing the curve of my hip. "What terrible thing will happen if we have sex?"

Nothing.

Everything.

"I'll get hurt."

I say it quietly, barely more than a whisper. But Sullivan snatches back his hand.

"You're right," he says. "I was being greedy."

Even that word...*greedy*...feels like teeth on the nape of my neck. My knees get weak and wobbly.

I cannot have sex with Sullivan Rivas, no matter how badly I'm tempted. Because I know myself. I'm not a casual person—

I've only had sex with four people in my whole entire life, and every one of them was a serious boyfriend.

I've never divorced sex from emotion, and now is not the time to try because I'm already completely out of control when it comes to Sullivan. When he's around, I get hot and cold flashes like I'm menopausal. I say things I shouldn't say. He convinces me to do things I never thought I would do.

Sullivan has probably had sex with a million people. He probably views it like sharing a stick of gum.

It wouldn't matter to him if we had sex, it wouldn't change anything.

But for me, it would be stripping off the last bits of my armor. And my armor around Sullivan is already weak—wet cardboard weak, limp spaghetti noodle weak.

I have to protect myself.

So I cross my arms over my chest and say, "We can't have sex." Telling myself as much as him.

Sullivan sighs. He picks up the knife once more, pressing it against the skin of a fresh tomato. "It's true...we shouldn't have sex."

That's what I just said, and yet, somehow, I'm disappointed.

I flee back to the Hibachi to bathe my face in smoke.

Stop it, you idiot. You're embarrassing yourself.

This attraction to Sullivan is not going away. In fact, it's getting worse.

I never felt this way about Trent, and we dated for over a year.

I liked Trent. The sex was decent. But I never obsessed over him. I never snuck glances at him, or took slow, shallow breaths of his scent, or swooned every time he ran his fingers through his hair...

This is some kind of juju.

A level of attraction that's quite inconvenient, actually.

Even now, I can't stop watching Sullivan through the kitchen window. I can't take my eyes off him chopping our salad.

What is it? Why does my whole body ache just from the shape of his shoulders? What is it about the proportions of this man, the way he stands, the way he tilts his head, the angle of his jaw, that calls to me, that whispers, *This one and no other...*

Already, his motion is smoother, the knife gripped just right. He's a fast learner.

His sleeves are rolled to the elbow. Each movement sends ripples up his arms, vein and muscle and smooth, brown skin...

A droplet of sweat slides down between my breasts and drops sizzling on the grill.

Sullivan glances up, our eyes meeting through the window. He's not mad about what I said—he smiles like I never said it at all, the right side of his mouth quirking up a little more than the left.

His crooked smile is his only flaw.

Of course, it's not a flaw at all.

It's what makes his smile exactly what it is—my favorite.

Instead of smiling back like a normal person, I duck my head like I just got caught.

My favorite?

No, no, no, no, no.

Sullivan cannot be your favorite anything.

Because you don't get to keep him. And you can't take another loss.

There it is. Plain as day. I didn't want to say it, but I have to.

You're a fucking mess, Theo, and you can't take another hit. For once in your life, protect yourself...

I sneak another glance at Sullivan.

He's frowning slightly, testing his new chopping technique on a carrot. As he concentrates, the tip of his tongue touches the center of his lower lip.

The smell of charring peppers reminds me of what I'm actually supposed to be doing.

"Shit!" I start flipping skewers as fast as I can.

The door to the pool house opens. Sullivan's father emerges, coming out into the fading twilight, blinking like it's full sun.

He's slightly better groomed than yesterday, in the sense that his hair is only half as messy and his eyes are less bloodshot. But his clothes still look like something picked rumpled off the floor, and his stubble is on its way to a full-blown beard.

As he stalks across the yard, I consider fleeing back into the kitchen. Staying put is more of a deer-in-the-headlights reaction than actual bravery.

"Theo, right?" he says when he reaches me.

"Y-yes..."

He's not smiling, not even a little bit. His blue eyes are coyote-pale and just as wild. I'm expecting him to shout at me again.

Instead, his mouth makes a twitching movement, a kind of painful grimace, and he grunts, "Sorry about the other day."

I can tell what it cost him to get that out.

He's like me...a sad, open book. That no one wants to read.

"It was my fault." I'll say anything to make his face less somber. "I shouldn't have woken you up."

"I ate the sandwich." He says it grudgingly. "After you left." Then, even more grudging: "It was the best BLT I ever had."

"Really?" Relief makes my bones go liquid. "I'm glad you liked it."

I really am glad. Food is magic, it feeds the body and the soul. That's why loneliness feels like huger.

Sullivan grins, coming out the back door. "Smelled those steaks grilling and figured you better apologize?"

His dad huffs, "I was going to apologize either way." Then admits, "The steaks moved up the timeline."

He watches me top each rib eye with a pat of butter.

Sullivan looks way more like his mom than his dad when it comes to coloring. She was sloe-eyed, coal haired, bronze skinned like him, while his dad has that shaggy surfer hair you only seem to see on men born and raised in California, with those eerie blue eyes.

But when he watches me, he looks just like his son.

It's that stare that blazes all the way through me. When they each fold their arms over their chests and lean back against the nearest tree, Sullivan could have another twin.

"Theo's staying with us for the week," Sullivan reminds his dad.

"I remember." *Doubtful.* "I'm Merrick, by the way." He pushes off the tree trunk and steps forward to shake my hand.

"Nice to meet you, Merrick." I grip his palm, which is rough and calloused. "Formally."

I feel a little awkward calling him Merrick, but "Mr. Rivas" would sound even worse.

Especially since Sullivan's dad doesn't look very old. He's battered and weary, but he must have had kids young—I doubt he's even fifty.

"So, are you two...?" Merrick lets the question hang.

"We're just friends," Sullivan calmly states.

I shoot him a look—I was under the impression that we were pretending to date in front of *everybody,* just to be safe.

Sullivan receives my look with a small smile that means...I have no idea what. I guess that we'll talk about it later?

"Okay," Merrick says, like he doesn't believe us.

Or maybe he doesn't care. His eyes have slipped away from us, toward the house. He's staring at the windows of the east wing, where he had his bedroom with his wife. With a jolt, I realize that you can see the portrait of Stella Rivas through the window, like she's gazing back at us.

"Where do you want to eat?" Sullivan asks me, as I transfer the rib eyes from grill to platter with a set of tongs.

Merrick steps down from the porch, like he's already planning to head back to the pool house.

Thinking fast, I say, "I hoped we could eat out here—it's such a gorgeous night."

I nod toward the ancient picnic table with its splintering bench seats.

Sullivan gives it a dubious look. It's covered in weeds.

But Merrick steps forward and starts ripping off the vines snaking up its legs.

"I'll get candles," Sullivan says, ducking back inside the house. He emerges a moment later with a motley assortment of half-melted stubs and lights them quickly as the sun sinks below the fence line.

I carry the platters out to the table, the pineapple wedges beautifully browned in their brown sugar glaze, the veggie skewers turned so the slightly charred side is hidden underneath.

Sullivan triumphantly places his salad on the table.

"I made that," he informs his father.

"Good to know," his dad grunts. "So I can avoid it."

"Theo supervised."

"How closely?"

"Close enough to know there aren't any bits of finger in it." I smile at Sullivan, dishing up an extra-large helping of salad as a vote of confidence.

Sullivan and his father totally ignore the salad and attack everything I made.

I laugh. "Aren't you even going to try it?"

"If I have room after the good stuff." Sullivan's mouth is full of steak.

"Sully's a carnivore," Merrick remarks. "Wouldn't eat anything green for the first ten years of his life."

Sully.

I like that. It suits him.

Or at least, this part of him.

Sullivan smiles at his dad. "I hope I've matured a bit since then."

"Oh yeah?" Merrick eyes the bits of pepper Sullivan pulled off his skewer and pushed to the side.

"Peppers don't count. But look…" Sullivan grabs a cube of cucumber out of the salad and tosses it in his mouth. "Impressed?"

I snort. "You showed him."

Merrick is suspicious of the pineapple wedges. "Hot pineapple?"

"It's good," Sullivan assures him.

His dad takes an experimental bite. Then heaps his plate.

Sullivan laughs though he's also offended. "You never take thirds of anything *I* make!"

Merrick scoffs, "Neither do you! How'd you come up with this, Theo?"

I tell Merrick the truth. "I had it at one of those Brazilian grills once—you know where they bring meat on skewers to your table? They only brought the pineapple by once, and that was the best thing in the whole place. So I had to figure out how to make it myself."

"Where'd you get the recipe?"

"No recipe—I just gave it a go for the first time today."

"Theo's really talented," Sullivan says.

"I can tell." Merrick shovels up his food like he hasn't eaten in a month. Maybe he hasn't—his clothes hang on him like he used to be bigger.

"What do you do, Mr—Merrick?" I stumble a little over his name.

He pretends like he doesn't notice. "I used to be a stunt man."

"That's how my parents met," Sullivan explains.

Merrick's eyes flick back toward the house. It's too dark to see inside the bedroom anymore, but I know as well as he does that the portrait's still there.

Stella Rivas is always close in this house. It's like Merrick lives next to her tomb.

And Sullivan lives inside of it.

I swallow the thickness in my throat. "How'd you get into that?"

Merrick doesn't answer, but then I see he's being polite, wiping his mouth with a paper napkin before he speaks.

"I was a race car driver first. But not quite good enough to make it to the top. I took a few precision-driving roles on film sets to make ends meet. One day the stunt guy they hired to jump off a roof didn't show up. So I said, I'll give it a go."

"You're brave." All the blood drains from my head just picturing that scenario.

"More like reckless and stupid." Merrick takes a monstrous bite of his steak. "I had no clue what I was doing. But gravity handled most of the work."

I notice he said he *was* a stunt double, past tense.

I glance at Sullivan, who looks nervous. He's probably worried I'll ask Merrick what's he's doing now.

I'm afraid I already witnessed it—he's slow-motion destructing, one day at a time. While Sullivan tries to hold his dad together with his bare hands.

"I don't know if I could jump off a roof," I say. "Like, not even for a million dollars. Not even if the check was sitting right there."

Merrick makes a choking sound that I eventually recognize as laughter.

"A million dollars! They paid me forty-eight bucks."

We all laugh then, at the pathetic-ness of that number and

the knowledge that, actually, if it were really needed...every one of us would make that jump.

I would if I had to. I'd jump every time.

Sullivan's eyes meet mine. He gives me a smile that shows that he has finally relaxed and let go of his worry for the day.

I smile back at him. I can't fix his dad. But maybe I can fatten him up—Merrick fills another plate.

Sullivan's empty skewers are stacked up like kindling next to the bones of two rib eyes.

I get deep satisfaction from feeding the two men.

It's primal, that need to be needed.

This is real, the food I cook, the comfort it brings, the beauty of the night that's impossible to ignore when our bellies are full and everything is settling.

Smoke drifts up from the candles. Pale, papery moths flirt with the flames.

It's been a long time since I sat down at a table with a family. This family is small and broken, but families are like books...the ones that are used and battered are the ones that were loved.

My family was just me and my mom. I'd give anything, *anything,* for one more dinner with her. I'd take all the splinters jabbing in my ass, all the smoke from the grill. Even if she looked sick, like Sullivan's dad. Even if she *was* sick, like right at the end.

Maybe it's a mercy when people go when they're hurting. But it's no mercy to the people who lose them.

I thought I was ready. Not even close. I could never have guessed how much I'd miss her. Or what it truly feels like to be alone...not one person on the planet who loves you. Who even knows your middle name.

"Come on, eat up..." Merrick nudges me with the platter bearing the last ribeye. "Let's put some meat on those bones."

"You should talk," Sullivan snorts.

"I'm an old man. Doesn't matter if I wither away."

Merrick isn't old by any stretch of the imagination, but there is something weary and ground down in the way he moves, like every part of him hurts.

When he passes the plate, I notice the faded tattoos on his hands, the kind that weren't done in any proper studio. They look like the sort a sailor would wear...or a prisoner.

The sky turns purple and faint stars emerge. The candles are failing, one poor, burned moth drowning in wax.

"You could put some fairy lights out here..." I glance up at the bare pergola. "That would be really pretty."

The yard would need a fuck of a lot more work than that to be "pretty" by common standards, but I like the wildness of it. With a little grooming, cutting away the dead undergrowth, it could be primeval instead of dystopian.

When it's time to clear the table, Sullivan takes a weighty stack of dishes into the kitchen and immediately fills the sink, rolling up the sleeves of his dress shirt and getting to work scrubbing everything clean.

Merrick stays outside, clearing the crumbs off the tabletop and picking up the paper napkins that blew away in the breeze.

When I join Sullivan, he tries to shoo me away. "You don't have to clean! You already did the cooking."

"I can dry at least."

He smiles at me sideways. "Well, I don't want to fight."

The slosh of suds is relaxing. Our hands touch as he passes me the rinsed plates.

I say, "Thank you. For the flowers."

I expect Sullivan to ask if Angus saw them, but he only smiles. "You're welcome."

I tell him the good news: "Angus asked if we could come to dinner this weekend."

"Oh yeah?" Sullivan rinses another plate and passes it to me. "That's good."

I assume he's pleased, but since he was already in a mellow state, it's hard to tell.

"Purple's my favorite color," I venture.

"I know."

I glance up at him quickly. "How did you know that?"

"That was the color of your prom dress. And those sneakers you always used to wear. And that notebook you sketched in..."

He's right.

If you would have asked me ten years ago, I would have said, *Sullivan Rivas barely knows I exist.*

Now I smile to myself, thinking maybe the flowers were a little bit for me after all.

16

SULLY

Long after I go to bed, I lie awake.

I can't stop picturing my dad when he said he only got paid forty-eight bucks to jump off that roof, wheezing with laughter, his eyes crinkled up.

He never told me that part of the story before.

He'd always just said it was the luckiest day of his life.

"You have to believe in destiny. There was no other way a roughneck like me would ever meet an angel like your mom."

I haven't heard him laugh like that in years. Or seen him eat like that, either. Theo's food is irresistible.

She looked like an oil painting in the candlelight—skin softly glowing, endless depths to those soulful blue eyes...

She makes you feel what she's feeling, just by looking at you. It's unnerving. And intoxicating.

I could tell my dad likes her. He barely likes anyone.

I like people okay—from a distance.

Theo's different. She gets under my skin.

She cuts through the bullshit. Won't play games with me.

I'm not doing anything...

Yes, you are.

I'm sweating beneath the sheets just thinking about it...how she looked at me. The feeling of being caught.

I can't seem to stop flirting with Theo.

I want to stop—when she asks me to. But then she says something in that soft, musical voice of hers or gives me one of her shy, fleeting smiles, and I can't help myself. I want to make her laugh, I want to make her blush. I want to shrink the space between us.

But then I think of the vulnerability in her face, the painful honesty when she said, *I'll get hurt...*

And I feel like a piece of shit for pushing it.

Because I really, truly don't want to hurt Theo.

The more I get to know her, the more I know that can't happen. She's had it rough enough already.

And most of all...

She doesn't deserve it.

Theo's kind, she's hardworking, she's talented, creative, genuine... Whatever goes on between us, whatever happens with this deal, when it's all over, I'm going to leave her better than I found her. That's a promise I make to myself, right now. And I *always* keep my promises.

I roll over, too hot to sleep. I need a glass of water.

Slipping out from the sheets, I pad down the hall, shirtless and barefoot in my boxer shorts. It's well past midnight; Theo must be asleep.

But when I pass her doorway, I hear a sound—a low, throbbing buzz.

I hesitate, bare feet sinking into the carpet.

Theo's soft moan rises over the buzz. The sound ebbs and swells in long, lazy swoops, her gasps and groans in rhythm with the hum.

Oh my god. She's using a vibrator.

And using it...pretty fucking hard.

"*Please…*," Theo moans. "*Oh god, please…*"

Holy shit.

This is the hottest thing I've ever heard, ten feet away on the other side of that door.

If Theo knew I was hearing this, she'd be mortified—I should turn around and head back to my room.

But then she gives another whimpering moan, and a wave of heat rolls over me, dragging me like a riptide until my ear is pressed against the door.

"*Ohhh…*," she groans. "*Ohh, yessss….*"

Jesus fucking Christ, this isn't fair.

I want to be a good guy, I really do…but I just can't leave. Not when Theo is panting and sweating on the other side of that door.

The buzzing increases. I don't know what she's got in there, but I swear she just turned up the dial.

Her cries are high and desperate and deeply erotic. It's primal the way they burrow in at the base of my skull and shiver down my spine…

I'd give anything to see what her face looks like right now. Whether her eyes are open or closed. How she's positioned on the bed…

Or even better…I'd give my car to know what she's thinking about.

"*Oh*!" Theo cries. "*Oh*!"

The buzzing rattles like ten thousand angry hornets.

I touch my cock through my pants. It throbs like a fever, heavy, swollen, and aching.

I'm going to walk away. In about five more seconds…

Theo's gasps come closer together. The vibrator makes a cyclical sound like she's rubbing it in circles somewhere highly interesting. I have never detested a door so much. While pressing my whole body against it.

The vibrator makes a short, spastic sound, abruptly falling silent.

"Shit!" Theo says, amusingly clear through the wall.

I smother my laugh. I'm praying with all my might that Theo has another set of batteries. There's no way she can leave me hanging like that. Or herself, either, I hope...

My heart is bumping in my ears and my cock is growling for more. Which might be why I fail to notice that Theo is not searching through her drawers but instead has crossed the room and opened the door. I learn this when I almost fall on top of her.

"Oh my god!" she shrieks. "What are you doing out here? Oh my god!"

She's wearing nothing but an oversized T-shirt, clutching two halves of a hot pink vibrator to her chest. Her face swiftly turns the same color.

I'm standing there like an idiot, cock tenting the front of my pants.

There's no getting out of this. No pretending it's anything but exactly what it is.

"I'm sorry. I was walking past, and I heard..." A grin sneaks across my face, I can't stop it. "Well, it sounded pretty fun in there."

Theo's eyes drop to my cock and somehow, someway, her blush deepens. I think most of the blood in her body is now in her face.

"What did you hear?" she asks weakly.

"Barely anything," I assure her. "Only...do you need fresh batteries?"

Theo takes several slow breaths with her eyes closed. "Is it possible to die of embarrassment?"

"Don't be embarrassed. It was the best ten minutes of my life."

Her eyes pop open. "You were listening for *ten minutes*!?"

"Well, maybe—" I stop myself and tell the truth. "Yeah, I was. Ten minutes at least."

Like a magnet, Theo's eyes drag downward. There's no hiding the effect she had on me. Her moans were... extremely exciting. Just her gaze resting there is making things worse.

Or better, depending on your perspective...my cock throbs and my whole body flushes warm.

Theo's forces herself to meet my eyes. She bites her lip and, very softly, she says, "You liked what you heard?"

I lean forward, arm across the top of the doorframe. "Extremely."

Theo's eyes drop once more, lingering on the obvious outline of my cock through my pants.

"*Jesus,*" she mutters.

I'll admit, it makes me feel good to note that what I'm packing is bigger than the pink thing in her hand.

If Theo was making those noises with her vibrator, I wonder what sounds *I* could get her to make...

Slow your roll, Sully. You just talked about this—literally two hours ago. You're not having sex.

Which means...I'll have to settle for second best.

"I've got some double-As in the kitchen," I offer. "I don't want you to go to bed anxious."

"How generous. Unfortunately," Theo says with great dignity, "it's broken."

Noooooooo...

"Would you like me to take a look?"

She considers then thrusts the two halves of the vibrator into my hands.

She must be desperate. Or this is her favorite.

The silicone is still warm from her body, which is highly distracting. I examine the motor, the casing.

"It snapped." I show her the piece. But can't resist adding, "Pressing a little hard, were we?"

She stares me down. "Don't make this worse."

I pass her the vibrator, deeply disappointed. "I don't think I can fix it."

My regret is real. What I wouldn't give to hear the finale of that particular show...

Then a wicked thought occurs.

"You know...I could help you finish?"

Theo's shoulders hunch as she clutches the vibrator to her chest. "We can't have sex. We just talked about this."

I know.

"It's not sex. It's just...a helping hand."

The corners of her mouth turn down, but I think she's hiding a smile, not a frown. "You're impossible."

"I'm flexible. And completely discreet...no one has to know that you let your fake boyfriend touch you for real."

We're all alone in the house. The silence is complete, the sense of isolation both safe and tempting. Theo's bedroom waits, the nest of her sheets already tousled and open...

I count the beats of her pulse in the hollow of her throat.

"Alright," she whispers.

Excitement flares, hot and swift. I tamp it down, slipping my arm around her waist.

"Come lie down."

I haven't been in here since Theo unpacked. I like how she's made the space her own—books on the nightstand, sprigs of lavender in a mason jar. The room smells fresh, like a living thing.

Theo's T-shirt barely covers anything, her bare legs flashing beneath. Her hair hangs loose down her back. When she gets ready for work in the morning, she twists it into a neat bun at the base of her neck. Unbound, it's black as tar and surprisingly wild. Her thighs are moon pale.

Her room is dim. Theo slips through the shadows, graceful as a deer. She reaches the bed and turns, eyes wide and nervous all of a sudden, like she's lost confidence.

But the scent of arousal rises off her skin and from every fold of her sheets... It curls in my nostrils and snakes down into my lungs, honey and spice, the sweet, animal smell of Theo...

I cup her jaw in my palm, and we fall into the bed together. Her hand touches my bare chest. Her palm is so soft that the moment she touches me, the rest of my skin wakes up, hoping to feel more.

My fingertips trail down her face, down her body, over the ancient cotton T-shirt to its tattered hem. My hand lingers at the border of fabric and smooth, pale thigh.

I know, I just fucking know, there's no underwear beneath.

I'm inches away from Theo's most sensitive, most vulnerable place.

I look upward first, checking her face while my hand hesitates.

"Is this okay?"

"Yes," Theo says, low, soft, and clear. "Finish me off."

I lift the hem of her T-shirt like a velvet curtain. What I find beneath is better than any Broadway show...

Theo has the prettiest pussy I've ever seen.

It's already warm and wet and swollen from the vibrator, lips flushing pink... She's delicate as a tea rose, soft petals and the shy little nub of her clit.

I part her thighs and stroke the back of my hand lightly over her silky mound. Theo lets out a long sigh, her hips lifting up...

I turn my hand over and slide my fingertips down her pussy lips, bringing my thumb back up to stroke under her clit...

Each touch sends shivers sweeping down her legs. Theo sinks into her pillow, back arching, chin tilted up. Her nipples point hard through the front of her T-shirt.

"You're so soft..." I murmur as I stroke her clit with my thumb. "You're such a soft, good girl..."

Theo curls against me in the nest of her bed. Her face turns against my neck, and she takes deep, slow breaths.

I stroke my thumb up and down, finding the wetness below, massaging it into her clit.

Her texture is like rose petals, like new, soft leaves...

I sink against her, breathing her in, Theo's scent and softness all around me, her sheets and naked limbs, and most of all, this melting pussy beneath my hand...

My fingers slide up and down, her little pink clit pinched between. I press and rub and tease and massage, watching the reactions on her face.

Theo is responsive, her gasps and sighs a kind of music. I don't know if she's leading or I am, but neither one of us can stop.

Her cheeks are flushed, her lashes fluttering. When her eyes open and lock on mine, I drown in blue.

"Don't stop," she begs.

"Not for a billion dollars."

I slip a finger inside her. Her whole body clenches, her arms drawing in tight, her pussy squeezing around my hand. She gasps like I hit her with a douse of cold water.

Impulsively, I kiss her.

I know I'm not supposed to—this isn't part of a "helping hand." But her mouth tastes delicious—warm and hungry and sweet. She kisses me back, her arms around my neck, her hands tangled up in my hair.

Kissing her soft lips while rubbing my hand between her thighs is a new kind of nirvana.

It's like I'm lying in a bed made of Theo, rolling around in her, drenched in softness...

Theo clings to me, making gentle, desperate sounds, humping against my hand.

I feel her climax building, her whimpers closer together. I recognize the tempo from listening through the door.

Her hair is wild and her eyes are glinting. Her fingernails dig into my arm. I've unlocked something inside of her, and now I'm determined to let it out.

My desire to make her come is all-encompassing—it seems more crucial than curing cancer or solving world peace. The only thing that matters right now is making Theo explode.

I slide two fingers inside her, my thumb rubbing circles on her clit.

Theo's kissing becomes wetter and wilder. I can taste it in my mouth, how close she is to the edge...

That taste is maddening, it triples my heart rate. Her scent rises off her skin. I smell it in her hair, her neck, her mouth, her pussy, those pheromones that mean only one thing...

I growl in her ear, "Tell me how good it feels..."

She turns to look at me, washing me in an ocean of blue.

"It feels like floating," she whispers. "Like when we swam together..."

Only now we're floating in pleasure, like sunlit water, linked everywhere we touch...

I kiss her on the mouth, and then I can't help myself, I drop down between her thighs and bury my face in that sweet, soft pussy. I make her come on my tongue with warm, wet licks that have her shrieking and bucking, her legs over my shoulders, her thighs locked around my ears.

I devour her sweetness, eating her pussy with her ass cupped in my hands, until I've lapped up every drop and Theo collapses, limp on the bed.

I lick her taste from my lips and run my hand over my mouth, smelling the last of her on my fingers, on my skin.

I pull up the covers, tucking her in, fluffing the pillows, making sure she's straight on the bed.

Theo's so relaxed that she looks drunk, with a sleepy smile and heavy eyelids.

"How was that?" I smooth the hair back from her face.

She closes her eyes, letting out a sigh that says so much more than words. "Fucking perfect..."

It's time to go, but I'm still sitting on the edge of the bed.

A post-orgasmic Theo is a sight to behold. The flush on her face would put a sunrise to shame, her hair slightly sweaty and her lips plump and swollen.

Her lashes lift and she smiles at me. "You know...it really isn't fair, how good you are at everything."

I grin, warmth in my chest. "Oh, you liked that?"

"You put my favorite toy to shame."

I smirk at the broken vibrator, like it knows I won. "Glad to be of service."

"But you know..." Theo tries to be stern, failing miserably as she smiles up at me, flushed and glowing. "That was a one-time thing."

"Right, of course."

I mean it when I say it.

But within moments of exiting Theo's room, I'm already longing to sneak back in again.

17

SULLY

I have a late appointment on Tuesday, so Theo drives herself to work. When I get home, she's already in the backyard with my dad, the picnic table heaped with platters of lemon-wrapped salmon, watermelon salad, and grilled asparagus.

My dad looks like he showered and maybe even combed his hair. With his fingers, at least.

The meal is mellow and relaxed. Theo and I sneak glances at each other, smothering our smiles. The memory of what we did last night is the best kind of secret, the kind that electrifies the most innocent interactions. Now I can't even sit near her without my skin prickling. I can't pass her a napkin without sparks zipping between our fingertips.

We said it was a one-time thing, but I already know how hard it's going to be to lie in my bed tonight, knowing she's just two doors away.

Theo is so fucking irresistible.

It's the way she's gentle and nervous...but when I touch her, there's a river roaring beneath the surface.

I barely dipped a toe in the torrent last night.

There's more, I know it. A hell of a lot more.

And I *want* it.

All day at work, I kept picturing the clock flicking over to midnight. Me slipping out from under the sheets, padding down the hall...knuckles rapping against her door...Theo filling the doorframe with her dark hair loose, breasts soft without a bra, T-shirt barely skimming the top of her thighs...

No, I can't do it again. That would set a precedent. Like now it's some nightly thing. She might feel like she had to say yes 'cause she said yes the night before.

I mean, I think she *enjoyed* saying yes the night before...

But that doesn't matter. I shouldn't have asked her right after I agreed we wouldn't fuck around.

I'm usually a lot better at keeping my word.

Goddamnit, Theo doesn't make it easy...

Look at her right now, in that deep blue top, the way it skims off her shoulders...

Theo has the loveliest skin. The light dances across it like abalone, bringing out a hundred subtle shades of blue and green and gold and pink within the cream.

She was made for candlelight, for dinners in the yard, for salty evening air that makes the bits of hair around her face go curly. She's talking to my dad, laughing, her voice music in the air, soft, soothing, and melodic.

Theo baked honey butter buns. She's already eaten four of them. I've had six, so I'm not judging.

As she butters a fifth, I say, "You look hungry..."

She glances at me under her lashes. "I'm starving."

She tears off a piece of bun and dips it in whipped butter. When she pops it in her mouth, she holds my eye, her tongue slipping out to lick a little butter off the edge of her thumb.

Well, shit.

Maybe Theo does want a visit after all...

I can't stop remembering the softness of her pussy lips.

Once I touched it, I had to taste it...

There was no turning back, like I'd jumped off a roof. The moment when I said, *Fuck it,* and buried my face in her pussy... the first taste of her velvety sweetness on my tongue...

I know she's thinking about it, too. She keeps chewing the edge of her lip, while her knees squeeze together beneath the table.

My dad can tell something's up. I don't think he was drinking today, or at least not as much—he's clear-eyed as he watches Theo and me a little too closely.

"You two went to school together?"

"That's right." Theo nods.

"Huh." He picks up an asparagus spear with his fingers and bites it in half. "Then how come I never saw you over here with the rest of the hooligans?"

"Dad—"

"I was a nerd," Theo says lightly. "Still am, really."

"You weren't a nerd." I don't know why it comes out harsh, like I'm mad at her.

Theo glances at me, eyebrow raised. "It doesn't bother me, Sully."

Her use of my nickname throws me off balance—nobody calls me that except my brother and dad. And my mom, before.

I like the sound of it on Theo's lips. It's softer than "Sullivan" —playful and affectionate.

Theo's not offended at the thought of herself as a nerd.

But I am.

"You weren't a nerd. You were just...yourself."

"Thanks," she says with very little enthusiasm.

"What I mean is...in high school, everyone's so desperate to impress, to prove themselves, to fit in...you never seemed to give in to any of that."

Theo shakes her head. "I just wasn't good at it."

I remember one lunch hour when I watched her read a novel in the cafeteria, the paperback propped open on her knees while she ate a microwaved cup of noodles. She never looked up once, never reacted to the shrieks or clatter of trays all around her, completely absorbed in her story.

I watched the emotions sweep across her face—excitement, intrigue, worry, relief...and felt jealous of how Theo had somehow escaped while the rest of us were still stuck at school.

"You stood out," I say. "Without even talking. That's why those girls wouldn't leave you alone."

What I'm saying is true. Some quiet people fade into the background. You never forgot that Theo was in the room. Or at least, I never did.

"Stella used to say that," my dad remarks, spearing a cube of watermelon on his fork and popping it into his mouth. "That some people have a kind of gravity that makes you want to watch them."

I look at him, surprised. My dad doesn't talk about my mom very much. Granted, he doesn't talk about anything much—eating dinner with me two nights in a row is rare. And chatting the whole time? Unprecedented.

Theo's meals make you want to linger. They demand to be savored with second helpings, with conversation. When we're done, the sense of satisfaction is so complete, all we can do is sit back and gaze up at the stars.

My dad is peaceful and relaxed, hands clasped loosely behind his head. Theo leans her chin on palm. Her eyes are as deep as the night sky, her cheeks glowing like the moon.

Softly, she says, "You couldn't take your eyes off Stella on-screen."

A shiver brushes over my skin. But my dad only nods. "Her more than anyone."

Usually, when my mom comes up, my dad gets this stunned, blank look on his face. It's like her name is wind that blows out the candle behind his eyes.

But tonight, candlelight dances golden across his skin. My dad takes a piece of soapstone out of his pocket and turns it over in his hand, rubbing its softness with the ball of his thumb.

"Directors were always asking her to eat food in scenes. Because whatever she was doing, it was mesmerizing. You put something in her hand, and whatever that thing was...it became something more."

He flips the stone, rubbing it with his thumb like it's a piece of glass and he'll clear the surface to see something beneath.

"In *Moonless Nights*, the director gave her a pomegranate. She ripped it apart, red juice running down her arms... They banned the movie in China, said the scene was too provocative..." My dad chuckles to himself, shaking his head. "They couldn't say why. But that was her power...she made you feel things."

There's a twist in my chest, a fiber twitching.

I look at Theo, at the emotions saturating her face. Her eyes meet mine, huge and shining with all her thoughts and feelings unexpressed.

Some people are an empty well. And some are a cup overflowing.

"I remember that scene..." Theo smiles. "I loved her from a movie. I can only imagine how you felt."

"I never had a chance," my dad says. "There was no choice about loving her."

He swings his legs over the bench seat and gathers up a stack of plates. "Thanks, Theo. I was looking forward to that all day."

"Will you come eat with us tomorrow?" she asks. "I'm making lasagna."

"You can *make* lasagna? I thought it only came frozen."

Theo laughs. "Prepare to be amazed."

My dad carries the plates all the way into the kitchen and sets them by the sink. He doesn't hang around to wash up, but I'm stunned all the same. That's the first time he's stepped foot inside the house in years.

"'Night, Sully." As he shuffles past, he says, too low for Theo to hear, "If you're not dating her, you're a fool."

I'm starting to think he might be right.

Dating Theo for real doesn't sound so bad...

But that could make things extremely messy between us.

I'm about to make my move with Angus. Our dinner Friday night will be our first meeting without his stooges around—the perfect opportunity to give him a good, hard push.

I can't distract myself with attachment to Theo. Emotion clouds judgement. I can't create a situation where I might have to pick between her and this deal.

Rationally, I know the right choice: keep things professional until Angus signs on the dotted line.

The problem is...I like her.

The more time I spend with Theo, the less I can deny it.

When she beats me home, when I pull into the driveway of a glowing house, cooking smells and music as soon as I open the door, and that swooping anticipation in my gut as I stride toward the kitchen, picturing how she'll turn, the smile that will light up her face...

Already I'm dreading her leaving at the end of the week.

Theo brings life to the house.

She opened all the blinds and cut back the wisteria covering the windows. She put the clippings in an old watering can, the purplish flowers spilling out like water flowing in reverse. She reads the news with her coffee in the morning and assaults me with the day's happenings the moment I enter the room.

I could get used to this.

And I'm not supposed to get used to this. I'm supposed to see it as a limited-time thing—in five more days, she's heading back to her cockroach-cleansed apartment. And a few weeks after that, we'll be parting ways forever.

But that doesn't mean I can't enjoy her lasagna in the meantime.

Theo's already got her hands in the soapy water. I scoot her to the side with a bump of my hip. "I'm washing."

"I already started!"

"Tough shit—my mom would kill me if I let you cook *and* wash the dishes."

Theo gives me a quick sideways glance. "Was it okay what I said earlier? About your mom?"

"Yeah, of course." Our shoulders brush as she takes her place beside me. Our knuckles touch when I hand her a dripping mixing bowl. "You liked her movies?"

She nods. "I used to watch *Snowbound* every Christmas."

That place in my chest twists again.

Reese filling a mug with more marshmallows than cocoa, my parents playing cribbage, Mom's chortle as she turns over her cards, me sweating in front of the fireplace because I begged to have it on even though it's sixty-six degrees outside. On the tinsel-wreathed TV, a younger version of our mother twirls through a snowy Central Park...

"Us, too," I say.

"Your dad wasn't upset? I shouldn't have—"

"He's not upset. It's been good for him, having you here. He likes talking to you."

"Really?" The tips of her ears turn pink.

I know this is a need for her, she told me frankly: *I like taking care of people.*

I could have guessed she'd try to take care of my dad. But never in a million years did I believe it would actually work.

"You saw—he was looking better today." I clear my throat. "I'm grateful."

Theo ducks her head. "I didn't do anything."

"He sure doesn't put on a clean shirt for *me*."

She laughs. "I like your dad. He's honest."

"That he is." I give her a beady look. "But why does that feel pointed at me?"

Her expression is saucy. "Guilty conscience?"

"I'm honest." I step closer. "With you."

She tilts up her chin, arms folded over her chest. "Then tell me what your dad said when he was leaving."

I'm electrified. "How did you know we were talking about you?"

She shrugs. "You're not that sneaky. And what gives? I thought we were pretending to be dating?"

"Not to him."

"I thought you said to everyone?"

"My dad doesn't know Angus. They're not gonna hang out."

She frowns at me. "Don't be patronizing. You made a big deal about it—how we couldn't tell *anyone* the truth."

"Well, you can't."

"But you just did!"

"I said *you* can't."

Theo stares at me, outraged. "How is that fair?"

"Because my best friend isn't Martinique."

She has to work hard to act like she doesn't know what I'm talking about. "Martinique wouldn't say anything..."

It's so unconvincing, I give her a long stare of shame while I shake my head. "Theo. I *met* her."

"She would nev—"

"I *talked* to her. She told me everything about you in ten seconds. She's the one who gave me your social security number; that wasn't even from a background check."

Theo stops trying to convince me and covers her face with her hand. She acts like she's doing it because she's annoyed, but I one hundred percent know it's because she's smiling.

"Look," I say. "I get she's your best friend. Personally, I find her delightful. But please, let's not risk our time, money, and probably one-and-only chance at this deal on Martinique's ability to keep her mouth shut."

Theo sighs and drops her hand. "Fine."

She's agreeing, but I don't like how defeated she looks. It's pathetic. Her shoulders slump and her head hangs down.

"What's wrong?"

"Nothing."

"Come on. Out with it."

She takes a breath then lets it out. "It sucks!"

"What?"

"Lying to her! I'm not going to call her up just to say things that aren't true. Now we're talking less and it's weird, and that's not fair! You can be normal with your dad, and I don't have anybody to talk to about...stuff."

"You can talk to me."

She rolls her eyes. "Not about everything."

"Oh, I see what the problem is...you want to gossip about me."

"Or vent." Theo shoots me a scowl.

There is nothing less intimidating than Theo's scowl. All it does is make me want to wrap my arms around her and kiss her on the nose, but that would not help our current situation. In fact, that would probably be the type of thing she'd vent to Martinique about: *My fake boyfriend gives me condescending kisses when I'm frustrated with him.*

"Why are you smiling?" she demands.

"I'm not smiling."

"You know I'm looking right at your face?"

"Alright." The grin breaks through. "You caught me."

"What's so goddamned funny?"

"You tell me—you're smiling, too."

"No, I'm not!" Theo cries though she absolutely is.

We're both grinning like idiots, soap suds dripping down off our hands.

"Get it together," I flick bubbles at her. "You'll give the whole game away."

She swats the dish towel into the bubbles, sending a big puff right into my face. "I'm the Mata Hari of secrets."

"You know they shot Mata Hari?"

"Well, shit." Theo's tea towel goes limp in her hands.

I hate that I told her.

THAT NIGHT, I lie in bed, fighting the urge to sneak down the hall.

Every time I toss and turn, I wonder if Theo's doing the same. I wonder if she's hot and restless like me, tormented by tantalizing memories of the night before...or if she slipped directly off to sleep.

Once, I even slide out from under the sheets and go stand in the hall, listening. But without the buzz of a vibrator, there's no way to know if she's awake on the other side of her door.

I trudge back to my room, cursing myself for being so weak.

Forget about Theo. Go to bed.

But I can't stop thinking about that loose, tattered T-shirt, which has somehow become the sexiest piece of clothing that's ever draped a female form...

I think how her breasts moved beneath the fabric.

I haven't seen them naked yet.

When I finally fall asleep, my dreams are fucking filthy.

On Wednesday, I arrive home to my dad manning the grill while Theo mixes up a pitcher of fresh limeade. This is surprising both because my dad can't cook and because he's wearing the pink, frilly apron.

"That's mine," I tell him.

"Finders keepers," he grunts.

He burned the garlic bread, but Theo eats it anyway to encourage him.

"You don't have to do that," I tell her. "You'll get sick."

She steps on my foot beneath the table, whispering, "*Be nice.*"

"*No...,*" I whisper back, loud enough for my dad to hear. "*He has to know; he burned the shit out of that...*"

"I probably had the heat up too high," Theo says. "I do it under the broiler at home."

"Don't make excuses for me." My dad takes a bite of the most charred piece of toast. It makes an awful crunching sound, black flakes raining down.

"You don't have to punish yourself!" Theo plucks it out of his hand, laughing, and replaces it with one that's less burnt.

Her lasagna makes me want to start some sort of Garfield-like religion. It's so good I'm starting to become suspicious of her.

"How do you make the best version of everything I ever ate?"

It's hard for Theo to accept compliments. She wants them, she needs them, but when she gets them, it's like hot, searing coals. She has to sizzle and endure.

She flaps her hand like it will cool off her face. "I was trying a new thing—cottage cheese instead of ricotta."

"It worked." I tilt my plate to shovel the last bites into my mouth.

Thursday, I come home to a yard lit with fairy lights. The lights are woven all through the pergola, gilding the leaves, casting a glow over the yard. Someone trimmed back the hedges and pulled up the vines so the space around the picnic table is clear. Even the firepit has been repaired.

Theo pops her head out. "I thought after dinner we could make s'mores!"

I grab her elbow as she carries plates from the kitchen. "Did you do all this?"

She's bright and buoyant, skipping across the yard in flat shoes. "It was your dad! He had the lights up when I got home. I did help him with the firepit."

This is crazy. They're both acting like it's totally sane, but no, I remember the last ten years, so I know my dad has not done one goddamned thing to clean up this place in all of that time.

And now, he's throwing fucking garden parties.

With Theo.

This is a bona fide miracle. And my patron saint...doesn't even seem to realize it.

Theo just grins. "I told you it could be pretty out here."

"A hell of a lot prettier than I thought."

I happen to be looking at her when I say that, and she happens to see it.

"You better not be saying that about *me*."

I know she's fucking with me, but I shake my head anyway. "Sorry, but no. I *always* thought you were hot."

"You did not."

"How do you know?"

"Because you were a dick to me!"

"I was a dick to everyone."

"Me even more."

I come close to her. It's the night that makes it feel meancing

—the candlelight flickering in the yard. "Maybe I just talked to you more."

Theo gazes up at me. Back then, when I'd get close enough to look into those big blue eyes, she'd shiver away from me. Turn and run.

This Theo is a little more rugged. She says, "You should go to therapy, Sully. It helped me a lot."

Oof. Bullet to the heart, what a sniper.

She winks at me as she brushes past. Her hand drags down my arm, her fingernails raking lightly on my skin.

Every inch of me is on fire.

I'm not going to make it until the end of the week...

18

THEO

I wish we weren't going out with Angus.

For one thing, I don't want to leave Merrick alone. He ate dinner with us every night this week.

Sullivan's trying to convince me that I don't need to cook anything for his dad.

"He won't expect it, he *can* actually survive on his own, he's done it before, poorly, but you saw, he's alive..." Sullivan smiles at me. "It's already been the best week of his life when it comes to food, so it's okay to take a night off."

He argues his hardest when he knows it's something I'm determined to do.

In this case, I already did it. The dinner's warming in the oven.

I only took a break to put on this gorgeous gown. It's the first time Sullivan's seeing it. I mean, his first time seeing *me* in it.

The effect is highly satisfying.

He grins and shakes his head, color rising up his neck. "Damnit, Theo. How am I supposed to talk to you in that dress?"

It's dark blue and sparkly. Mostly dark blue, just bits of

sparkle that glint when I move. But the dress's real power is how good it makes my ass look. It helps every place it touches, but there…it's doing something special.

"You bought it," I say like an accusation.

"Well…I was right."

It's the pause he drags out that makes me laugh, and the look on his face, gleeful surprise. With just the slightest edge of worry, like his creation almost got away from him. Like it still might.

Sullivan makes me laugh. He really *makes* me—like Merrick said, there's no choice about it.

I'm genuinely terrified that this whole Angus thing is about to blow up in my face, but a laugh is an atom bomb that kills everything else, for a while at least. I don't feel that stressed.

The way Sullivan's looking at me, what I actually feel is pretty sexy. Which is not a state I often attain.

It's fun. It makes everything feel like a game.

Sullivan plays this game constantly, it's the zone where he lives.

I know the dress is hot because I can see how it revs him up, gasoline in his veins. He can't stop grinning. "How am I supposed to work tonight?"

"I thought you considered problems like this…"

"I thought I did, too. But now…I've actually seen you. Who said you could look this sexy? I said dress up nice, not give a hundred people a heart attack. There'll be bodies falling all around…"

"Stop it." I smack his shoulder. "Don't make fun of me."

"I'm not." He grabs my hand and makes me look at him. "I've never been more serious. You look stunning. I'm stunned."

My smile sneaks out. "Be a little less surprised."

"I can't. You continually surprise me."

Something hot and fierce leaps in my chest. The strength of it startles me.

It's the way he's looking at me, delighted and even...interested.

Sullivan teases me for showing so much of what I feel, but so does he, when we're alone. Then, what he wants is written all over his face.

Or at least, that's how it seems.

I'm aware of the more chilling possibility...

Sullivan is just incredible at pretending.

Which is it?

The way he's looking at me right now feels real.

What went down in my bed the other night was the realest damn thing that ever happened to me.

But that's what scares me...

What if it only feels that way to me?

Sullivan catches me frowning. It must look like a rain cloud, sweeping over my face.

"What's wrong?"

I search for the question I'm willing to ask him.

"I was wondering...why you never came back to my bedroom."

His answer comes so quickly, it has to be true.

"You told me not to."

The look he gives me is full of so much heat, I'm not wondering if he means it. I'm wondering why the fuck I told him not to come.

"Well...I was wrong."

Sully throws back his head and laughs. The sound ripples over me like pure golden sunshine.

"Thank god, Theo. Fucking torture! I've never worked harder to behave myself."

My chest is full of flushing heat. That's real, his laugh is real, the way he grabs me is real, so he can kiss me, for a moment at least, before we have to leave.

I CARRY the dinner out to his dad.

Sullivan comes with me when he sees it's already made.

I'm barefoot in the tall grass of the yard, avoiding heels as long as I can. Plus, I like the coolness under my feet.

"I wish we weren't leaving him..."

"He'll be fine." Sullivan stops me, hand on my arm. "Theo, look, I'm incredibly grateful for what you're doing—"

"It's nothing."

"Not to me, it isn't." He grips my arm, looks me in the eye. "It's no small thing. He hasn't stepped foot in the house in ages. Hasn't sat and had dinner and laughed with me. But I don't want you to think...I don't want you to be upset if tomorrow...he's back to usual."

In the tension of his body, the rigidity of his face, I plainly read Sullivan's fear that that's exactly what will happen. If not tomorrow, then the day after. Or the day after that.

And maybe, it will. Merrick's grief is dark and endless.

But I know that after I lost my mom, it helped when I started to eat again.

I went to a cafe by the ocean and ordered bread. My mom taught me to make focaccia. She did well with any sort of food that rewards experimentation. She'd put the craziest stuff in her bread, and it almost always turned out better than mine.

The loaf I ate at the cafe was just rosemary. But it was the first thing I ate since she passed that actually tasted good. The salt, the crisp edges soaked in oil, the sweetness with the savory herb...

I took a bite, the salt hit my tongue, and the clear, pure light of the ocean was beautiful, and I was alive again. Even though I didn't want to be.

That's the power of food. It reminds you that things still taste good. And also, that somebody gave a shit enough to bring it to you.

"What's this?" Merrick says when I hand him the covered dishes. "I thought you were going out?"

But I notice he put on clean clothes anyway. And over his shoulder, I see a living space much tidier than the last time I came.

I don't want to get my hopes up any more than Sullivan does. But fuck, I hope his dad's going to be okay. I'll cook him a thousand meals if it helps.

"We are," I say. "But I wish we were staying here—Angus has the worst taste in restaurants."

Merrick snorts. "That doesn't say much about him hiring *you*."

I laugh because I've often thought the same thing. "It feels like when you're dating someone and all their exes are the worst. It's like, how did we end up together?"

"Angus has bad taste," Sullivan says. "It's his fatal flaw."

"What tipped you off? The croc hats?"

"He's close..." Sullivan smiles with strange satisfaction. "But he misses when it counts."

"And why, exactly, is Sully going to dinner with your boss?" Merrick inquires. "Seeing as how the two of you are *not* dating."

"Oh, we are to him," Sullivan says shamelessly. "It's all part of the play, Dad—getting a bit of business done."

Merrick shakes his head. "That's the stupidest thing I've ever heard."

"I promise you, it's working brilliantly."

"It always does," Merrick says. "Until it doesn't."

"He's a kill joy," Sullivan points his thumb back in the direction of his dad's door. "Always has been."

"Sully..." I wheel on him, heart racing with the knowledge that we're supposed to be at the restaurant in twenty minutes. "Calm me down. Tell me what you're going to do."

"It's simple. I'm going to talk to Angus and figure out what he actually cares about when it comes to this deal."

"Like what?"

"I don't know yet. But I promise you, it's there inside of him—the black swan."

"What the hell is a black swan?"

"The unknown unknown. The thing that makes or breaks a negotiation. It could be anything...a dream, a desire, a point of pride, an entrenched habit...but usually, it's an emotional trigger."

That makes zero sense to me.

"Angus is pretty rational when it comes to business."

Sullivan laughs. "I bet he thinks so. But we're all just animals, Theo—it's our passions that drive us. We make up the reasons later."

"Then what's my job?"

"Be part of the conversation, draw him out. And relax...it's just going to be you, me, and him at dinner."

But as it turns out, that's the first thing that goes wrong.

19

THEO

We meet Angus at Birch, a pretentious restaurant on Melrose obsessed with topping things with foam. The interior decor is supposed to look like a forest, so we wind our way to our table through a thicket of glowing white plastic trees.

Only, when we reach Angus' booth, he isn't alone.

I whisper, "Oh no..."

Angus' date turns, giving me a smile that only slightly rearranges the features on her highly-Botoxed face.

"Theo. What a surprise."

I notice she doesn't say it's a *nice* surprise.

Actually, I'm not sure how it's a surprise at all—I assume Angus told her we were coming.

But maybe not. Because he sure as hell didn't tell me that he's back to dating Jessica Kate.

"I'm Sullivan..." Sully holds out his hand.

Jessica gives him hers like she's bestowing a favor, laying it limply in his palm. But her eyes are sharp as they sweep his face, his suit, his watch, down to his shoes.

Jessica is a shark. Don't let the aggressive boob job, three-inch nails, or mile-long ponytail fool you—she's smart and she's ruthless. The fact that she's here right now is a huge problem.

Jessica could blow this whole thing out of the water.

And worst of all, she'd love to do it.

Because Jessica Kate is pure evil.

Angus knows it, too. Jessica has been making his life a living hell in a rotating cycle for about three years. He'll bump into her at some party or drunk dial her when he's desperate, they'll launch into another chaotic courtship spanning an average of two to six weeks until it implodes spectacularly. and the whole thing starts over again.

That's why Angus is giving me a look right now that's a mixture of guilt, excitement, and smugness—with a dash of terror. He's got his arm wrapped gingerly around Jessica's shoulders as they cuddle up in the corner booth.

I can tell it's going to be bad because she's already got him dressing in matching outfits. Angus' shiny green shirt is the exact same material as her space-age minidress. Also, he's drinking a martini. Jessica holds hers but never actually takes a sip. Like Angus' outfit, I'm pretty sure its only purpose is to match her dress.

"Jessica just moved back to LA," Angus says.

"Where were you before?" Sullivan asks politely.

"Dubai," Jessica says in her bored, drawling tone. "But it was hot."

"Dubai was hot?" I didn't plan to be sarcastic, but it slipped out. Maybe because Jessica's been taking a second and third look at Sullivan, repositioning herself in the booth so her body forms a sinuous curve with her long legs extended.

Unfortunately, Jessica has a highly tuned barometer for even the slightest degrees of shade. Her head whips around, her pale green eyes narrowing in on me.

"I don't suppose you've visited. I can't remember Angus needing his dry cleaning picked up from the Middle East."

Sullivan doesn't like that. It's subtle, but I catch it—the way his smile stiffens. He shifts his weight within the booth, his arm slipping down around my shoulders.

I'm not as bothered.

Taking shots at my job is one of Jessica's go-to moves. I'll admit, it usually upsets me. But tonight, it's not hitting quite so hard. The warmth and weight of Sullivan's arm is extremely comforting. And I can't help noticing how Jessica's eyes linger on Sullivan's hand cupping my bare shoulder—the way his thumb strokes across my skin.

Between Jessica's eyebrows, a place usually as smooth and featureless as fresh-fallen snow, a tiny line appears.

The sight of that small, forbidden wrinkle gives me a devilish bolt of glee.

Ignoring her, I say to Angus, "I don't know where I'm gonna get *that* shirt cleaned...is it made of birthday balloons?"

Angus laughs. "Fuck if I know. Jessica bought it."

"I can tell." When she shoots me a venomous look, I add blandly, "Because it's so stylish."

I let my hand drop to Sullivan's thigh.

His flesh is warm and thick and solid beneath my palm. I feel him shift again and, without even looking at his face, I know he's amused.

Jessica stares at my hand. So does Angus. It seems to irritate them in some subtle way, or function as a challenge.

Angus pulls his girlfriend closer and kisses the side of her neck. Jessica allows it, titling her head to the side to provide access, but otherwise showing no enjoyment whatsoever of his mouth against her skin.

Okay. How about this...

I snuggle closer to Sullivan and rest my head against his chest.

I play with the buttons on the front of his shirt in a way that's ridiculous and not how I would ever behave in a public place. But that's fine; I'm not the normal Theo right now—I'm the version of Theo who snagged a guy like Sullivan. And she can do whatever the hell she wants.

Jessica is highly suspicious.

She's met the normal Theo. She knows I have no game.

And she knows I've definitely never had a boyfriend this hot before.

"Sullivan...," she says. "What do you do?"

"Property acquisition."

Her eyes flash. "Isn't that convenient...Angus is looking for a property right now."

This is exactly what I was afraid of. As someone who built a career siphoning money off wealthy men, Jessica is extremely sensitive to anyone else attempting to milk her favorite cash cow. She's already on to us.

But all Sullivan says is a mild, "So I heard."

Jessica's pale green gaze darts between us. She's incredibly beautiful, but there's something reptilian in her stillness and coolness, in the smooth shine of her skin.

She knows this whole thing is fishy.

I'm starting to sweat.

"And you two have been dating for...four months?"

"Six," Sully corrects her.

"That's so weird that Theo never mentioned you."

She definitely knows. Shit!

Sully gives nothing away. His calm is uncrackable.

"Theo's a private person..." He trails his fingers lightly across my collarbone. "She's full of surprises."

Angus slugs back the martini in his hand and signals to the waiter for another. "Not to me—I can read Theo like a book." He snorts. "One with illustrations."

The illustration on my current cognitive page is a big middle finger thrust in Angus' direction. But I guess he's not quite as good at reading my mind as he thinks because when I focus on that image with all my might, all Angus does is smile at me.

I give the waiter my drink order. Sullivan does the same. Angus asks for another martini, but Jessica switches to bourbon like Sully.

"Sounds delicious," she coos in the softly sensual voice she usually reserves for asking favors of Angus.

"It is." Sullivan brushes the hair away from the nape of my neck with long, slow strokes of his fingers.

His touch is incredibly relaxing. I love sitting in the curve of his arm, in the warmth of our side of the booth. I feel safe and protected from Jessica, even though she's glaring at me from only two feet away.

I'm not sure what she's so annoyed about, but I'd guess it has everything to do with Sullivan. There are a lot of beautiful girls in the world, especially in LA. Not as many beautiful men—not like him. Sullivan stands out like a unicorn. I bet Jessica finds it offensive that someone as gorgeous as him is with a nobody like me.

Of course, Sullivan isn't actually *with* me at all.

But she doesn't know that.

She only suspects it.

And it seems to be driving her insane.

Mouth tight as an anus, she says, "Angus told me you two moved in together?"

"Not exactly," I say. "I'm staying at his place while my apartment's being fumigated."

"Ew." Jessica wrinkles her perfect little nose. "Your apartment has bugs? That's disgusting."

"Yup." My new mental illustration is a whole conga line of bugs punting Jessica out the nearest window. "Huge, disgusting cockroaches."

Jessica curls her upper lip. Most of her expressions involve only one feature because I think she has to focus really hard to move her facial muscles. "I can't believe you live like that."

The waiter brings my drink. I take a big, aggressive swallow.

"I love it." I set my glass down hard. "In fact, I'm going to miss those little bastards when they're gone."

Sullivan snorts.

Angus laughs, too, when he realizes I'm joking.

"Theo's not a diva like you," he says to Jessica. "She likes getting her hands dirty."

"I can tell," she sneers back at me, with a disdainful glance at my short, unpolished fingernails and grill-singed knuckles.

I deserved that one. I did take a shot at Angus' shirt, after all, and I do have the hands of a twelve-year-old boy.

Trying to make peace, I say, "Are you still modeling, Jessica?".

Jessica's various careers have included interior designer, TV host, music video director, and party planner, but I'm pretty sure the one she likes best is standing still so people can take pictures of her.

"No." She tosses her long, glossy ponytail over her shoulder, not noticing that it hits Angus in the face. "I'm a musician now."

"That's amazing!" Unbelievable, almost. "I didn't know you played an instrument."

"I don't," she says coolly.

"But she's a really good singer," Angus jumps to her defense. "And anyway, they do it all with auto tune these days."

"That's lucky." Sullivan somehow keeps a straight face. "Do you have an album coming out?"

"This week." Jessica lifts her chin. "It's called *Gilded Soul.*"

"I would *love* to hear it." Sullivan's fingers dance across the back of my neck, conveying his amusement where no one else can see.

Jessica, who normally sniffs out sarcasm like a bloodhound, is blinded by a pretty face.

She leans forward so Angus' arm slips off her shoulders, resting her elbows on the table instead, putting her breasts on display. She gives Sullivan a heavy-lidded look. "Come to my listening party next week."

My face goes hot, and my stomach gives a sick, clenching twist.

It seems impossible that Sullivan's eyes won't drop to those luscious breasts. I mean, she's practically serving them up on a platter. Even I took a look.

But Sullivan has superhuman powers of self-control. His gaze doesn't drop a millimeter, fixed firmly on Jessica's face.

"That sounds fun," he says. Without actually committing to attend.

That little line appears between Jessica's eyebrows once more. She slumps back in the booth, arms crossed over her chest.

I'm impressed.

Jessica is stunning, a ten out of ten in every way that I thought mattered to men. I know exactly how Trent would have behaved if he saw her walk by. I'd be afraid to leave them alone in a room together.

But Sullivan makes me feel like I'm the only woman in the world. Or at least, the only one who matters to him.

And even if it's pretend...he's still showing me respect.

My hand slides up his thigh.

His fingers tighten on my shoulder as he pulls me close to press his lips against my temple.

Angus watches.

He's already finished his second martini without even setting the glass down on the table.

"Maybe I *should* hire you," he says to Sully abruptly. "To help me find what I'm looking for."

I try to hold very still and not even breathe.

"Sure," Sullivan says, like he'd be doing Angus a favor. Like it doesn't matter to him at all. "What are you looking for?"

As Angus talks about what he envisions for the new campus, Jessica picks up a menu and peruses it in a way that makes it plain how boring she finds the conversation.

"You said you wouldn't talk business...," she complains.

"Baby, life is business." Angus tries to sneak his arm around her waist once more. "If you're not hustlin', you're dyin'."

"If that's all you're going to talk about, I'm going to sit with Theo."

Uh oh.

Jessica slides into the booth on my other side, right as the waiter comes to take our order. After that one-minute reprieve, we're tete-a-tete, only inches apart, close enough that her sweetly floral perfume fills my nostrils and her sparkly moisturizer rubs off her legs onto mine.

"So how did you two meet?" Jessica demands, making plain that the purpose of her cross-booth visit is further interrogation.

"High school."

"Hm." That's a mark in my favor, a tally in the "This Is Totally A Legitimate Relationship" column. "And you kept in touch all that time?"

"We bumped into each other at a party. He asked me to dance, and the next thing I knew...," my eyes meet Sullivan's, "...we were dating."

Sully grins. He's chatting with Angus but listening to us. I can tell from the angle of his body.

"Is it serious?" Jessica's eyebrow rises, her tone incredulous.

"Oh yeah," I say. "Extremely serious. He's completely obsessed with me."

Sully bites the edge of his lip, eyes still trained on Angus.

Jessica's rogue wrinkle reappears. I'm starting to love that little wrinkle. It's so determined. It has to fight against so much.

"Wow," she says, like she doesn't believe that for a second. "So like, he just knows everything about you? All your favorite foods, favorite songs, favorite place to get a pedicure?"

I know exactly where she's going with this.

She wants to catch us, right here and now, as the lying liars we are.

Unfortunately...she's right.

Even worse, Sullivan and I have not taken the time to memorize a list of each other's favorite things. Which I'm realizing now was a pretty big omission.

My eyes dart over to Sullivan. He's engaged with Angus and doesn't give me any clue what I should do.

I try to fudge it.

"Well, I've never actually had a pedicure, so..."

"You've never had a *pedicure?*"

Jessica gives me that LA Bubble look, like I'm a visitor from Planet Lame-Ass Loser. She'd be shocked to know I've also never taken a sound bath or put a two thousand dollar jade egg in my vagina.

"No, I haven't. But otherwise, sure—Sullivan is super considerate."

"That's great!" Jessica says with the biggest, fakest smile I've ever seen. "That's so sweet! So, like, I could test him right now, like the Newlywed Game?"

"Uh, I guess. But—"

"Okay, Sullivan," she interrupts his conversation midsentence. "What's Theo's birthday?"

"September twenty-fifth," he says at once.

Thank god—for Sullivan's memory and his research.

I don't know *his* birthday. But luckily, Jessica doesn't ask. She's too busy quizzing my fake boyfriend.

"What's her middle name?"

"Clementine."

Damn, he's good.

"What kind of pizza does she like?"

Will Sullivan remember?

"Mushroom," he says. "But she's not against pepperoni."

"I could have told you that," Angus says.

He looks annoyed by this game, or maybe just competitive.

When Jessica says, "What book is Theo reading right now?" it's Angus who shouts, "The Shining!" like he finally got his shot on Jeopardy. He's too pleased that he got the answer right to notice the filthy glare from his girlfriend. Smirking, he tells me, "I saw it in on your desk."

"Actually," Sullivan says, "she finished that one last week. Now she's reading The Silence of the Lambs." With a slightly subtler smirk, he says, "I saw it on her nightstand."

Now he's created a monster. Angus is determined to prove that he knows me better than Sullivan, thanks to four years of working together twenty-four seven.

"Favorite song?" Jessica fires off.

"'Party in the U.S.A.'," Angus guesses.

"I'd say 'Sunflower'," Sullivan says.

"Sullivan's right." I smile at him. That one's not too hard—I've been playing it all week long while I'm cooking. But I've also played it in my office a million times, and apparently Angus never noticed.

"Mom's name?"

"Uh..." Angus looks guilty for missing that one. As he fucking should.

"Diana," Sullivan says.

"Dream vacation?"

Now Angus is just firing wildly. "Tokyo?"

"Italy," Sullivan says. "For the *real* mushroom pizza..."

He doesn't know either, but that's a pretty good guess.

Jessica has lost control of this game; it's not turning out at all the way she planned. She shoots the questions faster, and Sullivan answers with ease.

"What's she afraid of?"

"Sharks, under-salted food, and letting people down."

"Biggest peeve?"

Sullivan smiles. "A lack of gratitude."

"Life's ambition?"

"To open her own restaurant."

Through gritted teeth, Jessica says, "Celebrity crush?"

"I know this!" Angus shouts triumphantly. "Adam Driver!"

"Based on what?" I laugh.

"Based on the number of times you saw that stupid dinosaur movie."

I don't bother to tell him I only went to watch Adam Driver battle giant space lizards three times, alone, because I was deep in depression.

Sullivan gives a solemn shake of his head. "Sorry, Angus, but I'm going to have to go with Reese Rivas for this one."

Jessica says, "Who the hell is Reese Rivas?"

Sullivan pulls up the IMDB page. "He's exactly her type."

He turns the phone to show the photo to Angus and Jessica.

Angus roars with laughter. Jessica looks confused.

"Oh my god!" Angus says. "You look just like him."

Sullivan nods. "That's how twins work."

Our food arrives, and Jessica returns to her side of the booth, deeply dissatisfied.

I, on the other hand, am feeling fantastic.

Angus has officially hired Sullivan.

And someone in this world knows my favorite song *and* my middle name.

20

SULLY

Dinner was a great success.

I knew it was a good sign when I saw that Angus brought his fake girlfriend to show up my fake girlfriend. That means he thinks we're in competition.

That became obvious when he tried to prove how much better he knows Theo—despite barely knowing her at all.

I was almost embarrassed for him, how bad he was at answering those questions. After working with her for four years? I bet the janitor's more observant.

Angus knows things about Theo—the things that matter to *him*. He just doesn't think much about what matters to her.

Which is a shame because it's really not that hard to make Theo happy.

She's not a simple person, but she is a pure one. Pure in heart, pure in desire. She likes fresh fruit, warm sunshine, walks on the beach, live music, breaking bread with friends, a good sleep after a long day...

She's not trying to fuck with anyone.

Which is why I'm not a fan of Jessica. She hasn't stopped

taking shots at Theo all night long. It's a good thing we're skipping dessert because it's starting to get under my skin.

I visit the bathroom before leaving the restaurant. When I come out, Jessica's lying in wait.

"Hi, Sullivan."

Ugh.

She positions her body in the tight space so it's impossible for me to get past without touching her or asking her to move.

She's beautiful but the sort of beauty I like the least, one that owes more to a surgeon's blade than to nature. She's got all the trendiest upgrades—the fox eye lift, filler in her lips and cheeks, a sculpted ski jump of a nose, and maybe even a shaved-down jaw, if she flew to Korea where that sort of thing is legal.

Her surgeon was an artist—the work is flawless. But that's exactly what gives her an android-like appearance, too smooth and stiff to show any real expression.

Theo's eyes are large and soulful in her heart-shaped face, and that face is always in motion, flushed with delicate tints of color, lashes fluttering, lips trembling, emotions flitting like ghosts, so quick I have to watch her constantly to catch them.

There's no comparison.

But if I have to compare...I don't have to think twice.

I do, however, have to figure out a way to shake off this girl with a minimum of drama.

"Did you enjoy your dinner?" I say, trying to sneak past.

Jessica did not eat one bite of her dinner as far as I could tell, pushing it around on her plate instead. That's the typical model diet: excuses and air.

"Not really," she says. "And you never answered my question."

"I thought I answered all your questions while you were auditioning for game show host."

"That was a test," she says, stepping closer but not letting me pass. "To see if you could actually be interested in Angus' errand girl."

I know she's trying to rile me up. It works better than it should—it's a struggle to keep my cool as I say, "Theo's not an errand girl. She's an extremely talented chef. Angus is a fool not to let her do her actual job more often."

"I'll tell him you said so."

"You do that."

We're staring each other down, the flirtatious vibe Jessica's trying to manufacture stretched to its breaking point.

"So?" she says.

"So what?"

"So are you coming to my listening party?"

"Sure. With Theo as my date."

She rolls her eyes. "You can drop the devoted boyfriend act." She fingers the buttons on the front of my shirt, gazing up at me coquettishly. "A man like you doesn't tie himself down to one woman—especially not one who spends her time in an apron."

"Jessica..." I take her hand and remove it from my chest. "Maybe you don't hear this a lot or maybe you just don't *want* to hear it, but I'm not interested."

Her nose wrinkles up in rage, as much as it's able to wrinkle. I use the opportunity to push all the way past her out of the cramped space.

When I return to the table, Theo is waiting, purse already slung over her shoulder. Where she's standing, she has a clear view over to the bathrooms, which means she almost certainly saw Jessica touching my chest. Angus, still seated in the booth, is blissfully unaware.

"I better order another drink," he jokes. "Women take forever to pee."

"Thanks again for dinner," I say, shaking his hand. Angus made a big production out of paying the check.

"I'm excited to see what you've got for me next week." To Theo, he says, like he's bestowing some big favor, "You can take the weekend off; I'm going to Bali."

"Have fun," Theo says in a restrained way that doesn't give me any hint as to her current mood.

It's only once we're alone, walking out to my car, that I can bring up the awkward moment with Jessica.

"I don't know what you saw, but—"

"I saw everything," Theo interrupts.

She pushes me against the brick wall of the restaurant, kissing me ferociously.

I kiss her back, hands thrust in her hair, tasting the sweetness of the wine on her lips.

When we break apart, Theo says, "You were perfect."

I laugh. "I don't think Jessica likes having competition in the 'fleecing Angus' department."

"No, she does not." Theo frowns. "She likes it best when she's the only one with an iron grip on his Amex. She's sneaky and underhanded, and she's never liked me, Sully—we need to be careful."

Every time Theo uses my nickname, it feels like a warm hand pressed against my chest.

I'm not surprised Jessica doesn't like Theo—people who avoid real work are always threatened by those who don't.

"So, I take it you don't want to go to her listening party..."

Theo laughs. "Only to hear how bad it is."

"Oh, that's my entire motivation—I *have* to know what sort of lyrics pour forth from a gilded soul like Jessica's. What do you think a solid gold soul is worth on the open market?"

Mystified, Theo says, "I've never even seen her *listen* to music."

"Do you think she dances? Will there be a video?"

Theo laughs. "God, I hope so."

On the drive home, I can't stop glancing over at Theo's legs.

Ever since the vibrator incident, I've been incredibly well behaved. I haven't knocked on her door once, despite fighting the urge about a hundred different times.

I'm not sure how I'm going to restrain myself tonight. Theo looks drop-dead, knockout stunning in that dress. The kiss outside the restaurant is still burning on my lips. I'll hire Jessica to lurk around the bathroom every single time, if that's what I get afterward.

I try to keep my eyes on the road, but they keep drifting back in Theo's direction. Around the seventh or eighth time, she smiles and says, "What is it?"

"Nothing...just admiring the scenery."

"The scenery?"

"Uh huh. It's very smooth and...shapely."

Theo's dimple peeks into view. She shifts in her seat, a movement that causes her skirt to ride a little higher up her thighs. *Little minx...*

She says, "This is one of my favorite drives."

"Mine, too."

I'm going the long way home so we can take the Pacific Coast Highway. There's almost no difference at all between the moonlight glinting off the deep, indigo ocean and that sparkling dress against Theo's creamy thighs.

Her hand lies on the seat between us, small, thin, and slightly battered—a clever-looking hand, one capable of all sorts of difficult and intricate tasks.

A hand that stole all over my body all night long, teasing against my chest, climbing up my thigh, twining in my hair, all maneuvers designed to distract and irritate Angus, but their real victim was me. My cock has been swelling and going soft for hours while Theo draped herself all over me.

I want to slip my hand into hers and link our fingers together. Such a simple act but strangely significant.

In a way, it feels like it would be crossing a bigger line than when I put my face between her thighs.

Holding hands is intimate. It's meaningful.

I could do it all night long while Angus was watching, but I'm not supposed to do it now.

I can't stop looking at her hand. I can't stop looking at her legs. I can't stop taking deep breaths of Theo's perfume, which smells a little bit like vanilla and cinnamon with an edge of something naughtier.

She's supposed to go home in two days.

Just two more days.

Is she looking forward to the peace and privacy of her own apartment? Or will she miss our dinners, our early morning coffee when we're both still puffy-faced and dreamy, our drives into work together?

I'm going to miss them.

In fact, how much I'll miss them is concerning.

For the last ten years, I've worked my ass off to make sure I'm never again drowning in that feeling of loss, of emptiness, of helplessness…

And now, just a few weeks into this thing with Theo, I'm already cut loose. Where's my discipline? Where's my planning? Where's my self-control?

Those are the anchors of my existence, and they're evaporating like they were never solid iron at all but only flimsy soap bubbles.

I was barely paying attention to Angus during dinner. The whole damn point was to dig down and figure out what's actually going to make him pull the trigger on a property. Instead, I lost myself in the game of jealousy and connection, taking all my pleasure from how good it felt on my side of the booth with Theo curled under my arm, proving that only *I* know what really makes her tick.

I was sloppy at dinner. Nonstrategic. I could have done way more to stay on Angus' good side, and I could have made an ally out of Jessica instead of an enemy.

I made mistakes because I was emotional and distracted.

Because of Theo.

"You looked stressed," she says.

"I'm not stressed."

Her eyebrow raises like a soot-black question mark. "I thought we promised not to lie to each other?"

Goddamnit. Why did I make that rule?

"Okay." I let out a breath. "I'm a little stressed."

"Why?" Theo sits up in her seat. "Angus hired you! He wants you to find a property."

"He *said* he wants me to find a property. But we're a long way away from signing on the dotted line."

Theo studies my face. "You don't think it was a real offer?"

I glance at her, impressed how quickly she's learning.

"You tell me...how did he phrase it?"

Theo thinks it over, remembering. "He said, *Maybe I should hire you...*You think he was exerting dominance? Trying to create an employee-boss dynamic?"

"We caught his interest and created this nice little competitive vibe that's got him all hot and bothered, but it only works as long as he feels like he's got the upper hand and he's getting what he wants."

Which is why I have to be very, very careful when it comes to Theo...

Angus is possessive of her. The only way this will work is if he thinks he won...

There are a hundred things that could still go wrong even if I play this perfectly. And I'm not performing perfectly, not even close—my head is full of the girl sitting next to me. Even in this very moment, my eyes are dropping irresistibly to those lovely legs.

I need to get it together. Stop treating Theo like my actual girlfriend and use her for what she is: a partner in crime in a delicate operation.

I can't protect her from Angus or Jessica, and I can't let myself get distracted when we're all out together. In fact, I shouldn't be distracted right now. No holding hands, and no looking at Theo's legs.

I fix my eyes firmly on the road.

Until about five seconds later when they slip sideways once more...

"Well...," Theo says, giving me a surprisingly devilish look. "If you're feeling stressed, would you like a helping hand?"

The good intentions I've been forming burst in an instant.

"Fuck yes," I say, wrenching the wheel to take the very next turn.

21

THEO

Sullivan pulls in at a lookout over the water. I'm nervous, all of a sudden, even though I just asked him to do this.

He turns to look at me, his hand resting lightly on top of the wheel, his dress shirt open at the throat, his eyes dark and liquid in the moonlight. The shape of his lips is so beautiful, I can hardly believe that I've kissed them.

The top's down on the car, but it still feels like we're in our own little bubble of air. All I can hear is my heart pounding in my ears, and all I can see is Sullivan.

He grabs my face in his hands and kisses me. The kiss feels forbidden, stolen, and all the more delicious for it. Our privacy in the car, away from Angus, away from the house, feels distant from even our own promises.

All the reasons I had to protect myself, to be careful, to guard my emotions, seem to belong to another time and place. Here and now, it's just the two of us under the stars with the surf crashing below. It's Sullivan's mouth on mine, his hands exploring my body...

I unbutton his shirt and slip my hand inside, touching his

warm, bare chest. My fingers fumble at the waistband of his trousers. But Sullivan stops me.

"Wait."

I'm already short of breath, panting a little like I'm running. "What's wrong?"

"Nothing, nothing's wrong. Only..." Sully winces slightly, like he has to do something he really doesn't want to do. "I don't want to hurt you, Theo."

"Then don't." I kiss him again, on his mouth, the side of his neck, that slice of warm, brown skin where I opened his shirt...

"But you said—"

"Fuck what I said. Don't you want this?"

"More than anything," Sully groans, and I can hear how much he means it. A thrill races up my spine, sparks crackling across my skin. I kiss him and kiss him, unbuttoning his pants once more.

"Then stop talking."

That's exactly what he does, using his mouth to kiss me instead, deep and warm and wet, until I'm drunk on his taste and dazed with his touch.

"Did you mean what you said?" Sully murmurs. "About helping me relax..."

"Of course. It's only fair to return the favor..." I've almost freed his cock from his pants. It's wedged beneath the zipper, thick and swollen.

But again, Sully stops me with a hand on my wrist.

"Much as I'd enjoy that, there's something I'd like even more."

"What?" I ask nervously.

"Another taste of this..."

Sully sweeps my legs up onto his shoulders, so my heels hang over his back. My skirt rides up almost to my waist, and he dives between my thighs, hooking one finger under the gusset of my panties and pulling them to the side. Cool air hits my bare pussy.

Sullivan's hot, wet mouth follows a moment later, making me gasp with shock.

"My mouth's been watering every time I think about it..."

He swipes his tongue up my slit, a blast of soaking pleasure that has my eyes rolling back, my head lolling out the open car window.

I cup the back of his head in my palm, feeling the thick, soft brush where his hair is cropped short, the longer, silky strands draped over my fingers. My legs are spread, thighs pressed against his ears. The warmth and pleasure of his mouth is so all-consuming, it feels like he's eating me alive.

He raises his head enough to lock eyes with me, his lips swollen and wet. "I fucking love how you taste."

He drops his head just a little, still looking into my eyes, and takes a long, slow swipe of my pussy with his tongue.

"Mm...," he growls. "Fucking delicious."

I've never watched a man eat my pussy before. I've always felt a little shy about sex in general, opting to do it in the dark. And Trent wasn't begging to head downtown, regardless of lighting.

But if there's one thing I know, it's the expression on a man's face when he enjoys what he's eating.

Sully is devouring my pussy like it's the most heavenly thing he's ever tasted.

His groans of enjoyment, his wild enthusiasm, and the aggression of his mouth sweep away any flimsy self-consciousness. It's so obvious how much he likes it that there's no room for me to be nervous and definitely no place for modesty—soon I'm singing like a songbird, crying out over and over as Sully makes a fool of me with his tongue.

Say a prayer for my poor, departed vibrator because it's completely been replaced—I'm coming like I never did even with my favorite toy. Waves of pleasure crash over me harder than the waves below, again and again until the beautiful dress Sully bought me is soaked in sweat and my thighs are trembling around his ears.

At last, he lifts his head, mouth swollen, dark eyes glittering with triumph. "Now I'm relaxed."

I give a laugh that's high and giddy, dazed with pleasure. "Are you trying to tell me you'd really rather give than receive?"

"A hundred out of a hundred times."

I'd call him a liar, but I'm pretty sure he just proved it.

And besides, Sully's kept his promise to be honest with me, just like I have with him.

Which is why when he asks, "So how was it?" I have to tell him the truth:

"That was the best hour of my life."

It's well past midnight when we get back to the house, but Sully and I are energized, neither one of us ready to head to bed.

"I'm not tired," Sully says.

"Me neither." I perch on the kitchen countertop, heels knocking lightly against the cabinets.

"What do you usually do when you can't sleep?"

"Read," I say. "Or make myself a snack. What about you?"

"Go out to the garage."

I smile. "Is that code for smoking a joint?"

Sully laughs. "No, though it could be...Can't smoke in the garage, though, that's where I keep all my machinery."

I perk up. "For woodworking?"

"That's right." Sully looks gratified that I remembered. "Haven't been out there all week. Someone's been distracting me..."

I like distracting Sullivan. I like when I have his attention.

That's what was so incredibly seductive from the moment he asked me to dance—those dark eyes fixed on me and me alone.

"Will you show me your workshop?" I beg.

He takes me around the side of the house to the three-car garage, which I'm realizing I've never seen opened because Sullivan parks in the driveway. He punches the code into the pad, making the door rumble up.

Inside is an entire woodshop, as neat and organized as Sully's room. Every single tool is either put away inside a drawer or hung inside one of those crime-scene outlines for wrenches and hammers.

Several pieces of heavy machinery stand against the wall, but I couldn't name the purpose of a single one.

"Want to make something?" Sullivan says.

"Make something?" I squeak. "I don't even know what any of this is!"

"You taught me how to cut a tomato—I'm pretty sure I can teach you to use a lathe."

"Okay..." I muster my courage, trying to view the tools as no more intimidating than a chef's knife or a saucepan and the machinery as just another sort of oven. "What can we make?"

"Something simple to start—how about a pen?"

I have no idea how we're going to make a pen out of wood, but I'm sure Sully does.

First, he helps me to select a block from the array on his shelf. I choose a dark walnut with a swirling grain. Sully helps me set it in place on the band saw. He puts his hands over mine, steady and firm, so the scream of the saw seems endurable and the open blade much less alarming.

Sawdust flies up as we cut the block in half, filling the air with sweet, burning walnut and dusting the front of my dress.

"I should have changed—"

"Don't you dare," Sully growls in my ear. "I'm not done looking at you in that dress."

I'm sure he can feel me shiver against his chest. I'm sure he can see the goosebumps on my arms and my nipples poking through the front of the dress.

I don't care if he sees. I don't care if he feels—I want him to. I lean back against Sully's warm body, letting his hands guide mine.

He walks me through an impossible number of complex steps, drilling a hole through the block, gluing in the brass casing, cutting away the excess wood, and, finally, turning the pen on a lathe. Even after that, the sanding and finishing takes another hour.

We talk all the while, Sully explaining the machinery and processes, describing some of his favorite projects of days past.

"I think I like making bowls the best. It takes forever to sand them, but that's what I love, the feel of the wood, the way you can bring out the color, the grain, the glow..."

I tell Sully how crepes are my favorite thing to make, blending the batter smooth, swirling it around the hot pan, peeling off the perfect, thin disc, turning it onto a plate, soft and silky.

"It's satisfying, that perfect golden brown..."

"Like oak," Sully says, grinning.

"Sweet smelling like vanilla..."

"Like cedar and cherrywood."

"You're going to make me want to eat this pen." I bring it up to my nose so I can inhale the freshly-sanded grain, so I can rub its silky smoothness against my upper lip.

But I would never eat it and never give it away or lose it. I'll keep this pen forever because I made it with my own hands, inside of Sully's, heads together, his lips against my ear.

He helps me with the final step, fitting the nib in place.

"There you are," he says softly, handing it to me.

"I'm never lending it to anyone." I laugh. "Not after all that work."

Woodworking makes cooking seem simple by comparison—even a project as basic as a pen has more steps than the fiddliest quiche.

Sully shrugs. "Everybody's always trying to get out of work, but that's like trying to avoid your vegetables. Work is good for the soul, like meat, like potatoes. You can't live on entertainment any more than you can live on chips and cotton candy."

"Agreed," I say. "But you've got to actually like your job."

Sully gazes around at the workshop he's already restored to neatness, sweeping up the sawdust, returning the tools to their rightful positions. His eyes are dark and distant.

"After we lost my mom, I threw myself into work because I had to. That's what saved me. Instead of becoming more angry, more bitter, more lost, I had to get stronger. I got on a schedule. I started reading every morning and working out. I took control of myself because that's the only thing I could control."

He takes several slow breaths. I see the fire in his eyes, and I see how hard he's worked to contain it, to use it as fuel instead of letting it burn free, consuming everything in its path.

That's Sully's demon: anger and rage.

Mine is cold, dark ocean.

When I lose myself, it's in the depths of drowning—sadness that drags me down.

My dreams saved me. But dreams are as unsatisfying as cotton candy if they never become reality.

Sully says, "I was working with an agency at first, I think I told you—my boss became a mentor to me, or so I thought. We were supposed to do the land deal together; we had a buyer lined up. I put all my savings into it. Then he stabbed me in the back."

I wince at the pain on his face, a betrayal that obviously still stings. "I'm sorry, Sully."

"It doesn't matter." He gives a hard shake of his head. "But I have to tell you, Theo, I can't swing the payments much longer, not on my own. We've got to close this thing with Angus."

"We will," I promise.

And maybe I shouldn't make a promise so difficult to deliver.

But I'm more determined than ever not to let Sully down.

22

SULLY

Sunday's supposed to be Theo's last day at my house. Her apartment is habitable again, and there's not really any reason for her to keep staying here.

Except that I want her to.

It's not because of my dad, either. No, I'm a lot more selfish than that. It's me who's dreading the slide back to silence, the empty coldness of the house, its echoing space. Eating meals alone or with my dad, usually in front of the TV. He won't want to keep dining outside on the picnic table when it's just him and me, and my cooking certainly doesn't deserve it.

And it's not just the company, like any warm body would do. It's the specific presence of Theo, the way she puts music on as soon as she walks through the door, the way she dances around the kitchen while she cooks and sashays down the hallways. She won't sing along to the music, not while I'm listening, but she sings in the shower, adorably out of tune.

I like how she calls Martinique after work even though they just spent eight hours together, to commiserate over the awfulness of Martinique's commute and her leering neighbors, who won't let her pass their front step without catcalling.

I like finding Theo's books scattered absolutely everywhere because she's almost never without a book in her hand, carrying them from room to room, forgotten paperbacks continually turning up between the couch cushions, on the porch swing, and even in the backseat of my car.

I love watching her read, how she scowls at the page or sometimes gasps out loud, how she bites at her thumbnail, more concerned for fictional characters than most people are for their real-life friends.

And I love, on a level so deep it makes my chest hurt, hearing her talk with my dad. Theo likes to sketch in the hammock in the yard. My dad does his carving on his front step. When their hobbies align, they chat to each other for an hour or more about movies, music, politics, and World War II documentaries.

He doesn't talk to me like that, or Reese.

Theo's different.

She listens, really listens, not just waiting for her to turn to talk. Her face is open and responsive, and though she rarely gives advice, whatever she says is delivered with such kindness and sympathy that it feels like things are already on their way to getting better.

They're out in the backyard together right now, my dad back at the grill for a second chance at ruining dinner, Theo setting out the fixings for fajitas.

I'm supposed to be chopping tomatoes, but it's a lot less fun without Theo's hand on top of mine.

"Don't let him ruin the meat!" I shout through the open back door.

"He's doing great!" Theo calls back, which I don't believe for one second.

"You worry about your tomatoes," my dad grunts. "And why don't you mix up some lemonade while you're in there?"

Theo says, "I already made virgin mojitos!"

She hasn't been serving alcohol with dinner. My dad exclusively drinks alone in the pool house, so it probably doesn't make any difference to him. But I don't think he's been drinking as much this week. His eyes are less bloodshot, and his movements are crisper.

Not that I'm getting my hopes up—it's only been a couple of days. But that's a couple of days more than usual.

In fact, this morning I saw several liquor bottles in the trash bin that were still half full.

It means nothing.

But also, it means everything.

We've barely sat down to eat, the table groaning with food, the yard lit up with fairy lights, when a familiar voice calls out, "What's with the party? I'm supposed to be the one surprising you!"

Reese stands on the back step, unshaven, hair a little longer than usual, looking rumpled from what I'm sure was a very long flight but delighted nonetheless at the sight of our backyard.

"Who cleaned up back here?"

"Merrick!" Theo says at the same time that my dad shuns the credit. "It was Theo."

I stand up to give my brother a hug.

He pulls me in close and slaps me on the back. I smell some exotic spice in his hair and feel the new muscle he's built. Otherwise, it's the most familiar thing in the world.

"Missed you, bro," he says. "Hey, Pops!"

He goes around to my dad's side of the table to hug him, too.

Theo smiles up at Reese. "Welcome home!"

"Oh no, you're not getting off that easy..." Reese's next stop is Theo's end of the bench. "Come on, hugs for you, too!"

Blushing brilliantly, Theo stands. Reese lifts her right off her feet, which he does pretty much anytime he hugs someone smaller than him.

Seeing Theo's small frame wrapped up in my brother's thick arms gives me a strange feeling. It's like watching her be hugged by me, but I'm also jealous.

Dad says, "I thought you weren't coming home for another two weeks."

"Filming wrapped early," Reese says cheerfully. "Don't know if I've ever said that before! Honestly, I think the director just wanted to get the hell out of there. He caught malaria *and* a tapeworm."

"Oh my god!" cries Theo. "Were you sick, too?"

"Nope!" Reese pats his flat stomach. "Healthy as a horse. I didn't even get the shits more than two or three times. Who's hungry?"

"Nobody anymore." My dad pulls a face.

"More for me, then." Reese grins, piling his plate with tortillas and meat.

"So, when does this show air?" Dad says. Despite his disgust at Reese's table manners, he still takes a huge bite of his fajita. Even my brother can't ruin Theo's food.

"Not for a couple of months," Reese says, talking with his mouth full. "But there's a viewing party for the pilot next week. I got you front row seats! You, too, Theo, you've got to come—pilot parties are the best, everybody's in a great mood 'cause nothing bad has happened yet."

Theo smiles. "What sort of bad things?"

"Oh, you know...terrible ratings, terrible time slot, director quits, star quits, network goes bankrupt, entire industry goes on strike...all the things that blew up my last six gigs."

Theo lifts her virgin mojito. "Well, here's to nothing bad happening..."

Reese touches his solo cup to hers. "For at least one entire season!"

We all toast, Reese draining his cup in one long draught.

"God, it's good to have ice again!" He holds his forearm up against mine. "You're pale as a ghost compared to me!"

I'd call my cafe au lait color a long way off pale, but my arm does look light compared to Reese's dark brown tan. He's covered in scratches and bug bites, too.

"So...," he says with a shifty look between Theo and me. "How come Theo's staying in the guest bedroom? Is that part of the Great Boss Fakement?"

"Sort of," Theo says, blushing furiously.

"How's that going?"

"Excellent," I say. "We've moved on to Phase Two."

"Phase Two, wow!" Reese grins. "Is that the part where you guys pretend to get married and have a baby?"

"No," I say with dignity. "No baby will be required."

"Are you sure? Because I don't think you've fully committed to the ruse. A big old belly would be really convincing..."

"Don't give him ideas." Theo shudders. "I can absolutely imagine Sully making me wear one of those fake baby bellies that are supposed to traumatize teenagers."

"I can imagine *Sully* doing that, too...," Reese says, with a wicked glance in my direction. It has not escaped his notice that Theo is using my nickname.

Not much escapes my brother's notice when it comes to causing trouble and harassing people. In fact, I'm starting to think it might not be such a great thing that he's back home.

My dad looks happy, at least. And I am, too. Though I can't shake the feeling that the presence of Reese is unlikely to help matters.

Reese is an agent of chaos. He likes things best when they're messy, unpredictable, and exciting. Which is the opposite of what this plan needs to be to succeed.

Plus, I just know he's going to give me shit about Theo. Reese has always had a soft spot for her.

Already he's watching us from the other side of the table, observing how Theo refills my drink and how I pass her the sliced avocado before she even asks because I know she likes to pile avocado on almost everything she eats.

"So how does it work?" Reese says. "Theo passes you the inside info, and you use it to charm her boss?"

"Not exactly," Theo says. "He's mostly been making Angus annoyed and irritable."

Reese laughs. "That's a novel approach."

I tell him, "It's working brilliantly, thank you very much."

"I bet," my dad says. "Until you get Theo fired."

"That's not going to happen."

My dad looks at me, unsmiling. "You don't know what's going to happen."

To ease the tension, Theo says, "We went out on a double date the other night with Angus and Jessica Kate."

"Jessica Kate!" Reese chortles. "I know her."

I groan. "Please tell me you haven't slept with her."

"Not a chance. She's got that look like she'd bite your head off and drink your blood afterward. Or take a pic of you naked and sell it to TMZ."

"Well, not *you* probably," I say. "But someone more famous..."

"Ha, ha." Reese lifts his chin. "Laugh while you can 'cause this show is gonna be—"

"Your big break, yeah, yeah." My dad and I could finish that sentence in our sleep.

"It will be!" Reese says with infinite confidence. Hope springs eternal in my brother's breast—or delusion.

"I can't wait to watch the pilot," Theo says kindly.

"Are you actually going to be in it this time?" My dad finishes his second fajita in one monstrous bite.

I explain to Theo, "Last time Reese made us go all the way downtown for a premiere, his scene was cut from the movie."

"Nobody told me," Reese scowls. "But it happens to the best of us. Did you know Harrison Ford played the school principal in ET? His whole scene ended up on the cutting room floor."

"Happens all the time!" Theo says. "Paul Rudd had the funniest scene cut from *Bridesmaids* — you can still watch it on YouTube."

"Really?" Reese delightedly searches his phone.

"Don't encourage him," I warn Theo. "He'll do this for hours."

"I don't mind," Theo says. "I love movie trivia!"

"I *used* to." I glower at Reese.

Reese smiles back at me, unperturbed. "Dad's got the best stories—stuntmen see the craziest shit. You ever miss it, Pops?"

"Hard to miss it when I still feel it every morning." Dad presses his hand against his lower back.

My dad picks up odd jobs now, mostly in construction. He hasn't worked anywhere steadily for more than a couple of months.

"So how did the double date go?" Reese circles back around.

"It was lovely, actually." Theo says. "Jessica couldn't bully me as much with Sully there."

She gives me a warm and amused look, the sort that's full of meaning and shared memory. Reese sees the look and shoots me one of his own that I pointedly ignore.

"Sully's a nice guy," Reese says, with way too much irony. Now he's getting a look from *me* that is quite unfriendly. "And how long will you be staying with us, Theo dear?"

"I'm going home tomorrow."

"What's the rush?" my dad pipes up unexpectedly.

"No rush." Theo looks pleased and embarrassed by all the attention. "Just, the fumigating's done."

"It might still stink, though," I say quickly. "There could still be fumes. It could be toxic."

Reese grins at me. "Solid point, brother." And then, to Theo, "Plus, I just got here! We haven't even had time to hang out."

I say, "Better stay a few more days to be sure."

Theo laughs. "You don't have to twist my arm—it's a hundred times more fun cooking in your kitchen than mine. Not to mention sleeping on a Tempur-Pedic mattress."

Heat spreads through my chest. I feel ridiculously relieved, like I just got a stay of execution. Theo is staying a few more days...maybe even another week. My mood soars, and I see my smile mirrored on Reese's face.

"Fantastic!" my brother says. "The house smells better, too—I could tell as soon as I walked in that there was a girl around. You ever notice that, how when it's just men, it smells like pee and testosterone?"

"Our house doesn't smell like pee," I say, offended. "Outside of your bathroom."

Reese shrugs. "Still smells better with Theo in it."

I can't argue with that.

After dinner, my dad lights the firepit so we can make s'mores again. With the fairy lights and the purple ironwood blooming and the sparks from the fire swirling upward, the backyard is almost magical.

Reese brings out his guitar and tunes the strings. "Why don't you get yours, Sully?"

"I haven't played in ages."

"So what? You worried you lost all your calluses?"

Softly, Theo says, "I'd like to hear you play."

Firelight bathes her face, turning her skin golden and her eyes blue green.

I can't refuse her request. In fact, the way she looks in this moment, I'd probably sign over the deed to the house.

"Well, if it's you asking…"

"Typical," my brother snorts.

When I return with my guitar, I'm shocked to see that my dad brought his out of the pool house. I can't remember the last time I saw it in his hands. It takes him a lot longer than Reese to tighten the strings, but when he's finished, the notes are rich and mellow and perfectly in tune.

He strums the chords of *Golden Years*. Reese plucks the riff. I join in, softly at first, the strings pressing into my fingertips because Reese is right, I've lost my calluses.

My dad sings the verse, his voice low and rough and husky. Reese joins in on the chorus. By the second verse, my fingers don't feel so thick and clumsy anymore. The guitar begins to feel like an old friend again, or like an old lover, my hands fitting against the shape they know so well.

The kindling pops, the smell of smoke and sparks and burned sugar swirling through the air. Theo's eyes are clear and luminous. After work, she changed into the sort of top that a milkmaid might wear, loose, white, and crinkly. Her dark braid hangs over one bare shoulder, bits of hair curling around her face.

"Come on," my dad says to Theo. "You know this one, join in."

She shakes her head hard. "I can't sing."

"Liar," I say. "You love singing."

Her eyes go wide, and she presses her lips together like a song might accidentally leak out, shaking her head even harder. "I'm terrible."

"You can't be worse than me," Reese coaxes. "Come on, let's hear it!"

"We'll play loud," my dad says, strumming harder. "We won't even hear you."

Winking at Theo, I say, "I already heard you in the shower..."

Theo is bright pink, but she's smiling. She can't hold out for long against the combined pressure of all three of us and the pull to sing along to David Bowie.

Reese belts the chorus extra loud and extra off-key. Laughing, Theo joins in, quietly at first but picking up steam when she sees that no one's judging her.

Her voice is soft, melodic, and lilting, as soothing as her speaking voice. It's never going to win American Idol, but it blends in a strangely lovely way with my dad's rough growl and Reese's enthusiastic tenor. Soon I'm singing, too, which I almost never do, but tonight it feels right.

Tonight feels golden and full and like everything's going to be okay—sensations I haven't experienced in a very long time.

Usually, I feel dread and pressure. Usually, I feel like there's a hole in my guts that can't be filled.

Theo can't replace my mom. But somehow, she creates a balance that allows the rest of us to be something like we used to be. She's a center we can orbit around. A reason to be out here together, feeling happy and alive once more, if only for the night.

I don't want this to end. I don't want her to go back home because then the spell will break, and I'll be like I was before. Everything will be like it was before.

At least, until the deal with Angus is done.

Then, everything will change forever.

I'll be loaded instead of broke and scrounging. My dad will have security, and he won't have to take construction jobs with his degenerate prison buddies. I'll be able to afford to send him to rehab, assuming he'll agree to go. And Reese won't have to take every shitty gig that comes his way—he can do character roles in indie films or stage plays or even try writing a script like he's always talking about.

Those are the dreams that have motivated me for years. But now that I'm the closest I've ever been, I don't feel the same sense of certainty.

Maybe it's because this thing with Theo isn't working out how I expected. My plans have already twisted and changed so much...I can't see clearly to the end anymore.

I look at Theo across the fire, and I begin to worry that it's inevitable; I'm going to have to choose between hurting her and saving my family. Because if there's one thing I've learned, it's that you can't get everything you want. There's always a trade-off.

I'm not okay with either of those options—I'm not okay with hurting her, and I'm not okay with letting my dad and my brother down. They depend on me. I'm the only one who can fix this.

Which means I have to make this work.

Somehow, I have to make this work.

Reese catches my eye. I haven't seen him in three months, but it feels like he's already inside my head again. Like he's reading my thoughts from across the firepit.

He leans his head in the direction of our dad, raising an eyebrow as if to say, *"Check out the old man strumming and singing again...what have you been feeding him?"*

I give Reese half a smile and half a shrug in return, which means, *"I don't know what's going on, but let's not do anything to jinx it."*

It's only later, in the house, that we can actually talk.

Reese and I are washing the dishes while Theo takes a shower, which she often does at night as well as in the morning. She says the cooking smells get in her hair, but honestly, I kind of like when I catch the hints of nutmeg or rosemary or fennel that mix with the natural sweetness of her scent.

Reese barely waits for her to leave the room before he says, "Okay, what the hell is going on?"

I make a serious business of scrubbing out a pot so I don't have to look at him. "I told you what's going on."

"Not with Angus," Reese says. "With you two chuckleheads."

I'd like to play dumb, but that won't work with Reese, and it'll really piss him off. We don't lie to each other.

So instead, I say, "It's gotten a little complicated."

Reese snorts. "Who could have seen that coming?"

"Oh, shut up. I said a *little* complicated—we're still on target."

"Oh really...what target is that, exactly? Because I don't remember the part of the plan where you two move in together and play house."

I grit my teeth. "That was an unexpected detour, but it's working perfectly. Angus is jealous as hell, Theo's right here where I can keep an eye on her, and I didn't hear you complaining when you were eating your sixth taco."

"Oh, I'm not complaining," Reese says cheerfully. "I'm just pointing out that you're way off the reservation. You think you're in the middle of a carefully cultivated Sullivan plan, but this is starting to look a hell of a lot more like some bullshit *I* would pull. And you know how that always ends..."

"This is nothing like one of your plans."

"And why is that?"

"Because I'm completely in control."

"Oh, okay..." Reese nods and wipes a rag around the pot. "So you and Theo *weren't* giving each other eyes all night long like she took an edible and you're a plate of nachos."

"We've been getting to know each other. We work together really well."

"You *work together really well?* Oh Jesus, it's worse than I thought."

"What's that supposed to mean?"

"It means you're delusional, big brother."

Unlike most twins, Reese delights in the fact that he was born second by four whole minutes. He loves being the younger brother so he can foist anything unpleasant onto me.

But now, apparently, he's decided it's his turn to give advice.

"I'm delusional?" I give him a withering look. "Remind me who spent the last three months pretending to be a Centurion in the Sumatran jungle."

"Ah," Reese says with a maddeningly superior expression, "but the difference is, *I knew I was pretending.*"

"I also know I'm pretending. So does Theo. We're not actually dating."

"But are you fucking?" Reese cuts right to the chase.

"No, we're not."

Technically true but avoidant of what happened just last night.

Reese isn't fooled. Shrewdly, he says, "Not having sex, or not messing around?"

I attack the cheese grater with the Brillo pad, tempted to do the same to my brother's arm. It's obviously been too long since I gave him a good, hard snakebite.

"We messed around a little bit," I admit.

"I knew it!" Reese is insufferable when he guesses right. He digs his elbow into my ribs and wiggles his eyebrows at me. "How was it?"

I can't smother the smile that spreads across my face.

My brother crows and punches me on the shoulder. "You dirty dog! Gettin' freaky with Theo Mahoney—"

"Seriously, shut up or I'll dunk you in the dishwater."

"Try it! I've been doing two hundred push-ups a day. I bet I could shot put you over the house."

To prove it, he tries to put me in a headlock. It's true that Reese has been working out nonstop with Hollywood's eighth-best trainer, but I haven't been skipping the gym. A scuffle ensues that slops dirty dishwater all over the kitchen floor while we each try to waterboard the other, ending only when we're both soaking, Reese's shirt is torn, and Theo is standing in the doorway, staring at us.

"What are you two doing?"

"I'm welcoming him home," I say, still strangling Reese with my right bicep.

Reese breaks my grip by giving me what we lovingly refer to as a "sack tap," which means he slaps me in the balls.

"Ow, you little bitch-bastard!"

"Look who's talking!" Reese dances around me with his fists up like an old-timey pugilist. Unfortunately for him, his heel comes down in a puddle, and he slips and falls on his ass.

I laugh at him, while also groaning with my hands cupping my balls.

He laughs at me from the floor. "Hope you didn't want kids."

Theo shakes her head at the pair of us. "I don't understand siblings."

Reese
RIVAS
CALIFORNI
LOS ANGELES
CALIFORNIA

23

SULLY

Despite Reese's guilt trip, I wake up Sunday morning determined to keep Theo for at least a couple more days.

I make the strategic decision to order a shit ton of groceries to be delivered bright and early in the morning—all her favorite things, plus a whole bevy of tempting new ingredients.

Theo unpacks the bags like it's Christmas morning.

"Where did you find rambutan? And look at these raspberries! They're practically the size of a plum!"

Theo holds up a palm full of raspberries that have got to be modified with at least one gene taken from Arnold Schwarzenegger.

I grin. "What should we make for dinner? Do you want to experiment with some more diner dishes? I got some bison meat; I thought it might be cool to try a gourmet burger or some kind of twist on a meatloaf—"

Theo beams at me. "Or an open-faced sandwich! I have this incredible recipe for a vinegar-based barbecue sauce..."

I never thought I'd be anything better than dismal at cooking, but Theo's an excellent teacher. With her help, I actually whipped up a pretty passable guacamole on fajita night. Even my dad managed to grill the carne asada without burning it.

Theo makes food fun, and she never takes it too seriously—when I fuck something up, she manages to make it edible again, or she chucks it in the trash, shrugging and saying, "Now we know what doesn't work."

As she's neatly slotting the groceries into the fridge, she gives me a shy glance. "You really think I should stay a few more days?"

"You'd be doing me a huge favor if you did. It's really been helping my dad, all these meals together..."

That's true even if it's not the only reason I want her to stay. Or even the one that matters to me most.

"Is Reese okay with it?" Theo bites her lip. "He'd probably rather have his own space—"

"He's got half the goddamn house! He can't even hear us from over there. Not that there's anything to hear."

Theo gives me a swift look. I didn't visit her room last night, and she didn't visit mine.

I stayed in bed out of guilt.

Theo might have been worried about Reese—or maybe she just didn't want to come.

"Trust me," I say. "He likes having you here. We all do."

"Okay." Theo's face relaxes. "I'll stay a couple more days."

The elation I feel is so swift and overwhelming, it's a little frightening. I shouldn't be this excited.

And yet, I find myself saying, "What are your plans for today? For once, I don't have a single appointment...."

"Angus is in Bali," Theo says, smiling. "Which means I'm also completely free and unoccupied."

"A whole entire day off! My god, what will we do with this kind of freedom?"

"We've got to do something..." Theo bats her lashes at me. "Otherwise, we're wasting it."

"I know what we should do." Reese strolls into the kitchen and takes an enormous bite out of one of Theo's freshly baked blueberry muffins.

I snatch the other half of the muffin out of his hand and pop it in my mouth. "Who said you're invited?"

Reese grins, chewing lustily. "Me, of course."

REESE'S GENIUS plan is to spend the day at the Santa Monica Pier. Starved of decent food for the last three months, he demolishes two hot dogs, a burger, a frozen lemonade, and a funnel cake, and then regurgitates thirty-eight dollars of food into the nearest trash can after his third ride on the Pacific Plunge.

I expected Theo to be timid, but she surprises me by immediately getting in line for the tallest rollercoaster.

"Are you sure?" I say, gazing up at a structure that looks like it was designed by a drunk carny well before modern safety standards.

"I'm not worried." Theo winks at me. "There are no sharks on rollercoasters."

Even so, she looks a little nervous as we near the front of the line.

"Having second thoughts?"

"Not a chance!" She grips the railing in both hands. "I'm doing this."

Nobody is pressuring Theo to take this ride, but it's obvious she's trying to prove something to herself. Her lips get pale and her knees get wobbly, but she climbs into the car anyway.

As our rickety ride climbs the first rise, Theo gives me a concerned look. "Are *you* afraid?"

I wouldn't say I'm scared of rollercoasters, but they do make me nervous. It's the complete lack of control—I don't even like riding in other people's cars, let alone a train of tin cans zooming around a wooden track.

But *afraid?*

"Of course not."

"I thought you promised not to lie..." Theo teases. "Your knuckles are white."

I look at my hands gripped around the bar. "You could pry those off with a crowbar, easy."

Theo laughs. "Don't worry, I'll keep you safe."

She puts her arm around me right as our car tips over the edge and goes plunging down.

Someone's screaming. I'm worried it's me until I realize it's Reese right behind us.

The car whips around hairpin turns, swoops and dives. Theo's shrieking with pure, unadulterated glee. Her hair is a black whirlwind, her eyes sparkling bright.

As we flip through the last loop, there's a moment where gravity swaps and we're floating in space. Theo turns and time seems frozen, suspended, her hair a cloud around us, her lips parted, her hand clutched to my chest.

The urge to kiss her is overwhelming.

But Reese is five feet away, and in that fractional hesitation, the moment passes. The car loops around, and we coast out of the final bend.

Theo can't stop laughing, giddy and weak-kneed from a ride that felt near suicidal.

"They have not tightened the bolts on that thing in at least twenty years," I mutter, gratefully departing the janky little cart.

"That's what keeps it spicy," Reese says. "The fact that about once every four years, one of those things goes shooting off the rails."

We head to the arcade next, where Theo proves surprisingly adept at Space Invaders, and Reese and I resume our ancient grudge match as Ryu and Ken. I redeem my manhood by winning Theo a stuffed panda in the shooting gallery.

Theo won't set the panda down for a second, lugging him around on her hip like an extremely lazy, black-and-white toddler. Even when she waits in line for more frozen lemonade, she won't let Reese hold Mr. Pipps.

"I can be trusted to babysit a panda," Reese says crossly.

"You *just* lost your sunglasses in the arcade five minutes ago," Theo points out.

"Fine," Reese sulks. "I'll win my own panda. Sully, lend me twenty bucks."

"No way—you already wasted thirty on that game."

"I'm right there! If I would have hit two more targets—"

Theo takes the opportunity to sneak away to the lemonade line, panda still safely tucked under her arm.

Reese stops complaining to note, "She's turned into quite the little spitfire, hasn't she?"

"Yeah, she's changed a lot since high school. We all have... except for you." I give Reese his own elbow to the ribs.

But Reese turns and fixes me with a surprisingly serious look. "She likes you, Sully."

"Yeah, I like her, too."

"Then what the fuck are you doing?"

Heat rises up the back of my neck. "We already went over this last night."

"Yeah, and the more time I spend around you two, the less I think of this so-called plan. This is going to blow up in your face spectacularly, take it from an expert in impulsive fuckups."

"There's nothing impulsive about this. I spent months planning—"

"But did you really consider the consequences?"

"Of course I did."

"Then I repeat, what the fuck are you doing?"

I'm starting to get annoyed with Reese, but I press down my anger. I know he has my best interests at heart even if he's being a condescending fuck right now, not to mention a huge hypocrite.

"I told you," I say through stiff lips. "I've got it under control."

"You can't control this shit. Not even close!"

"What are you talking about?"

"Oh, I don't know, like number one, she falls in love with you and you ruin her life. Or number two, she makes all this delicious food for our dad and then he goes back to being a depressed alcoholic as soon as she leaves. Or Angus finds out and fires her and makes it his mission to ruin the rest of her life...do you want me to keep going?"

"No," I say, but Reese continues anyway.

"Or how about, you somehow manage to pull off the impossible and actually get this deal done, only for Angus to find out what happened afterward, so he can sue you for fraud. There's a lot of things that could go wrong—you're playing Russian roulette with a litigious billionaire."

"You can't sue someone for pretending to date your assistant."

"Well, I guess it's okay, then."

I glare at Reese, my heart thundering.

This might be the first time in our lives that my brother is lecturing *me* on the right thing to do. The fact that even *Reese* thinks this is dangerous does have an effect on me.

When Theo returns, barely managing to balance three frozen lemonades along with her stuffed panda, the mood is unmistakably tense.

"What happened?" she says, blinking at my scowl and Reese's stiff posture.

"Nothing," I grunt.

Theo gives me a hurt look because that breaks our rule against lying.

24

THEO

I can't remember when I had more fun than our afternoon on the pier, but the mood in the car on the way home was strained.

That's the second time I've walked in on Sully and Reese squabbling. Maybe that's just their dynamic, but I can't help feeling like it's got something to do with me.

There was a definite vibe like they were talking about me when I walked up with the lemonade. They both shut up instantly and gave me that awkward look like they were worried how much I heard. Sullivan seemed pissed and Reese wouldn't make eye contact.

They both relax over dinner, which we eat outside in a yard almost entirely cleared of debris after Merrick and I spent most of Saturday hauling out four trash bins of dead branches and undergrowth.

Sully wouldn't like it if he knew how much work I've been doing around the house—he told me to take it easy and relax on my rare weekend off. But he's a hypocrite because he was at appointments all day on Saturday, and anyway, I love hanging out with his dad.

My dad took off when I was eight. But he wasn't that great a father to begin with. Honestly, it was kind of a relief when he was gone because at least I didn't have to hear my mom crying in her room as much.

Once it was just the two of us, we were poor as hell, but our apartment was quiet and calm. If my mom said she could come to my school play, she'd be there, and if she had to work, that was okay, too, because at least she was honest about it.

My father was nothing but a chain of broken promises: birthday gifts he talked up for months but never actually bought, outings that were supposed to be fun and special that turned out to be me sitting in the car while he popped into the pub for "just a minute" to have a drink with his friends.

My mom was the only person I could count on. She never let me down. She never would—until cancer took away that choice.

You'd think it might bother me being around Merrick. I'll admit, the smell of liquor leeching from his skin does induce a queasy mix of dread and nostalgia. But yesterday when we worked in the yard, all he smelled like was clean sweat and smoke. And in every other respect, he's nothing like my dad.

My dad was a bragger, a liar, a fantasist. When I was really small, I adored him because he could tell the most incredible stories. He'd have my mom and me rolling with some anecdote about how he avoided a speeding ticket or some prank he pulled with his buddy's lunch pail.

But later, I started to pick up on the hints that he was unfaithful to my mom, and I guess, in a way, to me, too. After he left us, he remarried and had three more kids. Or so I heard from the only aunt who still talks to him.

Drinking aside, Merrick's nothing like my dad.

He's honest—sometimes brutally so. He's quiet and somber,

but when I bring up a topic of interest, he's intelligent and insightful.

And most of all, I can tell how much he loves his sons. The way he talks about Reese and Sully shows how intimately he knows them, their strengths and their weaknesses, their passions and plans.

He's not lazy, either. He might be broken and fucked up and nonfunctional at times, but when he's sober, he works like a beaver, head down, shoulders hunched, completing Herculean tasks in a day.

I don't want to fool myself that I can "fix him" just by cooking him dinner, but I can see for myself that he's doing better now than he was a week ago.

I was relieved when Sully asked me to stay a few more days. It probably won't change anything, not long-term. But also...maybe it could.

I've got to figure out what's going on with Reese, though. If he doesn't want me here, it's not cool for me to stay.

I corner Sully after dinner, pulling him into the music room and closing the door.

"What were you fighting about with Reese?"

He shifts in place as if he's considering how much to tell me. I look at him, narrow eyed, because if he won't answer me honestly, I'm going to be pissed. We made a deal. In fact, the whole thing was Sullivan's idea!

At last, he sighs. "Reese was giving me shit because he's worried about you."

Warmth spreads in my chest. I always liked Reese—more than Sullivan, actually, though of course I feel differently about that now that I've become better acquainted with Sully's best traits. But I appreciate that Reese is looking out for me.

Though really, the expression on Sullivan's face might be just as responsible for the warm and wobbly feeling I'm experiencing. He looks so concerned, it's kind of adorable.

"I'm not going to get hurt," I say, mostly to make him feel better.

I don't actually have any idea what's going to happen to me. This thing has already expanded so far past what I imagined...I couldn't predict the ending any more than I could predict what people are going to be wearing on Rodeo Drive in the year 2080.

But I don't feel quite so terrified anymore.

This week has been one of the best weeks of my life. I cooked some of the most delicious meals I've ever made and ate them under the stars with my new favorite people. I didn't have to spend hours in traffic in my crappy car or even visit my shit apartment. Instead, I worked out with Sully in his gym, slept on a memory foam mattress, played cribbage with his dad on the back steps, read a stack of Stella's old thriller paperbacks, and got tipsy on wine coolers and played Sully in Mario Kart until two a.m. on a work night.

And best of all, I didn't cry once. Not over some frustration at work or some slight from Angus or some unpaid bill or some shit Tinder date.

It was a brilliant week, one that boosted me up beyond what I would hardly have believed possible.

I think the real difference was that I didn't feel lonely once. Sullivan was always right there, down the hallway or only a phone call away.

And maybe I should be terrified because all I've bought myself is a couple more days. This has an expiration date; it will end eventually. And Reese is probably right that when that happens, I'll be fucking devastated.

But I was already miserable before.

Now, at least I've had an incredible week.

I wouldn't give that back for anything.

And I'll take all the additional days I can get. Even if I know it's only temporary. Even if it will hurt like hell when it goes away.

I'm okay with that now. Because it's better than never having this week at all.

Sullivan isn't so easily convinced. He's still got that pained look on his face. "Reese might have a point. If Angus figures out that you lied to him—"

"He's not going to find out."

Sully's jaw flexes as he considers, hands stuffed in his pockets. At last, he says, "You haven't said anything to Martinique?"

"No, of course not. I promised you I wouldn't."

"Okay."

He looks stressed and uncomfortable, which I find endearing. Sully wasn't stressed at all when we started this thing. But now he's worried about me.

"It's going to be fine," I assure him. "You're taking Angus out this week—knowing how convincing you are, you could wrap this whole thing up by Friday."

Sully lets out a barking laugh. "No pressure!"

I shrug, saying simply, "I believe in you."

Sullivan tilts his head, searching my face. "Thank you. That means a lot, actually."

"I'm not rushing you, but I am feeling confident. I've never seen Angus so wound up. I thought you were crazy when we started, but after that double date, I'm feeling more than ever like this might actually work."

Sully finally smiles, that smile that seems to dissolve every bone in my body as it spreads across his face. "You're the convincing one—how do you flip my mood around so fast?"

He makes a move toward me like he might sweep me into a hug but stops himself.

I try to hide how much I brightened and even opened my arms.

Now we're both avoiding each other's eyes.

Sully's smile fades. "We probably should quit with the hookups, though. It could make things…complicated."

"Right," I say, cursing with all my soul the heat in my face. "I was thinking the same thing."

That's a filthy fucking lie, which breaks our agreement.

"Okay, I wasn't thinking that at all," I admit. "But you're still probably right."

"It's for the best," Sullivan says unhappily.

He shifts his weight, his hands hanging at his sides, his fingertips almost grazing mine.

I look up into his face, the urge to reach up and touch that shock of thick black hair falling down over his eye almost overwhelming.

But I resist.

And so does he.

We both go to bed alone like good little conspirators.

25

THEO

Monday morning, Sully offers to drive me to work again, which is swiftly becoming one of my favorite things about our arrangement. I hate driving and I love being chauffeured around like a princess. It makes my morning immensely less stressful, especially after a peaceful half hour of reading headlines to Sullivan in the sunny kitchen nook while he uses his fancy espresso machine to make the best goddamn latte I've ever tasted.

Or at least, it's peaceful until Reese comes strolling in in his boxer shorts with his hair sticking straight up, as well as about twenty percent of his morning wood.

"Reese, what the hell!" Sully shouts.

"Oops, shit, I forgot," Reese laughs, pulling open the refrigerator door to hide his lower half. "Not that it's anything Theo hasn't seen, huh, Theo?"

Actually, I have *not* yet laid eyes on Sullivan's equipment though I can't deny that I've imagined it approximately nine thousand times.

In fact...I'm not entirely annoyed with Reese for giving me a new data point to enhance my nightly fantasies.

"It's a little different when it's on your body," I note, peeking out from between my fingers.

"It's not different at all," Reese promises solemnly. "We measured."

"Stop talking," Sullivan says. "And go put on pants. And a shirt."

"And a *shirt*?" Reese groans like he's being sent to a gulag.

"Sorry about that," Sully says while his brother exits the room, still grumbling.

"No problem at all." I shoot him a mischievous look. "You're lucky Reese didn't come out stark naked—he seems the nudist type. Then I'd know all your secrets..."

Sullivan scowls. "Don't give him any ideas."

"Want a muffin for the road?" I made banana chocolate chip this morning.

"Better not," Sullivan pats his stomach while giving the muffin a wistful look. "If I don't watch it, I'm going to become the chonky twin."

"Don't worry, girls like a little junk in the trunk."

"Oh yeah?" He grins at me. "In that case, grab two."

ANGUS IS BACK in the office, looking tanned and hungover.

"Theo!" he barks. "You're late!"

Actually, I'm six minutes early. "Late" to Angus has nothing to do with agreed-upon times and everything to do with when he happened to arrive.

"Sorry," I say because that's easier and more effective than arguing or, heaven forbid, pointing to the clock.

Not good enough. Angus jeers, "Getting in your morning snuggles with Sullivan?"

It used to bother me when he'd act like this. But there's something incredibly powerful in holding a secret of my own. Nothing he says gets to me in quite the same way when I know I hold the trump card.

"Yup," I say blithely. "Sully loves to spoon."

Angus' scowl is perversely thrilling. I'm really starting to love pissing off my boss.

"You're in bright and early," I remark. "I guess that means Jessica *isn't* a fan of spooning."

His face falls in a way that's kind of tragic. "Not really," he says in a small voice.

Jessica is so mean to Angus, I could almost pity him—if I didn't remember what an ass he was to the rest of his girlfriends, not to mention his ex-wives.

Jessica and Angus play the exact same game; she's just better at it.

Angus asks, "Are you coming to her listening party?"

"What night is it?"

I'm stalling, trying to come up with an excuse why I cannot possibly attend this event. Sullivan might welcome the chance to mock Jessica's almost-certainly horrific debut album, but I would prefer to stay far away from Angus' girlfriend until they break up. Which should be any minute now.

"Sunday," Angus says.

"Ooh, I wish I could, but—"

"I need you there," he says flatly. "To make sure everything runs smoothly. Jessica's really counting on this party to turn heads. Her single hasn't been doing quite as well on Spotify as she hoped."

"Oh no..." I say while making a mental note to tell Sully he doesn't even have to attend this party to enjoy the warbling beauty of Jessica's "gilded soul."

"Tell Martinique I need her there by four o'clock to wrangle the caterers."

"You got it."

I hustle off to give Martinique the shit news, feeling guilty because that's exactly the sort of job that would usually be assigned to me.

"It's fine," she sighs. "I don't have any plans this weekend anyway. I broke up with Raymond."

"Which one was Raymond?"

Martinique has a new boyfriend every other week. I haven't heard much about this one because we haven't been chatting as often since I've been staying at Sullivan's place. Mostly because I can't tell her any of the things I want to tell her.

"He's the orthodontist," Martinique says. "And that was the entire problem—he would *not* stop telling me how pretty I'd be if I fixed my teeth."

Martinique has the sort of incisors that turn in slightly, and they happen to be fucking adorable. I want to drive to Dr. Raymond's office and write something nasty across his windows. Something like, *How dare you try to improve my flawless friend!* But that probably wouldn't fit—I'm not very good at graffiti. Or writing "Happy Birthday!" in a card without squishing in the last three letters.

"Well, he's clearly insane."

Martinique laughs. "I mean, they are crooked."

"So what? Who wants Chiclet teeth? Your smile is gorgeous!"

Martinique gives me a sideways hug, laying her head on my shoulder. "Can I hire you to follow me around and hype me up?"

"I'm pretty sure that's what Angus already hired me to do."

She snorts. "He doesn't need any extra hyping."

"Neither does Jessica." I sigh, thinking how insufferable she'll be if she actually becomes a pop star.

"Guess it's a good thing I'm not bringing Raymond to the party anymore if I've got to be there at four. Sucks that it's back to the dating apps, though. I'm so tired of swiping."

"You know...," I say. "Sullivan's brother just got back into town."

"The twin?" Martinique's eyes light up with interest.

"The one and only. Or, I guess...one of two?"

"I'm in!" Martinique says at once.

I laugh. "I haven't even told you what the plan is yet."

"I'm assuming it has something to do with me banging this gorgeous brother as a rebound from my douche-magouche boyfriend."

"I was just going to invite you to his screening, but if banging somehow occurs...I doubt anyone will complain. Except maybe the neighbors."

"Aren't you and Sullivan the neighbors?"

I pause. "Yes, actually. Plus their dad, Merrick—he lives in the pool house."

"Oh yeah? What's the dad like?"

"Gruff, smart, funny."

"Good looking?"

"Very, actually."

"Hmm..." Martinique says, eyebrows rising. She's always liked older men. "You've got a whole harem, don't you? Thanks for sharing...is the hot dad coming to the party as well?"

"Probably...," I say with squirming discomfort. I don't think Sullivan would be thrilled about Martinique hitting on his dad. Also, I kind of feel like I should mention the fact that Merrick is a raging alcoholic, but I don't want to talk about him that way, not even to Martinique. "But I don't think he's on the menu—Merrick is...a widower."

"Oh, I gotcha." Martinique drops the idea at once. Her dad died when she was a baby, and her mom never remarried either. "Well, that's fine—if the brother looks anything like Sullivan, he's fine as hell. And I'm not completely against actors. For a hookup, at least."

"You're so benevolent."

"I try. But there's only so much of me to go around... Speaking of which...you must have popped your Sullivan cherry by now. How was it?"

"Uhh..."

"Oh my god. *You still haven't slept with him?*"

"Could you shriek a little quieter? There might be a couple of people in the office who haven't heard you yet."

"I'm sorry," Martinique says, just as loud, "but that's outrageous! What the hell are you waiting for?"

I really, really, really hate this part of it.

Martinique is my best friend. I've never lied to her before. It's not fair that Sullivan is making me do this.

Still, I promised not to tell her the truth.

Biting my tongue and cursing Sully, I say, "We fooled around a bit..."

"That's better than nothing," Martinique says grudgingly. "Though I'm still pissed at you for waiting so long to tell me! What happened? I want to know everything."

"It's kind of embarrassing..." I'm remembering the moment when I opened my bedroom door, hot and bothered and clinging to the pieces of my vibrator, only to run smack into Sullivan.

"Perfect." Martinique gleefully settles down on my desk to hear the tale. I bet she'd pay fifty bucks for a bucket of popcorn right now.

I tell her everything I'm allowed to tell, which is mostly the sexy bits, while Martinique howls with laughter.

"And he loves to eat pussy?" she sighs. "He really is perfect.

What the fuck are you doing not banging his brains out? I know you like him..."

I press my lips together, nodding. I like Sullivan too much.

"And I know you're attracted to him..."

"Extremely."

There's no point denying that part. And I don't have to—I'm allowed to be attracted to my fake boyfriend.

"Is it nerves?" Martinique says. "Are you worried because you've only had sex with four people and he's probably slept with, like, six hundred gorgeous women?"

"Well, I wasn't before, but I am now, asshole."

Martinique snickers. "With that face and that hair and that body? For sure he's got a triple-digit body count."

I'm not supposed to sleep with Sullivan in any case, but the thought of all the women he must have dated, and how beautiful and successful and smart they probably are, makes me feel like shit.

I got dumped by Trent Borgeeno. Trent fucking sucks. If I'm not good enough for him, I don't know why I think there's a snowball's chance in hell that Sully would want to date me for real.

Martinique sees the look on my face and becomes immediately repentant.

"But who cares!" she says unconvincingly. "That doesn't matter! Sullivan's crazy about you. He's going to love fucking you even if you barely know what you're doing and your blowjob technique is B+."

"You should get a job as a motivational speaker."

"Maybe I should." Martinique buffs her nails on her shirt, completely missing the sarcasm.

I appreciate the encouragement, but Martinique can't give me advice because she doesn't know what's actually going on. She thinks Sullivan is "obviously crazy about me" because she doesn't know this whole thing is a scam.

To ask her what to do, I'd have to tell her the truth. And I promised I wouldn't.

So I'm right back where I started—wondering if the reason Sullivan has pulled back again is because he's scared of his feelings...or only of mine.

26

THEO

I'm feeling nervous as hell because today is Sully's first time out alone with Angus. He's taking him around to several properties, though not the one Sullivan owns himself. He says he's saving that for last.

I have no idea if Sully's scheme is genius or unhinged, but Angus is wearing a suit today, and that has to mean something. Whether he loves Sullivan or hates him, Angus obviously sees him as someone to impress.

Angus makes a huge, big deal all morning long around the office, telling everybody how my boyfriend is "working for him now" and what a big favor it is to me.

"What are you gonna get me for Christmas for this?" He waggles his eyebrows.

"It depends. Can I put it on the corporate card?"

"I don't know how you're going to put a foot rub on the corporate card."

The idea of touching Angus' feet, which are the same texture as his crocodile hat, makes me want to throw up almost as much as one of his protein shakes. Angus' feet are the only thing that could give me sympathy for the trials and tribulations of Jessica Kate.

"You're going to have to get Sully a knighthood if you want me to touch your feet."

"Done!" Angus says in a way that seriously alarms me.

"That was a joke—I'm not rubbing your feet even for a knighthood."

Angus pouts. "They're not that bad."

"Your last two pedicurists quit."

"Sondra moved."

"To Anaheim."

"She said she doesn't like driving the freeway..."

"She doesn't like shaving your bunions."

Negging Angus is so much fun. I should have been doing this all along. What was I so afraid of? Getting fired? I should have fired myself.

Whatever happens, when all this is over, I'm not working for Angus Tate anymore. If Sullivan taught me one thing, it's that I'm worth more than that. Even if I'm a liar and a dropout and a hot mess, I respect myself more than Angus does.

Martinique is in a foul mood because Angus has been making her work directly with Jessica on the party planning.

"She's got me hand sorting green M&M's into bowls! I told her you can buy them all in a single color, but she says those taste weird."

Jessica loves green the way that Angus hates yellow.

"Maybe they really are soulmates."

"The devil and the devil's mistress," Martinique says darkly.

"Don't let Angus hear you call him the devil's mistress."

She snorts. "Jessica hates *you*, by the way—she won't stop talking shit. You must have really pissed her off at dinner."

I think of the moment when Sullivan removed her hand from his chest, and I feel a hot bolt of triumph.

"If Jessica Kate had good opinion of me, that's when I'd be worried. I only care what people think of me when I admire them."

"Does that include me?" Martinique bats her eyelashes.

"You more than anyone."

"Well, I think you're wonderful. And I'm not just saying that so you'll help me sort M&M's."

"I will help you, though."

"Thank god," she sighs.

SULLY ARRIVES at noon to pick up Angus.

By that point, almost everyone in the office is hanging around their desks to get a look at my boyfriend.

"Oh my god!" Leanne the accountant says. "He looks just like that actor! Aren't you worried he's going to cheat on you?"

I'm more concerned with the shocked expressions I'm seeing all around me. Not a single person says, "*What a lucky guy...*"

Dating Sullivan is not exactly easy on the ego. Until he locks eyes with me and his whole face lights up, and he comes striding straight across the room. Then I feel like a million bucks.

He cuts though the gauntlet of staring eyes, not stopping until he sweeps me up in his arms and hugs me. He gives me a chaste kiss and sets me down, saying, "I missed you extra today."

It's possible that the entire thing is a performance. Probable, even.

But in that moment, I make a dangerous choice:

I pretend it's entirely real.

I look up into Sully's eyes and let myself pretend, just for a minute, that the warmth on his face, his excitement, his hands still gripping my arms, are one hundred percent genuine. I pretend that Sullivan loves me desperately, and three hours apart really did make him ache to see me.

I've never tried heroin, but the oxytocin that floods my body as I look up into his dark eyes has got to be the exact same thing. The moment I give in, I already know I'm lost. Say no to drugs, kids...just one hit can hook you forever.

I say, "I missed you, too."

And something even worse happens—I realize I'm not lying. Not even exaggerating.

I missed Sully and I'm ridiculously happy to see him.

The smell of his skin and his shaving cream is giving me dopamine. The devilish look on his face makes my mind race. I'm suddenly jealous that I'm not going on his outing with Angus because I love watching Sullivan work.

And even though I know the whole damn office is watching and this is entirely inappropriate, I seize his face in my hands and kiss him. I kiss him because I want to. Because I *need* to. And this might be my only chance.

Sullivan's arms go around my back. His hands slip into my hair. Our bodies press together.

It's only a few seconds, but the passion, the intensity, is all out of proportion. When we split apart, Sullivan is flushed, my heart is racing, and Martinique hoots at us.

"Do you two have an OnlyFans? I'm ready to sign up."

"Sorry," I say, embarrassed. I'm not sure if I'm apologizing to my colleagues or to Sullivan.

The expression on Angus' face is hard to read. He looks fixated, upset, but something else as well...something that almost looks like longing.

I don't think Angus is attracted to me, not in any serious way —he's always treated me like a peon, not a prospect. But I'm beginning to think that he's powerfully jealous all the same. Not of me, exactly, but of what he thinks exists between me and Sullivan.

It's the one thing he's never had—someone who actually adores him.

"*Whew.*" Sully pretends to wipe his forehead. "Remind me to visit you at lunch more often."

"I wish you would." I lay my hands on his chest in a ridiculously soppy way.

I'm playing it up for Angus, but also, I've jumped all the way in the deep end. I tell myself I'm method acting while I gaze up at Sully like I love him. While I take deep, head-spinning breaths of his cologne.

This is fine. This is totally okay. Just a couple more breaths...

"Alright, break it up," Angus snipes. "Time to go."

"See you tonight," Sully says, tucking a piece of hair behind my ear and giving me one last quick kiss on the cheek. Only then does he turn his full attention to Angus. "I've got some great places lined up."

"I hope so. The ones Corgus showed me were shit. Sloppy seconds from Bezos? Kill me first."

Sully catches my eye and gives me an approving wink. I almost explode with pride.

When they're gone, Martinique grabs my arm in both hands. "Yeah, I'm definitely going out with the brother. Identical, you said? Like, all the way down?"

"Reese is a little messier."

"Perfect," Martinique says serenely. "I'm a fucking slob."

SULLY WARNED me that he'd probably be out late with Angus, so I drive myself home after work and start planning dinner for what will probably only be Merrick and me—Reese is out at a casting.

I find Merrick shirtless and filthy in the bottom of the pool, a huge pile of weeds tossed up along the rim. I change clothes into something scrubbier and drop down to help him.

Merrick doesn't bother to try to stop me—he's well aware that I like working with my hands as much as he does. He passes me a pair of gardening gloves, and we work in companionable silence for the first hour, the only sounds the soft cadence of our grunts, shuffles, and dripping sweat.

Merrick seems slower than usual, sweat pouring down his back, hands shaking as he tears up another deep-rooted weed.

Even so, by the time the sun dips toward the fence, we've cleared out the entire pool.

"Are you going to refinish it?" I ask. "Actually put some water in?"

"Would you and Sully go swimming if I do?"

"Of course!"

"Then I will." He leans on the handle of his shovel, wiping his forehead with the back of his arm. The golden streaks in his hair glint in the late sun. The hair on his arms is golden, too, against his nut-brown tan. His chest and arms look a little fuller than they did a week ago, a little less depleted. His blue eyes are clear.

His face, though...his face is full of sorrow.

Quietly, Merrick says, "I should have done this a long time ago."

"The second-best time to do it is today."

"No, it's not." He shakes his head, shamefaced. "The second-best time would have been a little less long ago."

He gazes around at the yard and house that still need an immense amount of work—the walls stained, the roof missing shingles, ivy and kudzu growing everywhere, swallowing the pool house.

"I have no excuse," he says miserably. "I'm a fucking disgrace.

Stella would be ashamed of me. She never would have believed I'd let this happen. That I'd do this to the boys..."

My heart is breaking, and I don't know what to say, so I say what I know for certain is true:

"Those boys love you. Sullivan *loves* you. He'd never be ashamed of you."

"Sully..." Merrick says his son's name with such a painful level of love that tears spring into my eyes though I blink hard to hold them back. "Sully deserves so much better."

His hands grip the handle of the shovel until his knuckles go white and his shoulders shake with emotion, with the thing he's trying so desperately to hold inside.

"It all fell on Sully. I should have been there for my boys—I'll never forgive myself for that."

Merrick drops his head and drops the shovel, too, his hands covering his face. Without thinking, without even knowing what he's talking about, I put my arms around him, and Merrick falls apart.

He sinks to the cement, and I sink down, too, still holding onto him like I can somehow hold him together through sobs so wracking they feel like they'll shake him apart.

"I'll never, never forgive myself for what I did. They needed me. They shouldn't have lost us both. And when I came home, the evidence of how hard it had been, how awful it was...I could see it everywhere, all around me, and it was overwhelming. The idea of trying to fix this place, trying to make it like it was...it seemed impossible, and wrong, even. Because it can never be like it was, not without her. To even try to fix it was a lie. But I should have, I should have...why did I let them live like this?"

I hold Merrick, smelling the smoky scent of his skin, a little bit like Sullivan's and a little bit like my dad's because of the faint hint of bourbon.

"It's okay," I murmur, rubbing his back. "It's going to be okay."

Through the bits and pieces I make out, coupled with the smeared tattoos on his knuckles, I gather that Merrick spent some time in prison after his wife's death, and he feels guilty as hell about it.

"Stella meant everything to me...but I lost control...I can't imagine what it was like for my boys, here alone..."

Maybe I shouldn't ask, but I have to know. "What happened?"

His voice comes out hoarse and choked from the hollow of his arms. "I chased him down, strangled the life out of him...for taking Stella from me."

Now I understand...the stalker at the door. Merrick must have killed him.

Which means that Sully lost his mom *and* his dad for a time when he was only eighteen.

I hug Merrick with all my might. "You didn't want to leave. You came home as soon as you could. My dad never came home. He was an alcoholic. He'd cheat on my mom, break her heart. He'd lie to me and let me down. And after all of that, what I really hate him for is leaving. He abandoned us, he didn't care. I would have rather had him there, the terrible man that he was, than the rejection of him leaving me, knowing that he didn't love me."

"But I did leave them..." Merrick moans.

"You didn't abandon your sons—you avenged their mother. And they already forgive you for it. Your boys are strong and capable because you and Stella loved each other and raised good men. They were able to handle themselves *because* of you. Look what a good job you did—give glory to your wife by enjoying them for her."

"I can't," he sobs. "I let them down. I let them down."

I don't know what comes over me. Maybe it's the stress and pain I've seen on Sullivan's face. Maybe it's the hope he's barely allowed himself to feel this week. Maybe it's my resentment at my own father.

I grab Merrick by the shoulders and force him to look into my face, practically shaking him.

"Then stop letting them down!" I bark. "Sullivan doesn't care what happened before—do you hear me? He loves you! He loves you so fucking hard! The ONLY thing he cares about is you getting safe and healthy again. If you care about him, you'll stop punishing yourself."

Merrick blinks at me with eyes that are definitely bloodshot now, but from tears, not the bleariness of alcohol.

Miserably, he says, "I can't do it. I've failed so many times. I'm weak."

"There's nothing weak about how you feel about your sons. Do it for them if you can't do it for yourself."

It hurts me to say that. My dad didn't love me enough to change. He didn't even love me enough to stay.

But Merrick is different than my dad. I've seen for myself.

He *does* love his sons. And love is a powerful motivator.

"Anyone can change anything they want about themselves if they're willing to do the work. Look at me—I was a scared little mouse, now I'm fleecing a billionaire. I was a broke-ass bitch, but I'm going to open my own restaurant. I was a lonely loser, and now I'm...friends with the hottest person I know."

Even with his face swollen with tears, Merrick has to scoff at that.

"*Friends,*" he snorts. "You two are ridiculous."

Hope leaps in my chest even though we're supposed to be talking about Merrick.

"You think Sully likes me?"

I'm nakedly transparent, but Merrick is kind. He stands up, holding out his hand to help me do the same.

"He's crazy about you, kid."

Now I could cry from pure elation.

Hearing that from Merrick means a hell of a lot more than

hearing it from Martinique—Merrick sees us when we're not pretending.

And he knows his son. So unless Merrick's just being nice... maybe, just maybe...it could be true?

I'm scared for him to see how happy that makes me. I'm scared to even feel it.

So I try to play it cool even though I have never, ever been anything close to approaching "cool."

"Well, good," I say. "'Cause, you know...I kinda like him, too."

Merrick makes a soft sound that I eventually recognize as a laugh.

"I know, kid. You're pretty obvious."

27

SULLY

The first outing with Angus goes even better than I hoped. I take him around to a couple of properties that might fit the bill. If he decides to take one of those, I'll make a nice, fat commission. But the real goal is to sell him my land. If I can hook that particular whale, I'll pocket almost twelve million dollars.

I got the land for a steal, but I had to max out every dollar of leverage I could beg, borrow, or steal. I'm mortgaged to the hilt, with ruinous payments I won't be able to float for much longer. I need to close this thing with Angus within the month.

The real trick will be making sure that Angus picks *my* property and no other—and that's where Theo comes in. I need to tie the land to Theo in his mind so he feels like he has to have it. So in the end, he feels like he's getting everything.

It's a risky little play, but so far, I've got Angus right where I want him. He would not stop asking questions about Theo's and my relationship the entire time we were out.

It amuses me even while it stokes my disgust. Angus had Theo working right next to him for four years, and he never gave a fuck about her. He's only become obsessed now that he thinks someone else wants her.

It's classic dog in the manger psychology, and it's exactly what I was counting on, but it still pisses me off. It's only now that I've pulled Theo out of the mud and cleaned her off that Angus realizes he was trampling a diamond under his feet the whole damn time.

I love letting her sparkle. I bought her a new dress for Reese's premiere even though Angus won't be there. This one was just for me—to see the smile on her face when she tries it on.

Theo twirls in front of the mirror in my room, which is the only one that's full-length in the house, outside of my parents' old room. The dress has that '50s silhouette that looks so pretty on her, with a sweetheart neckline. I'm wearing a button-up grandpa shirt to match her vibe.

"I love it!" Theo's smiling so brightly.

It's easy to make her happy. I can't stop doing things to make her smile.

I set a fresh stack of thrillers on the bed. "Since you burned through all my mom's."

"Not *all* of them..." Theo gives the books a guilty, hungry glance. "But more than I'd like to admit in a single week."

She pounces on the thrillers, devouring the blurbs.

"Murderous housewives! And this one's about a codebreaker... and one set in Alaska! I can't wait to read these!" She throws her arms around me and hugs me with her cheek pressed against my chest, her head tucked under my chin. "You spoil me."

She fits in my arms like puzzle pieces only wish they could fit.

I hold her like that, close my eyes, inhale.

And then...

Fear detonates, spattering everything with glittering black ink.

Happiness is dangerous.

It makes everything seem bright and shining and safe when it isn't, not at all.

It's the loveliness of Theo in this moment, the way she looks up at me, blue eyes, heart-shaped face, like a valentine in my arms, that makes me suddenly afraid. I know what happens when you adore someone like this.

I let go of her and step back. It's abrupt—she blinks up at me curiously.

I say something, anything, to fill the space.

"It's nice of you to come to this thing of Reese's. I should warn you, it might be bad..."

"Worse than Mounties Getting Mounted?" Theo laughs.

The fact that she remembered that dumb joke makes the wrong look come over my face. I'm supposed to be laughing with her. Instead, I swallow hard. "No, you're right—nothing can be worse than that, we'll be fine."

Theo takes my arm, walking with me out to the car.

I'm a robot with a glitch, all my systems shorting, blinking.

It's a date...

It's not a date.

She's my girlfriend...

She's not your girlfriend.

What I'm feeling is too much, what I can say is too little.

I'm glad I took the top down on the car because I know I'd be sweating otherwise. I flip through the dials, let the first clear song play. *Paradise* streams from the speakers. Theo tilts her head back against the seat and smiles at me.

My hand drops down on the nape of her neck. Theo blinks at me slowly like a cat, warm and sleepy. I rub my thumb gently against the tension at the base of her neck until it melts away.

We're driving down the Pacific Coast Highway, which is the most glorious highway in America; I'll put it up against any other. Take a drive at sunset and see the coast bathed in pastel turquoise and lilac before flaming down in melting shades of orange and red.

Theo's skin reflects every color like a pearl, her eyes as clear as the ocean. I can't stop sneaking glances at her, knowing that, like the sky, she'll only look exactly this way just once.

Her hand slips into mine. She interlocks our fingers and squeezes.

"Are you nervous? For Reese?"

I let out my breath and admit the truth. "So fucking nervous. If this thing blows up in his face—"

"It won't."

She sounds so certain.

"If it's not this, it'll be the next thing," Theo says with quiet confidence. "You remember that freshman showcase where Reese did the improv set with all the props? Even the teachers were pissing themselves, he had the principal rolling...None of us were surprised when he got *Rocko Rocks!* Reese is right about one thing...he was made for the screen."

Theo makes you feel what she's feeling.

She believes in Reese. She believes in me. She thinks tonight's going to be beautiful, and maybe it is...because it sure looks beautiful from where I'm sitting.

The coast spools away behind her, Theo's dark hair alive in the wind. Salt air in our lungs makes it feel like we're sailing, not driving.

I say, "I think I want him to succeed even more than he does. How did this happen? I don't want to be so invested."

I meant it like a joke. I said it sort of laughing. But Theo sees right through me.

"You take care of him," she says simply, her fingers gripped with mine.

For better or for worse, whenever I've locked eyes with Theo Mahoney, she's *always* been able to see right through me.

"I was cleaning out the pool with your dad," she says softly. "He told me what happened when he was sent away. How you were left alone—"

"I was fine," I say sharply. "We were fine."

"Your dad feels—"

"I know how he feels, I know how fucking bad he feels. I thought the guilt would kill him in prison. It *is* killing him, right now, just slower."

I didn't mean to grip her hand so tight. When I see the pain in her face, I let her fingers go.

I grip the wheel instead so my hands won't shake.

"That's why I'm doing what I'm doing, everything I'm doing... to show him that I'm fine, we're fine, we're fucking fantastic. Because if he can see we're thriving, then he doesn't have to keep hurting himself..."

The words tumble out too fast. My arms are rigid on the steering wheel, my whole body hard like wood, painful, tight...

"I'm not supposed to be the one taking care of everybody. I was the fuck up, the asshole. You knew me...you know what I was like."

Theo's soft hand touches my thigh.

The rest of me softens, too, all the parts that seemed so stiff and wooden.

"It will happen," she says. "Reese will get his shot. Your dad will heal. And you were never a fuckup, Sully."

Theo knows what I was.

Aggressive. Angry. Even before my mom died.

There was always a devil inside me to balance the angel on my brother's shoulder. In my teenage years, the devil took hold.

I'm ashamed of how I behaved then. I had poor self-control.

I take Theo's hand, gently this time.

"I am sorry. For how I treated you."

She looks at me, her eyes huge and luminescent. She lifts our linked hands and presses her lips against my palm, closing my hand like she's closing away the kiss.

"Thank you," she says. "That was so long ago, and it doesn't matter at all, but it makes me feel good anyway. Is that silly?"

"No." I shake my head, smiling at her.

"Isn't it funny...," Theo says softly, her skin glowing in the silvery light glimmering off the water, her eyes deep and shadowy. "I was scared of you. But even then, all I wanted was for you to talk to me..."

Her hand strokes playfully up and down my thigh.

In the twilight, with her hair pulled back, she looks young and dewy and more than ever like the Theo I knew, shy and delicate and oh, so tempting...

I can't help but feel a bit like the old Sully.

Low and husky I say, "When you used to wear that one sundress, the blue one with the straps, I'd stare at your back for an hour in Trigonometry."

Theo shifts in her seat, knees pressing together. "That one time you bumped into me in the hallway—"

"Excuse me," I interrupt. "But you bumped into *me*."

"Whoever it was...," Theo says, smiling. "Do you remember what you said to me?"

I remember like it was yesterday. The smell of sweat, sneakers, and Abercrombie cologne interrupted suddenly by something else—sweet, warm, and delicious. I collided with her, and while she was a fumble of books and papers, blushing and shaking in my arms, I realized I was holding the soft and surprisingly sensual body of Theo Mahoney.

She's like a doll, I thought, startled by the porcelain clarity of her skin up close, the thick, dark lashes, the pink tint that flushed her cheeks. Some people startle you from across a room—Theo shocked me with how beautiful she looked at the distance of a magnifying glass.

I let her go with some snarling line—

"Careful, Mahoney—that was second base."

It comes out sounding exactly the same, like no time at all has passed.

Theo shivers, her eyes glowing in the last of the light.

"That's right," she says. "That's exactly what you said."

"Why was I such an ass?"

There was no need to be aggressive. But I hear it again now, edging my tone...*Careful, Mahoney*...that craving she pulls out of me...

"Can I tell you something?" Theo says.

Her fingertips dance up and down my thigh.

"Later that night, in bed...that was the first time I ever...you know."

I capture her wandering fingers, gripping them tightly in my hand. "Are you serious?"

"Oh, yes," Theo says, tinting pink.

"You had your very first...experience...thinking about me?"

"Well...thinking about your hand landing on my breast."

"This hand?" I slip it inside the front of her dress, catching a handful of her warm, bare breast. It's the left breast, the same one I touched back then.

And yes, of course I remember the sudden and tantalizing softness, unmistakable even and because of how unexpected it was, a breast in my hand out of nowhere. Arousal hit me like a hammer strike. Who knows what I would have done if we weren't in a crowded hallway...

Now we're only in a car. Theo's nipple is hard and hot and stiff as I drag my thumb across it.

My arm lies across her chest, pinning her to the seat. Her eyes meet mine like we're locked in combat. I pinch her nipple between my finger and thumb. Theo's lips part, and she breathes fast and shallow.

"We can't," I say while her eyes glaze, while she squirms against the seat.

"Definitely not..." Theo says, pressing her cheek against my shoulder, arching her back so her breast fills my palm. "We shouldn't."

She leans against me, and my hand drifts lower, down the softness of her body, dropping to her lap...

I keep my eyes on the road like that means I can touch her anywhere I want. Like it's not breaking the rules as long as I'm not looking...

My fingertips slide up the silken softness of her inner thigh. Theo shifts in her seat, her knees parting slightly.

My fingers steal a little higher, and I discover something very interesting...

Good girl Theo Mahoney isn't wearing any underwear.

The velvet softness of her pussy lips is the most exquisite surprise. I slide my fingertips back and forth...wetness weeps like oil.

"We are absolutely not supposed to do this..." I rub my thumb over the soft, slippery button of her clit.

Theo's voice is soft and dreamy, her expression much the same.

"This is fine," she says. "We should put it in the contract, anything but sex..."

My thumb keeps stroking soft circles, all the way around.

"Anything but sex is completely on the level?"

Theo nods, slow and sleepy. "I think so. Nobody gets hurt from a little fooling around..."

"Better give you just one, then..." I say. "For luck..."

I rub her softly, that wet and melting pussy that comes alive beneath my fingers, shivering, clenching, telling me everything about how Theo likes to be touched, right there, right under my hand...

And even though we both know this isn't in the contract and probably shouldn't be, I make Theo come in the passenger seat, watching her skin flush, her eyes glaze, her thighs clench, her head tilt back, and every shivering gasp roll through her until there's a very good chance we're going to end up in the ocean because I can't take my eyes off her..

When I'm done, she's panting, gripping my wrist with both hands. Her cheeks are glowing, and her hair is a lot less tidy.

She catches sight of herself in the side mirror and laughs. "Everyone's going to get one look at me and know."

"You've got that freshly-fucked flush, don't you?"

She starts to get nervous. "I hope I un-pinken..."

"Theo..." I lift her hand to my lips and kiss it. "You look perfect."

She does. But I should not have done that because that was the same hand I used to touch her, and it smells like Theo's pussy. Now I'm even more turned on when we're supposed to be entering a movie theater in twenty seconds.

Theo also did not expect the theater to arrive so fast. She hastily tries to fix her hair.

Camera lights are flashing. The number of famous faces is a hell of a lot more than at the Mountie show.

"Look at that!" I say. "An actual red carpet."

"Could it be?" A grin spreads across Theo's face. "Could this actually be—"

"Don't say it," I interrupt. "Don't jinx it."

Instead, Theo slips her hand back into mine.

As we step onto the carpet, we're blinded by flashing lights.

Shouts of, "Reese, Reese!" and "Rocko!" show that I'm being mistaken for my brother. There's a ripple of confusion and surprise when I join him, followed by a fresh burst of camera flashes.

My brother's grinning fit to split his face. If nothing happens beyond this, at least I know in this moment Reese is happy.

He sweeps Theo up in his arms, hugging her. "Can you believe all this? Wait until you see the pilot, Theo, it's so fucking rad. My character's got this tragic backstory, you don't find out until season two, but it's real dark stuff, it's why he acts out, you know, when he feels—"

"We're going to watch it in two seconds," I remind him.

"I know, I'm just setting the stage..."

"*Shh*," I say loudly as the theater lights go down.

Reese takes his seat, gleeful as a kid.

I'm feeling pretty excited, too, until the show begins to play, and I realize that my brother has found a way to fuck me over spectacularly once again.

28

THEO

The lights go down, plunging the theater into darkness but not into silence because the premier is packed, and most of the actors are still chattering excitedly with their guests. It's only once the episode begins to play that a flurry of shushes quiet the last whisperers.

I'm sitting between Sully and Reese, a rather overwhelming pair of bookends. Sullivan is intimidating enough all on his own, and while Reese is a friendlier presence, the ways in which he's like and unlike his brother can be disorienting.

Martinique was furious that Jessica duties kept her away from her date. Since Reese is tagging along to the listening party, she only has two wait a few more days to meet him.

Merrick likewise cancelled, citing illness. Sully seemed to think that was only an excuse—apparently it's like pulling teeth to get his dad to attend even the most minor of social events. I suppose a glitzy premiere is about the worst thing imaginable for him—sure to dredge up bittersweet memories of attending the same sorts of events with his wife.

But I don't think it was an excuse this time. He really did look exhausted and ill when we finished cleaning out the pool the other day.

Reese is the exact opposite—so incandescently excited that it would take something close to a zombie apocalypse to ruin his night.

Sully is adorably nervous. I think he'd give a kidney to secure a second season for his brother's show.

From the very first shot, I have a feeling that no organ donation will be required. The pilot is stunning.

It's lush and gory and dramatic. Reese is almost unrecognizable in his Roman armor—he has to nudge me and point to himself on-screen before I cotton on.

"That's weird..." I say to Sully under my breath. "He looks like you."

"Almost identical, some people say."

"Oh, shut up, you know what I mean."

I've always been a believer that you never know if someone's good looking until they speak. It's expressions, those momentary flashes of thought and emotion, that truly shape a face. Despite being identical, I never thought Sully and Reese looked alike because Reese looks friendly and easygoing, while Sully looks like he's up to no good.

But Roman Reese is a whole different beast. He doesn't look easygoing at all. He's intense and determined. Ruthless, even. With that iron jaw and burning gaze, he's never more closely resembled his twin.

It's a little eerie, actually. I stare up at the screen, transfixed.

Reese's character is part of some raiding party that captures a village. The onslaught is bloody and brutal, much worse than what I usually watch. I can't handle horror movies, and even the John Wick films make my stomach turn.

I don't want to offend Reese, however, so I try to look pleasantly interested through the onslaught of broadswords splitting skulls and arms lopped off with axes.

Sully, seeming to notice my hands twisting in my lap, or perhaps the faint sheen of sweat on my upper lip, lays his hand across the back of my neck once more and gently rubs.

It's like he's pressing a button that releases all the tension in my body. I close my eyes partway, letting the on-screen blood and screaming blur while waves of pleasure roll down my back.

Now Reese's character has captured some sort of barbarian priestess. This is better because it means the murdering has stopped. I wouldn't say it's all the way to kosher, however, because there's a definite dub-con vibe in Roman Reese's tent while he orders the priestess-girl to give him a bath. The bath is imperative; he looks like Carrie after prom night, but I'm guessing he has ulterior motives...

I sneak a glance at Sully, wondering if I'm supposed to be turned on. A bunch of people were getting killed a second ago, but now there's sexy torchlight, and this is HBO.

Roman Reese looks pretty hot in his loincloth. More hot than I want to admit in this moment.

I am not attracted to Sullivan's brother. I know that sounds crazy because they're identical, but trust me...it's sugar and salt. They're not the same.

I happen to like salt.

With that intense, hungry look on his face as the priestess strips off her clothes, the man on-screen looks pretty fucking salty. His body is lean, tanned, and muscular...exactly like Sully's.

The firelight flickers across his chest. His dark eyes watch the priestess. She's pale, raven haired, freckled...from the right angle, she looks a little bit like me.

I sneak another glance at Sullivan.

He shifts in his seat. There's something very uncomfortable in the set of his shoulders.

"This is the good part...," Reese murmurs.

The priestess is sponging down the Centurion, water rolling down the divots between his abdominal muscles. Reese's abs are ten feet tall right in front of my face. Only they don't look like Reese's abs—they look like Sully when he comes out of the gym and goes straight to the kitchen to refill his water bottle, towel around his neck, sweat running down his chest...

Now it's me shifting in my seat, trying to get comfortable. This theater is hot. Someone should turn on a fan.

I don't know how much the priestess liked her old job in the pagan temple, but she seems highly invested in her new position. She's sponging down every last inch of Roman Reese, and she is not hurrying. She runs her cloth down the thick slabs of muscle on his back, pausing at his loincloth.

She gestures, asking if she should remove it.

Yes, yes, get that thing out of here...

Sully clears his throat.

The priestess unties the loincloth and pulls it away, revealing the two round, full, gloriously bronzed globes of Reese's ass. The crowd hoots and cheers.

I'm taking slow, shallow breaths, trying not to react, trying not to stare, trying not to move a millimeter in my seat.

I can feel Sully next to me, rigid, his hands gripping the seat rests. His breath comes out in short bursts through his nose.

The camera pans down Reese's body, making a landscape of every swell, every bulge. Reese was working hard in the jungle, and hard work pays off...he looks spectacular.

My brain is having a fiesta. It won't stop connecting things that shouldn't be connected.

Reese is an even better actor than I thought, his expressions, his voice, his mannerisms completely altered. He's not *exactly* like Sully but similar enough that when he seizes the priestess and crushes her in a kiss, my heart swoops with the strangest mix of excitement, arousal, and even jealousy...

I know it's Reese, but I can't stop seeing Sully. And as he pulls off the girl's dress, baring a pair of milk-white breasts with pale pink nipples, I can't help seeing myself. This is exactly how our bodies would look together, naked, entwined...

My face is burning, there's no way I can hide it. I don't want to look at Sully and make things worse, so that means I have to keep staring at the screen.

Roman Reese throws the girl down on a pile of furs, revealing a full-frontal shot of his erect "war hammer." The theater erupts in deafening cheers. Reese is grinning. Sully says, low and furious, "I'm going to kill you."

I'm staring with all my might, storing away every millisecond. I don't care if it's wrong.

In fact, it's definitely wrong, but I don't give a damn. This is the hottest thing I've ever seen, and I'm not missing a moment of it.

Roman Reese ravages the priestess to the sound of pounding drums. It's the most gloriously graphic sex scene I've ever had the pleasure of witnessing, as if HBO and the director made a deal for the benefit of all heterosexual womankind.

The director must have had a crush on Reese or a vendetta against Sully because I've never seen so many lingering shots of sweat-drenched pecs and thrusting buttocks. It seems to go on for an hour, and yet, I never want it to stop.

Even the noises the priestess makes sound perversely like my own. It's brain-bending, the jumbled shots of dark hair, pale thighs, hungry lips, and clutching hands. All uncannily familiar, as if the fever dreams that grip me each night have been plucked from my head and broadcast across the movie screen.

Sully sits in painful discomfort next to me. I can only imagine what he's feeling as an entire theater of people ogle what is essentially *his* naked body on-screen.

I feel awful for him, but apparently that's not enough to stop me from also being extremely turned on.

And I don't mean just a little bit.

I am red-faced, squirming, knees together, hoping I don't soak the seat in a theater full of people with my fake boyfriend and his brother sitting on either side of me.

So yeah, it's bad. And it's not getting better.

Roman Reese is putting on a clinic. He's having sex in ways I didn't even know people could have sex.

Sully has settled into a kind of sullen endurance where he stares expressionlessly at the screen as if time has no meaning.

I'm indulging a fantasy where, eventually, Sully forgets that any of this ever happened and dresses up like a Roman for Halloween. Or maybe just borrows that loincloth from Reese...

Finally, it's over. The scene cuts to the Roman leader, and presumably the priestess is allowed to get some sleep.

Reese turns to us, grinning.

"Pretty cool, huh? That actress' name is Maddy. She's thinking of opening a smoothie shop."

"That's great," Sully says through gritted teeth. "You'll have something to eat through a straw after I break your jaw."

"You look mad," Reese observes. "You kind of sound mad, too."

"Bingo," Sully hisses. "Two for two."

It's very lucky for Reese that there are about four hundred witnesses in the theater, and he's safe on the other side of me. He shrinks back in his seat, looking distinctly nervous.

"I told you it was for HBO—"

"You didn't tell me you were going to show *our dick* to the western hemisphere—"

"*Shh!*" someone says.

Sully throws a glare over his shoulder that kills the possibility of any further *shushes.* Or, probably, of that person pooping for the next three days.

I feel bad for him, I really do.

But also, when this episode is up for streaming…

I'm going to watch that scene a hundred times.

29

SULLY

I know I've said it before, but this time it's serious...by tomorrow morning, I'll be an only child.

Theo's trying to calm me down as I stalk toward the car. She stumbles a little in her high heels, struggling to keep up.

"It's not so bad..."

"Yeah, you're right. It's only full-frontal nudity that's about to be broadcast to the *entire fucking country.*"

Even though my brain is blazing, I still remember to open her door for her.

Theo slips into the passenger seat, conscientiously buckling her seatbelt.

"You're right," she says quietly as I take the driver's side. "It totally sucks; I'd be humiliated."

That takes all the fire out of my furnace.

I sigh and start the engine. "I know he's not doing it to fuck me over. Hell, I'm happy for him. I just wish he'd think once in a while about how this shit affects me. It would be nice to at least get a head's up."

Theo's smile creeps back. "You'd rather not find out alongside four hundred other people?"

"Shockingly, no. Especially not—" I break off.

"Especially not what?" Theo says quickly.

I mutter, "Especially not with you right there."

The mood in the car shifts. Theo's voice is pitched lower than usual when she says, "Why not?"

Heat prickles the back of my neck. I'm finding it hard to look at her, though usually, I can't resist.

"I was embarrassed," I admit. "I hate that feeling."

Actually, I *loathe* that feeling. I'll do almost anything to avoid it. It makes my guts churn and my skin flame. It makes me want to shake my own brain out of my skull just to get away from it.

And with Theo right next to me...it was unbearable. I would have stormed out of the theater if it wouldn't have ruined Reese's moment.

Theo turns to face me, her bare legs pointed in my direction, her elbow resting on the open windowsill, dark hair spilling down over her shoulder.

"Trust me, Sully...you have nothing to be embarrassed about."

I force myself to meet her gaze. It's steady, intent, and the opposite of mocking. Theo's not laughing at me. Not even a little bit.

She doesn't look disdainful.

She looks...interested.

Heat spreads up my neck and all down my chest. My body warms and relaxes. My hand unclenches on the wheel. The breeze rolling in through the window is cool and sweetly scented with magnolia.

I don't know how she does it, but Theo can be more convincing than me at my best.

It's the strength of her conviction. She believes what she says —and she makes you believe it, too.

And if Theo doesn't think I looked like a fool...who else's opinion matters? She's the one I want to impress.

"I wouldn't have taken you if I knew it was going to be...like that."

"Why?" Theo says, her voice still low and husky, sending shivers across my skin. "Because it's already hard enough to behave myself when I'm only imagining what's under those clothes?"

She lets her eyes roam up and down my body. For the first time in my life, I think I might be blushing.

I grunt, "That doesn't seem fair. You've seen me all the way naked, and I've only seen you mostly naked."

"I never saw *you* naked."

"It's the same."

"You promise?" Theo says.

She's giving me a look that is nothing like the looks that came before. This is a whole other Theo—heavy eyes, hungry gaze... If not for that seatbelt across her chest, she looks like she'd dive across the seats and devour me.

Maybe I shouldn't be quite so mad at Reese.

I'll admit, there was a part of that scene that was pretty fucking hot. Roman Reese had his priestess bent over, taking her from behind. The girl was pretty enough, but I hadn't paid much attention to her until that moment, when I realized she looked a bit like Theo. Not in the face, but from the rear view...there was some definite similarity. And Reese, of course, looked almost exactly like me.

I didn't feel turned on at the time, steeped in rage and humiliation, but now that scene flashes through my brain. Theo's giving me her ravenous stare, and I'm remembering the very real glimpses I've gotten of her naked body, the taste of her mouth, the feel of her skin. It all swirls around my head, mixed up with graphic images of what we might look like fucking.

But we can't fuck.

I promised Theo I'd stop trying, promised her I'd stop even thinking about it.

I shouldn't have made that second promise—it's damn near impossible. But I can at least keep the first one.

So even though everything inside of me is pulled toward the gravity on the other side of the car, though all I want is to flirt back with Theo, put my hand on her thigh, kiss her at the next light, even...I keep my eyes fixed on the road and turn the music on instead.

I say, "Thanks for talking me down off the ledge. I really don't want to ruin this for Reese."

"I know you don't." Theo shifts so she's facing forward now, too.

She says it softly, lightly, but there's a hint of disappointment.

I can't look at her to confirm. Can't look at her at all because my self-restraint is shredded.

Even facing forward, I can still smell her perfume. I can hear her soft breathing. I can feel every time she moves.

A thousand invisible threads seem to connect us all over, so every moment she's tugging at me.

We're quiet the rest of the drive home, but my mind isn't quiet. It's screaming at me to say something, do something, satisfy this want, even if all I can do is put my hand on her knee to give myself a taste of that butter-soft skin...

Keeping my hands to myself is torture.

I don't know what Theo's thinking. She's withdrawn and almost seems upset.

When I pull into the driveway, she goes right into the house without waiting for me, without looking back.

I let her go because I'm exhausted with the effort of concealing my feelings and resisting what I want. I'm low and miserable, wondering how I got myself in this mess. A month ago, my plan seemed brilliant. Now it seems devised by my worst enemy.

I pause outside Theo's closed door, wondering if I should knock. But what would I say?

I imagine the conversation:

I'm sorry I was so upset.

I'm sorry I can't keep my hands off you.

I'm sorry I'm going to kiss you again right now...

That's why I can't knock. Because I can't be trusted.

Theo made the right choice. She went straight to bed so there's no question of us reenacting any of what we just saw on-screen.

I should do the same.

I trudge off to my own bedroom to begin the highly unappetizing process of brushing my teeth and washing my face so I can roll into bed completely alone.

I'm glaring at myself in the mirror, mouth full of toothpaste, when I hear a soft sound at the door. So gentle, I'd hardly notice if some part of my ears weren't straining, waiting, hoping for what they're not supposed to get.

I open the door.

Theo is standing there, completely naked.

30

THEO

The car ride home was an uneasy tangle of temptations. I could tell Sully was upset and wanted to give him all the sympathy he deserved, but it was difficult to castigate Reese for creating my all-time favorite piece of cinema.

I felt terrible for Sully, that was true, but once he relaxed a little, lust came roaring back. The vibe in the car turned flirty, and I thought he was cheering up...

But then he flipped the music on and didn't say another word to me.

Now I'm lying in bed, frustrated and confused.

Maybe he just doesn't like me. Or at least, not the way that I like him.

Or maybe he was too upset from what happened, and I'm being a selfish ass.

I flop on my other side, punching down the pillow, trying to get comfortable.

He said he was attracted to me. He wanted to sleep with me. Didn't he?

I'm the one who told him to knock it off.

What the hell was I thinking?

I flop on my other side, hot and itchy all over.

Is Sully being a gentleman? Is that why he shut me down? Or is that just wishful thinking...

I can't get comfortable. I can't still these swirling thoughts.

My arousal should be fading, but it isn't. I'm horny and pent-up, and I don't even have my goddamned vibrator. This feeling of throbbing want isn't dissipating. In fact, it's only ramping up.

I roll out of the bed, stripping off the oversized T-shirt I sleep in, planning to take a cold shower.

But my feet are not paying attention to what my brain decided. They're not headed in the direction of the bathroom at all. Instead, they stride for the door, and my treacherous hand wrenches it open. I'm heading down the hall, naked as the day I was born, without a thought for if Reese might have come home.

There are no thoughts in my head at all as I knock on Sully's door—just one irresistible impulse.

The moment Sully answers, I grab him and kiss him.

We tumble onto his bed, his scent all around us. Sully is only wearing a pair of boxer shorts; I yank them down, rabid to see all of him.

This won't make any sense because the visual was almost the same, but the sight of Sully naked is ten times more arousing than Reese. Then, I felt conflicted, guiltily turned on...now I'm looking at the real, actual Sullivan, and there's nothing like the real thing.

He's fucking gorgeous.

The fact that I get to put my hands on his body, that I get to touch this chest, this stomach, this back, this ass...the fact that he's kissing me right now, moaning into my mouth with that low groan that's the most delicious mix of pleasure and longing...

It seems so impossible, and yet, exactly right. This is where I'm meant to be, this is what I want. Offer me the presidency, a pool full of gold, the entire Taj Mahal, and I'd pick this instead.

His hands are all over my breasts. He takes one in his mouth, sucking the nipple in a way that makes my back bend and my eyes roll back.

"Oh my god, Theo...oh my god..."

He stops himself for a moment, our legs tangled together, his hand in my hair.

"Wait, wait...," he says, making a little space between our mouths. "You don't want to do this..."

"Yes, I do."

He looks into my eyes carefully. "Are you sure?"

"Sully, if you don't take me right now, I'm not going to make it through the night. I *need* you."

I don't know who this person is who seizes Sullivan and kisses him like she's trying to suck the soul out of his body, but she's right—I *need* this.

My lust for him is storm clouds filled to bursting. We can't go back to blue skies until the rain comes pouring down.

It's reckless and the opposite of what I said I wanted, but I don't care anymore. I want him. And if he rejects me after, if this whole thing is over, it really doesn't matter. Because the truth is, I'm already going to get hurt. I was lying to myself when I thought it was possible to escape unscathed.

I'm already crazy about Sully.

I have been this whole damn time.

That was the lie...pretending this was ever fake.

I want him so badly that I'll take whatever I can get, even if it's only playing pretend for a few more weeks. I'll throw myself into the fantasy and live it so fully that I'll at least have the memories after he dumps me.

I could live for years off how good this feels right now, his hands on my breasts, his lips on my neck...

It's so much better than I imagined, than I ever *could* imagine...while it's flaming on my skin, searing in my lungs, surging in my belly, I'm going to burn with every moment.

His hot mouth drags down my neck, his tongue laps at my breast. Our legs are tangled up together, the burning rod of his cock digging into my hip. I wrap my hand around the shaft and squeeze. Sully's whole body goes rigid, and he groans, crushing me in his arms, devouring my mouth.

We roll across his bed, tangled in the sheets that smell so strongly of his scent, it's driving me mad.

"I snuck in here once...," I confess. "And touched myself in your bed."

"Naughty girl...," Sully growls against my neck. "When was this?"

"My first whole day here."

His wicked laugh bubbles through my blood. "What were you thinking about?"

"The look on your face when Angus touched my arm..."

Sully makes a low sound in his throat—he knows exactly what I'm talking about. "I hate when he acts like he owns you... when you belong to *me*."

Something clenches in my belly, hot and thrilling.

"Say it again...," I whisper.

"What?"

"That I belong to you..."

Sully wraps me up in his arms, hands tangled in my hair. He looks into my eyes and holds me there.

"You're *mine*," he growls. "Mine and no one else's."

His cock presses against me, hot and throbbing. I part my thighs. "Then take me."

With those deep, dark eyes fixed on mine, Sullivan slowly slides inside. He pushes in, bit by bit, a heat and friction so unbearably intense that it rides the line of pain and pleasure.

He's slow, achingly slow, giving me time to stretch around him. His eyes are locked on mine, his lips brushing my mouth. I breathe him, taste him, and take him in, a millimeter at a time.

It seems an age until our bodies meet. Time stretches, flexible and elastic. The air is honey thick, perception melts. My body becomes his body and his becomes mine, linked together, one creature, bonded by this all-consuming sensation.

If this is sex, then I guess everything I did before was just pretending. Because I've never known anything that felt like this.

Sully's powerful enough to crush me, but he holds me like precious porcelain. He gathers me up in his arms like a doll, lifting me, sliding me down on his cock. I'm on top now, gazing down into his face, but he's still in control. His hands circle my waist. The tilt of his wrists shifts my hips. He rocks me, makes me ride him.

His body surges beneath me. He lifts his hips, thrusting into me, and pulls me down with his hands. My palms are flat on his chest. My hair hangs down around us like a curtain.

His hands explore my body, running up and down my sides. He cups my breasts in his hands, lifts them, plays with them. His thumbs slide across my nipples, teasing them, pulling them into points.

"These breasts, this body, those lips..." His burning eyes stare up into mine. "You're a goddess, Theo. I worship you."

I've gotten pretty good at knowing when Sully is lying.

When he gazes up at me now, what he says is the pure, unvarnished truth—he looks at me and sees something divine.

There it is, reflected in his eyes: what I can be at my best, my strongest, my most ethereal—what I am right now, in this moment, because of him.

When Achilles' mother wanted to make him immortal, she held him over a fire. I'm bathed in Sully's flame, in the heat from his body, the fire in his eyes. It surges through my veins. I burn and burn, knowing when this is over, I'll never be the same.

Sully grips my waist, fingers digging in. He thrusts up into me, harder, faster, making me trot on top of him, making my breasts bounce.

Each thrust pulses through my body. Each breath lights me on fire.

I ride and ride him while he worships me with his hands.

Then I lock my fingers through his, and I lean down to kiss him, drowning him in thick, dark hair. His hands grip mine, and he turns to whisper in my ear, "Come for me, baby girl..."

I kiss him deeply, using the taste of his mouth to tip me over the edge.

I tumble down and down and down through a staircase of mirrors, a thousand sensations splintering and twisting, a kaleidoscope of color turning in on itself.

Deep inside me, I feel the rush and roar of Sully's climax. His arms lock around me and his mouth melds with mine.

He is me and I am him, one brilliant bolt of pleasure...

And then I'm back in my body again, wrapped up safe and warm in Sully's arms.

I WAKE to knocking at the door and fall out of bed in a tangle of sheets that still smell like Sullivan though he's nowhere to be found.

That's strange because I'm still in his room and it's still the middle of the night.

Even stranger, I open the door to find Reese instead of Sully. His hair is a mess, and he looks distraught.

"Can you come help us?" he begs. "Dad's really sick."

31

SULLY

The sight of Theo is such a relief, I almost feel like crying. My dad has been shaking and vomiting for hours, sweating so heavily that his mattress is drenched.

"We've got to call an ambulance," Reese mutters.

My dad grips Reese's arm, fingers digging in though his whole hand is shaking. "No," he grits through his teeth.

"Dad, you're a mess. We've got to—"

"*No.*"

Theo takes one look and seems to understand what's happening.

"Get a bowl of cool water and a clean cloth," she says to Reese. "Also, some towels. Sully, please bring a jug of ice water. And do we have any sunflower seeds?"

"Uh...maybe?"

"If we do, bring them. Also, some bananas."

"What for?" Reese says.

"They raise dopamine levels. My dad said it helped, the once or twice he tried to quit."

Theo doesn't point out that they obviously didn't help enough to prevent her dad sliding right back into drinking.

Either way, I'm grateful to have something to do. I run across the dark yard to the kitchen, rummaging in the pantry until I find a pack of mixed nuts that includes sunflower seeds. I sprint back to Theo, arms laden with bananas, ice water, and clean glasses.

She's already sponging my dad's face. Reese paces next to the bed.

"We've got to get him to a hospital—" He tries to whisper it, but my dad thrashes, knocking the bowl of water out of Theo's hand.

"*No! No hospital!* If I die, I'm dying right here."

It looks like that's going to be sooner than later. Waves of tremors wrack his body, shaking him so hard that his teeth chatter. His hands are claws drawn up to his chest, and his feet convulse against the bed, his eyes rolling back.

"Hold him!" Theo cries. "Try to get him to drink some water."

I hold my dad while he shakes and shakes. His body burns from the inside out, a feverish heat that has me sweating.

"It's going to be okay..." I hold him until my arms ache. "It's going to be okay..."

When the tremors ease, Reese lifts a cup of ice water to his lips. My dad swallows a few sips, then vomits all over his pillow.

"Move him to the couch," Theo says. "I'll clean it."

Reese and I carefully lift our dad over to the sofa while Theo strips the bed. There are no spare sheets, so she remakes the bed with fresh blankets, laying a towel over the pillow in case he vomits again.

"What's happening?" Reese whispers, eyes wide and terrified.

"Alcohol withdrawal," Theo says.

"Withdrawal?" Reese is confused.

"I think he stopped drinking," I say. "Or he's trying to."

"We really should get him to a hospital," Theo murmurs. "Withdrawal can be fatal."

But that's the one thing my father won't accept. As Reese and I try to lift him once more, he fights us so violently that it seems like insisting will do more harm than good.

"I'm not leaving," he rasps. "I'm not leaving her."

My mother is buried in the Rose Hills Mortuary. But my dad acts like she still inhabits the house.

I say, "You need help—"

"I need to stay right here."

I look at Theo helplessly.

"Let's get him calm and cleaned up," she murmurs to me. "Then we'll see."

I've never passed a longer night. I don't know what I would have done if Theo hadn't been there. She obviously learned a thing or two from her mom, the nurse, because she's steady and undeterred by the sweat, vomit, and urine we're cleaning up all night long, not to mention the useless lumps of dread and exhaustion that Reese and I have become.

Finally, as dawn breaks, my father falls into a heavy sleep, half a banana in his stomach, bathed once more by me and Theo, who treated his naked body with dignity and respect, and sleeping on sheets freshly laundered by Reese.

Reese stays in the pool house, napping on the couch so he can keep tabs on our dad.

I feel empty, hollowed out.

Theo's so tired, she can barely stagger back to the house. I put my arm around her waist to help her up the steps.

We pause outside her bedroom door.

I want to thank her, but there's no words big enough.

So I sweep her into my arms and hold her like she's the most precious, precious thing. Hoping she can feel how goddamn lucky and unworthy I feel.

"Theo," I croak. "I...just, thank you. *Thank you.*"

"He's going to be okay," she whispers in my ear.

I turn my face against her neck. Blame it on the exhaustion, but that's when I break down.

Theo pulls me into her room and into her bed.

I wrap my arms around her and cradle her there in the nest of blankets, her back tucked against my chest, her head under my chin.

It feels like Theo's slipped all the way inside me to fill that empty, hollow space. Her warmth becomes my warmth. Her breath becomes my breath. Her calm becomes my peaceful oblivion.

Sooner than I would have thought possible, I'm drifting into dreamless sleep.

32

SULLY

The next day, I cancel all my appointments to stay home with my dad. Theo can't skip work, but she drives home over her lunch hour to check on us, insisting on whipping up a pot of homemade chicken soup even though my dad's still too sick to eat much.

He only finishes half a bowl but seems cheered by Theo's visit. He spends the rest of the afternoon reading a biography of Winston Churchill that she borrowed from Martinique for his enjoyment.

By Thursday, he's feeling a little better, and by Friday, he's up and out of bed, looking pale and exhausted but more clear-eyed than I've seen him in years.

He threw away every drop of alcohol in the pool house, and Friday night, he attends his very first AA meeting even though he's barely recovered enough to stand up on his own. Reese goes along with him, for physical and moral support.

Theo's late coming home from work. When she still hasn't pulled into the driveway by eight p.m., I'm fighting the urge to drive to her office to throttle Angus. I swear he keeps her late on weekends on purpose, punishing her when he doesn't have any plans of his own.

But when she finally pulls in, it's not Angus who delayed her but rather the fat, fluffy puff ball in her passenger seat.

Theo unbuckles the seatbelt restraining the most enormous Saint Bernard puppy I've ever seen. She can hardly lift him out of the car, fur spilling over her arms, the puppy grinning up at me with his tongue hanging out.

"New boyfriend? Just like that, I'm replaced."

Theo laughs, nuzzling her nose against the puppy's ear. "He's not for me. Though, if I hold him another hour, I won't be able to let him go."

"Please tell me he's not for Reese. You can't have an untrained dog taking care of a puppy."

"Actually...," Theo says nervously. "I was planning to give him to Merrick. I was reading this book on addiction, and it said it can help to replace a bad habit with something positive instead."

"Okay..." I'm slightly concerned about how my dad's going to take care of a puppy when he can hardly take care of himself. But I suppose I can check in, help with walks or feeding or whatever. It'll certainly help to distract him and give him some company when Reese and I are out. "What's his name?"

"Bernie Sanders," Theo says at once. "Apparently, he only answers to his full name."

I kind of doubt he answers to anything. This puff ball clearly lives to eat and snooze.

"Where'd you get him?"

"Leanne, the accountant, has a Saint Bernard that got unexpectedly frisky with the neighbor's dog—poor thing was so old, she hardly thought that was a possibility anymore. She only had the one puppy, but he looks healthy enough."

"He looks like he ate the rest of the litter."

"Bernie would never do that," Theo says, snuggling him with all her might.

Bernie's lucky he's a gift to my dad because he's already hogging way too much of Theo's attention. I'm mildly jealous.

"What about me?" I growl. "Where's my cuddles?"

Theo tilts up her chin to give me a kiss over the top of the dog's fluffy head.

She slept in my bed the last two nights—not that we got much sleep. I could almost thank my dad for getting so sick because there's been no talk of Theo going back to her own apartment, and I'm sure as hell not going to bring it up.

In fact, with this puppy here, I could see her staying another week at least, just to help Bernie get settled in. I give the dog's head a nice scratch behind the ears, willing to forgive him anything if he earns me a few more days with Theo.

"Where's Merrick?" she says, already heading around the side of the house.

"In the pool house with Reese. They just got back."

I trail after her, taking the opportunity for a long look at Theo's ass in her work clothes. She's wearing the dark suit she wore the day she met me at the pizza place, which feels like a hundred years ago.

It's the same suit, but Theo looks different as she tosses a grin back over her shoulder at me. She's left her hair down, loose and wild, and even the way she walks has a little more sway in it. Maybe that's for my benefit because she knows I'm right behind her. I hope it's for my benefit.

Bernie is coating her in dog hair, but Theo doesn't seem to care. She's buoyant and bouncing, bursting into the pool house without knocking, calling out, "Merrick, I brought you a new friend!"

I've got to see this. I would not say that my dad is a person who likes surprises or gifts. I'm not even sure how much he likes dogs.

He looks slightly stunned as Theo deposits the huge, fluffy puppy in his arms. "What's this?"

"Bernie Sanders the Second," Theo says.

My dad looks down at the dog in bemusement. Bernie responds by enthusiastically licking his face. Not one or two licks but an attempt to wash his whole, entire face.

Reese pouts. "You never let *me* get a puppy."

I remind him, "You couldn't even keep your goldfish alive."

"I had George for two years!"

"There were six different Georges," our dad says.

"*What?*"

"Every time one would go belly-up, your mom would sneak an identical goldfish into the tank."

Reese makes a strangled sound. "Oh god! Poor George."

I ask, "Which one?"

Reese covers his face with his hands.

Theo gives me the look that means she thinks I'm being too mean to my brother. She doesn't know how much he needs it—everybody else lets him get away with murder.

Goldfish murder especially. Six times, Mom?

"Better stay away from Bernie," I warn Reese. "There's only one of him."

"But I want to hold him," Reese says wistfully. "Look how fluffy he is..."

Dad makes a shelter of his arms as Reese reaches for the dog. "He likes it right here."

Bernie Sanders has already curled himself into a ball, big brown eyes blinking sleepily.

My dad strokes his head, slow like a hypnotist. In minutes, the puppy is snoring. Dad keeps petting him anyway.

Theo's trying not to smile too much, which makes her dimples pop. She's pleased and proud of herself, and she should be. My dad's gazing down at the dog with the kind of look I never thought I'd see again on his face. Poor fool's already falling in love.

"How was the meeting?" I ask him.

"Good," he says. "I'm going back tomorrow."

My twin, incapable of finding anything dull, says, "Me too! The stories these guys have to tell—I'm getting so much inspiration for my screenplay."

I nod along with him. "I'm glad their pain can become fodder for your work."

Theo gives a soft snort, but Reese is oblivious. "I know! And I can drive Dad—two birds with one stone."

"I didn't quit drinking just to die in a fiery wreck," Dad says. "I'll drive myself."

"Got a little out of practice, all those months in the jungle." Reese has the grace to look sheepish. "Sort of forgot about turn signals."

"And braking," Dad says.

"If we'd get a Tesla already, I wouldn't have to do any of that. That's the first thing I'm buying when the show gets picked up for a second season."

"Good idea." I slap his back. "Make sure you spend your whole, entire paycheck and don't put any in savings."

"Is that sarcasm I hear, beloved brother?"

"It's resignation."

"We'll see who makes it to twenty million first. Then I'll be paying *your* bills."

"Can't wait. You still owe me fifty bucks from the last time you wanted to take out some Tinder date." *Not to mention five figures of other assorted loans.*

Reese only grins. "Put it on my tab. By this time next year—"

"Yeah, yeah, I know, you'll be sipping Mai Tais on Leo's yacht."

"Wearing matching swim trunks." Reese smiles blissfully.

"I met Leo," Dad remarks. "At a party in San Trope. He kept staring at Stella's tits."

Despite living in LA all her life, plus four years in Angus' star-studded orbit, Theo has an adorable weakness for celebrity gossip. Her eyes go wide. "Were you mad?"

"Nah. I was doing the same thing. The way she looked in a swimsuit—I'd have to fight half the boat."

I glance at Theo right as she looks at me, and I know we're both remembering me dunking Angus.

She smothers a laugh with her hand, her faced flushed and lovely. The softness as her fingers drag down her lips, the way her eyes linger on me...I think the memory pleases her, and she's even more pleased that I'm thinking of it, too.

That was the moment I first lost control—when I deviated from the plan. And I haven't looked back since.

People tell themselves lies. Lies to explain why *I couldn't do this* or *it wasn't my fault...*

I try to look at myself honestly. Through the lens of what I actually do, not what I intend.

And if I apply that standard, it's pretty obvious... I've been chasing Theo this whole time.

Plan? What fucking plan...I want her.

That day, I was the guy with the most gorgeous woman on the boat on his arm. Theo was stunning. She *is* stunning. And Angus about lost his mind realizing what he had right next to him all this time.

I've been laughing at him ever since.

But maybe I'm the fucking idiot.

Theo's right here beside me, making my life what it's never been—glowing. So what am I doing playing games?

I want to stop all of this, the pretend, the show for Angus... even the deal itself is beginning to feel tainted. If pretending to date her was to my benefit, *actually* dating her should be even better, but it isn't. I can't toy with Theo anymore, not with the way that I feel about her. I can't use her to bait Angus.

It's gone way beyond distraction or sub-optimal choices.

I'm afraid.

Afraid that if I fuck this up, I might lose her.

I don't even *have* her right now—not really. Because of this goddamned contract.

There it is, written in ink, signed by us both—what we're actually here for.

For me, safety and security for my family. A way to take this stinking pile of straw, this fucking property I was saddled with in a deal gone bad, and spin it into gold by selling it to Angus.

There's my dad sitting right there, puppy on his lap, with one beautiful, precious, shining day of sobriety behind him. If he lost the house now, he'd spiral down worse than ever.

But he's only here because of Theo. I know that in my soul.

I spent years taking care of him.

Theo made him feel again.

She put a crack in his heart with that sandwich, and then she wrenched it all the way open again. Even though he knew the pain of it could almost kill him.

She showed him the good things still here—not Mom, but dinners in the yard and sweating in the sunshine and holding something soft, that needs you, on your lap.

And maybe it was one thing Theo did or everything, or maybe it was just finally time. But no matter the reason, it wouldn't have happened without her.

And whatever's coming my way tomorrow, if my dad falls off the wagon, if I get hit by a bus, I want Theo here with me. Just like I want to be there for her.

I love taking care of her, God, I fucking love it. Getting what I want feels great, but getting it for her is transcendent. It takes an ordinary moment and turns it into something I know I'll play in my head again and again like a favorite film, the light in her eyes, the look on her face, the way she turns to me...

Maybe I can have it all, Theo and the deal...

But if I've learned anything, it's that there's always a trade-off.

And I can't make this trade.

33

THEO

Sunday starts out lovely when I wake to Merrick playing with Bernie in the backyard but swiftly slides downhill when I remember that tonight is Jessica Kate's popstar party.

Martinique has been complaining about it all week. She's been non-consensually assigned to the only assistant position on the planet worse than mine.

Jessica is a ruthless taskmaster, running Martinique ragged all over the city when she isn't grilling her for information about Angus or, apparently, about me.

"She was asking me a million questions yesterday," Martinique gripes as I help her wrangle the catering trays into Angus' walk-in refrigerator. "All about where you went to high school, and how long you and Sullivan have been dating, and where you worked before this. You better be careful, Theo—she has it out for you."

My stomach does a slow, uneasy roll. I feel incredibly grateful that I never spilled the beans to Martinique, no matter how many times I was tempted. Much as I love my best friend, I'm not sure how well she'd stand up to Jessica's week-long interrogation if she knew the truth.

I could not, however, resist telling her that Sully and I finally slept together.

"Tell me everything!" she squeals. "Every single detail!"

"Not *every* detail..." I'm already blushing.

"All the good ones," Martinique insists.

I give her a play-by-play until we're both flushed and giggling. Martinique gets a determined look in her eye.

"If he's that good, I'm definitely sleeping with his brother tonight." Her mind's already leaping several years ahead. "Maybe we'll marry twins! Wouldn't that be amazing?"

Unbidden, the image of a ring pops into my head. Sully waiting at the altar. Coming home to his beautiful, broken-down mansion, not for a week but for forever...

Martinique stops laughing when she sees the look on my face. "What's wrong? Too soon to talk about wedding bells?"

"No..."

"Because you look like a woman in love."

In love?

Sick, sinking fear takes hold of me.

I can't be in love with Sullivan.

Insanely attracted to him, completely infatuated with him, maybe... But not love. That would be...devastating.

"I'm not in love," I say.

There's just one problem. Over the last few weeks, I've become a lot more aware of what I sound like when I lie. And that...felt like a hell of a whopper.

Martinique isn't buying it either. "Not in love? Or not ready to admit it?"

"Both. Neither."

"Uh oh." She gives me a pitying look. "You've got it bad."

"I don't. I'm not." I swallow hard, shaking my head in swift, short jerks. "I'm not in love."

Lies, lies, lies.

Martinique can tell I'm distressed, even if she's not sure why. She puts her hands on my shoulders and looks into my face. "Baby girl, why are you so upset?"

It feels more like panic, this pressure in my chest that keeps expanding until it seems like I'll pop.

I can't fall in love with Sullivan.

Because as much as he might enjoy flirting with me and even fucking me, there's no way he's going to let himself fall in love with *me*.

But when I picture him right now, the pull I feel could separate my soul from my body.

I want him. I need him.

I love him.

"I'm not upset," I say. And then I burst into tears.

AN HOUR LATER, I've told Martinique everything.

I know I wasn't supposed to. I know I promised. But I couldn't hold back anymore—I need my best friend's advice.

"Holy shit," is her first brilliant response.

"I'm going to need a little more than that."

"This makes so much more sense! I was so pissed at you for not telling me you had a boyfriend—I should have known there was something going on."

"I'm sorry."

"I'll forgive you—if you come to karaoke with me."

Martinique loves karaoke to an unreasonable degree. I know exactly what she's asking for because I've endured it several times—six solid hours of terrible singing and worse Jell-O shots,

Martinique refusing to leave until we've performed "Umbrella" and "Cheetah Sisters" together.

"You got it," I say without hesitation.

Sensing her advantage, she closes in for the kill. "Three times."

"That's blackmail!"

"I learned from the best—the best being your boyfriend."

"Ha, ha, ha."

"This is incredible. You're like a spy..."

"I'm not spying. It was supposed to be just an introduction... now it's gotten a bit more complicated."

"I'll say." Martinique smirks.

"What should I do?"

"Tell him how you actually feel," she says at once.

"I can't do that."

"Why not?"

Just the thought makes me feel like I stepped up to the edge of a diving board with a pool a hundred feet below.

"Because I don't know if he feels the same."

"And how are you ever going to know unless you ask?" Martinique says with maddening practicality.

"I was thinking I'd just wait and observe, kind of see how it goes..."

"Perfect. That should get you right where you want to be by the time you're both eighty."

I sigh. Martinique makes everything seem so easy and so obvious. It isn't—not for me.

"I'm not you, Martinique; guys don't just fall all over themselves trying to date me—"

"This one does."

"He's pretending."

"He's not pretending."

"I just told you—"

"Babe, nobody's that good an actor. I've seen how he looks at you."

I want to believe that. God, I want to believe it with all my soul. But Martinique is biased. She once told me I looked stunning in the same romper that Angus said made me look like a toddler with a saggy diaper.

Martinique can tell I'm not convinced. "He wouldn't be hooking up with you if he didn't like you," she insists.

"It's not that I don't think he likes me at all..." I sigh. "I just don't think he feels...quite the same as me."

I don't see how he could.

The way I feel is outrageous, over the top, and out of control. It's too much, too soon, all-encompassing and all-consuming.

I don't just *like* my fake boyfriend...

I'm head over heels in love with him.

34

THEO

When everything's set up for the party, I leave Martinique at Angus' house and drive back to Sully's place to change my clothes.

Sullivan, ever punctual and ever prepared, is already dressed in a gray suit, his hair still slightly damp from his shower, skin flushed and face freshly shaved.

The sight of him puts a painful twist in my chest, part pleasure, part longing. It's like the last day of vacation—I've never appreciated what I'm looking at more, while already aching for how soon I might lose it.

"How's Merrick doing?" I ask.

"Excellent," Sully says. "He ate all the leftover soup *and* the spaghetti from last night."

"I was going to have that for breakfast," Reese complains, joining us in the kitchen.

"Then maybe you should have woken up before two," Sully says.

Reese gives him a blank look. "But it's Sunday?"

"Nice outfit," I note.

Reese is wearing grandpa trousers and penny loafers, an open shirt covered in silver sequins layered over a white undershirt and several chain necklaces.

He gives me a grin as bright as his shirt, slightly lopsided to the left, the opposite of Sully's. "I call it 'Disco Sleaze.'"

"Martinique'll love it—she's crazy for vintage clothes."

"What else is she into? I tried stalking her Instagram, but it's private."

Answering is easy—my BFF is nothing if not vocal about her preferences. I could probably write a fifty-page guidebook for Reese on the Republic of Martinique.

"She loves fashion and baking. She makes the cutest birthday cakes for everybody she knows in their favorite flavors—reason enough to be friends with her. And she's a water baby, can't get enough of swimming and surfing..."

"Hold on, hold on!" Reese pulls out his phone and starts taking notes.

"You haven't even met her yet," Sully says.

"I want to be prepared! You never know when a blind date might turn into 'The One.'"

"Better tell him what she *doesn't* like," Sully says. "Or he'll show up with a bouquet of edible underwear."

I laugh. "That might be right up her alley."

"Really?" Reese beams. "Because I do have some fuzzy handcuffs—"

"See?" Sully shakes his head.

"Things Martinique hates..." I list them off on my fingers. "People who interrupt, people who ask what's happening during movies, people who don't shut your door on the way out, small yappy dogs, big stinky dogs, expensive avocados that are already brown inside..."

"Well, that last one should be illegal," Sully says.

Reese types frantically. "I think we might be soulmates."

"You interrupt all the time," Sully points out.

"When have I ever interrupted you?"

His twin gives him a beady look. "Do you want that list alphabetical, or—"

"See, never!" Reese shouts.

Sully gives a slow shake of his head. "Don't use that joke on the date."

I can't decide if Martinique is going to love Reese or hate him. On the one hand, Reese is an adorable goofball. On the other hand, Martinique has never dated anyone for longer than a month. Reasons she has broken up with men include talking to their mom too little, talking to their mom too much, snoring, and ordering her appetizer for her.

Reese should be safe from most of those, but I'd need a month to list off the rest of Martinique's pet peeves and the drive to Angus' house is only twenty minutes.

Sully takes the wheel, Reese squished into the tiny backseat.

"Holy shitballs!" Reese says when we pull up to Angus' place. "That's a proper villain's lair. His house looks like it would beat the shit out of our house and take its lunch money."

"Somebody already beat the shit out of our house," Sully says.

"You don't want to live here," I tell Reese. "It's like wandering around inside a sculpture."

Angus' house is cold and impersonal. He didn't decorate any of the rooms, and that's exactly what it feels like—like a staged set always waiting for some glossy magazine shoot.

But Reese scoffs at the idea that this level of luxury could be in any way unpleasant. "Think of the parties I could throw here!"

Sully gazes around at the rager already in full swing. "Yeah, all you need is a gold-digging girlfriend..."

"Can I apply?" Martinique says, popping into view.

Martinique looks like a tiny firecracker in her tight red dress and heels with her glossy cap of black hair.

Reese lights up at the sight of her. "All I need is some gold to dig."

She smiles back at him. "Pizza and Netflix are solid gold to me."

I smother a snort. Martinique must really like the look of Reese because she ripped a strip off the last guy who took her to a second-tier steakhouse. She's got Tiffany tastes on a Target budget, and usually it's her boyfriends who make up the difference.

I warned her that Reese is indeed in the ninety-nine percent of actors who are broke, but she agreed to the date anyway, based mostly off hotness and the ridiculously slim likelihood that it might lead to us marrying twins.

She doesn't seem to be regretting her choice. She links arms with Reese. "Want to buy me a free drink?"

"As many as you can handle."

Blowing us a kiss, Martinique disappears into the crowd with Sully's already-stunned brother.

"Nice work," Sully says. "You gonna get a job as a professional matchmaker?"

"Let's see how they feel by the end of the night before I start switching careers."

"If chef and matchmaker don't work out, you could be a full-time party planner." He gives an appreciative nod to the sparkly green decorations plastered all over every inch of the house. "This is incredible."

"That was mostly Martinique—"

"Don't try to be modest with me, I know your touch." He indicates the upside-down forest of emerald tinsel dripping from the ceiling, spangled with fairy lights. "I know who came up with that."

I flush with pleasure, as much from the look he gives me as the way he recognizes my fingerprints. Sully makes me feel special. He makes me feel like the things I create are valuable, that *I'm* valuable.

"We went all out—I'm hoping if things go well tonight, that'll put Jessica in a good mood, and then Angus will be a in an even better mood for your meeting tomorrow."

Bright and early Monday morning, Sully is finally showing Angus the property he owns. Everything rides on this—tomorrow, Angus has to fall in love.

Sullivan seemed confident every step of the way, but now his expression is uneasy.

"What's wrong?"

"Nothing." He shakes his head. "You're exactly right. Tonight, the plan is to soothe and flatter Angus and make sure Jessica feels like the Queen of Pop."

"Shouldn't be too difficult..."

But as I gaze across the sea of faces, I spy something strange: a familiar face I haven't seen in a very long time.

"Is that Amber Patterson?"

Sully looks where I'm pointing, his thick black brows drawing together. "Yeah, it is."

Amber attended Piedmont Prep the same year as us.

"I haven't seen her in ages. Wonder what she's doing here?"

"Hm." Sullivan scans the crowd, his frown deepening.

Angus grabs my arm. "There you are! I've been looking for you! Good to see you, Sullivan."

The two men shake hands, Angus gripping and pumping Sully's hand like he's trying to dredge up water in the desert. He looks like he's had a few drinks already, face flushed and eyes glassy. From the mile-wide grin, I assume Her Majesty is pleased with the party so far.

"Where's Jessica?" I ask.

"Out by the pool."

I spy her through the windows, lounging in a green spangled

bikini, holding court to a bevy of admirers, including Corgus, who struggles to maintain the strained smile plastered across his face.

"She looks happy."

"She is," Angus says with visible relief. "I paid—I mean, I managed to get her single playing on the radio."

"Congratulations," Sully says.

He does an admirable job of masking any sarcasm, but there's something tight in his face. His shoulders are stiff, and he's still searching the room.

I touch his arm, wanting to meet his eyes, to get some sense of what's bothering him, but Martinique interrupts.

"Can you help me with the caterer? I failed high school Spanish."

I only got a B+, but that's been good enough to coordinate with Consuela, Angus' favorite go-to for authentic tacos and street corn.

I sometimes suspect that Consuela speaks excellent English but pretends not to so she never has to talk to Angus. It's a good strategy, and I'm not going to blow her cover, no matter how bad I am at pronouncing "*servilletas.*"

By the time I get back from the kitchen, Angus has dragged Sully off somewhere, and the party is more packed than ever. Despite the cathedral ceilings and the open doors to the backyard, the main floor is sweltering. I'm sweating in my dress.

A pack of Jessica's modeling friends cackle together, ogled by a skinny, freckled guy who looks oddly familiar. He kinda resembles the kid who used to sit beside me in math class—

"Theo?" A damp hand touches my elbow.

I turn to meet a face I haven't seen in eleven years—my prom date, Davis Verger. He's broader than he was before, more muscle and more flesh. His hair has thinned a little, and he changed his horn-rim glasses for contacts, but it's definitely him.

"Davis?" I choke, feeling a strange unsteady lurch, like time is folding back on itself. "What are you doing here?"

"What do you mean?" he laughs. "You invited me!"

Dazed, I gaze around at the throng of strangers mixed up with fellow Galactic employees, friends of Angus and Jessica, and a few familiar faces...too many familiar faces.

Davis Verger, Amber Patterson, Jody Westbank, that kid from algebra...my stomach clenches tighter and tighter as I recognize my old classmates. It's not just one or two of them...it's a whole goddamned reunion.

"What do you mean I invited you?"

Davis falters, blue eyes crinkling up into new crow's feet at the corners. "You sent me an email? It was your name on the invitation..."

"Right, of course." My heart is thudding, and my mouth is dry. "Sorry."

"Is something wrong?"

"No, nothing's wrong..." My eyes dart around, finding uninvited classmates.

"Good," Davis says with relief. "Because I was really excited when I got your message. I've been wanting to look you up for a while now—"

"Uh huh..."

I'm barely listening, trying to figure out what the fuck is going on. There's no way Martinique invited these people, and I know it wasn't me. Which leaves only one possibility...

"What the hell?" The venom in Davis' tone makes my head snap up. He's gazing across the room at Sullivan, who happens to be glaring right back at us. "What's *he* doing here?"

I swallow hard, trying to clear space in my throat. "Sullivan's my boyfriend."

Davis whips around, lip curling up. "You can't be serious. You're dating *Sullivan Rivas?*"

"Is that so hard to believe?" Anxiety makes my voice wire tight, strung through with something else—something deeper and more constricting.

Davis is talking to me like the old Theo. Looking at me the same way. And that makes me *feel* like the old Theo, the nerd, the freak, the charity case...the one Sullivan would never date.

"It's a little surprising," Davis says.

"And why is that?"

"Because he's an animal, Theo! You saw what he did to me."

I did see. Sullivan grabbed Davis by his shirt collar, wrenched him up out of his seat, dragged him out behind the gym, and beat the ever-loving shit out of him. Without a word. Without even a warning.

At the time, I thought it was evidence that Sullivan was just as mean as he looked. It certainly tallied with his rudeness and his perpetual foul mood.

But it doesn't synch up at all with what I know about him now.

"What were you fighting about, anyway?"

Davis' expression is shocked and hurt. "Nothing, I told you! He attacked me out of nowhere. I thought we were friends!"

That doesn't make sense to me—even if the look Sullivan's giving Davis from across the room seems like we might be on the verge of a second-round beatdown. Sully was an asshole in high school. But I only saw him punch first once.

"He didn't say anything? Even after?"

"No!" Davis insists. "We never talked again. My parents wanted to prosecute, but I—" He pauses, corrects himself. "I told them not to."

"Why not?"

"Because we *were* friends before. And I figured he had it bad enough after what happened to...well, you know." Davis shrugs uncomfortably.

Sullivan's mom had just been murdered. Maybe that's why he snapped. But something still feels off.

The heat in the room keeps climbing. Sweat slides down my spine. I see Carl Blythe, Marcus Ferguson, a girl from my PE class...familiar faces distorted by age and weight and new hairstyles. The decade gone by is a carnival mirror, twisting and warping my classmates.

Why are they here? What's happening?

Sullivan is trapped on the other side of the room with Angus, not listening as my boss yaks in his ear, his dark gaze returning again and again to me and Davis.

He looks angry.

It feels like the room is shrinking...I know this is a trap, but I have no idea when the teeth will snap shut.

"How long have you two been dating, anyway?" Davis sidles closer. "Because if it's not serious—"

"Excuse me." I just spotted Martinique. Cutting through the crowd, I grab her by the arm.

"Hey!" she chirps. "Have you—"

"There's a shit ton of people here from my old high school."

"What do you mean?"

"Her, her, him..." I point with my eyes while Martinique, ever subtle, turns her whole body and squints like she's trying to read an eye test.

"I didn't invite any of those people."

"*I know,*" I hiss. "It was—"

"Enjoying the party?" Jessica purrs, cutting through the crowd like a green-sequined Moses.

I sometimes think Jessica is the source of all those Hollywood baby-eating rumors—the more evil she looks, the more beautiful she becomes. She's really outdone herself today with the glitter makeup and the waist-length hair extensions. In her platform shoes and kimono robe, she resembles a space empress, like she should be carried around on a palanquin by several brawny, shirtless men.

It's intimidating. Even Martinique looks terrified. "I asked Consuela if she had any more—"

Jessica cuts her off like she doesn't exist, her pale eyes locked on me alone. "I thought you'd be impressed by how many of your old friends I managed to track down."

"I'm all the way to stunned."

If Jessica put the same level of effort into her music as she does into being spiteful, the single playing on repeat all over the house might be tolerable instead of torturous.

She smiles like a cat, mouth curving up, green eyes wide and unblinking. "I've been talking to them all night long...digging up dirt on Theo Mahoney. But it's tragic, really...half of them don't even remember you."

She gives me a pitying look, but there's no pity in it, not really—just amusement and disdain.

"I can't say I'm surprised to confirm that you were a nerdy, awkward loser. I mean, not much has changed, except that somebody's learned to dress you better."

Her eyes flick down to the ocean-colored dress that was one hundred percent selected and paid for by Sully. My face burns.

That's too much for Martinique. "You know what, Jessica—"

Jessica wheels on her with eerie speed. "You better think carefully about the next words out of your mouth. Angus is already *this close* to firing you the next time you show up late." She snaps her fingers in Martinique's face. "So, unless you want to wear out those knock-off shoes applying for jobs, you better get your ass back to the kitchen."

Martinique goes still, either with fear or with rage. Knowing her, it's the latter. Her small fists are clenched at her sides, and I bet she'd like nothing more than to tell Jessica exactly what she thinks of her.

But I also know that my darling, generous, exuberant friend is fucking terrible at budgeting and tends to have five bucks left in her account at the end of the month. If she gets fired, she'll lose her apartment. So I catch her eye and give a tiny shake of my head.

"You got it," Martinique grits through her teeth, stomping off for the kitchens.

Jessica watches her go, soaking up Martinique's frustration and humiliation like the world's most fucked-up sponge. Only then does she turn her venom back on me.

She taps a long, sparkly green fingernail against her shel-lacked lips.

"Where were we? Oh yes...your depressingly dire high school career. It was no surprise that you were a complete nobody and even less surprising that you've always been pathetically broke. What was funny was how nobody seemed to remember you with Sullivan?"

Every part of me feels scoured by sandpaper, skin stripped off, exposed.

"I never said we dated back then."

"You weren't even friends."

"We knew each other."

"I don't think so." Her voice is low and soft, but it drags across me like claws. "I don't think you knew him at all. I think he looked you up a couple months ago when he realized who you were working for. I think he's using you to get close to Angus. And I think this whole thing where he pretends to be *in love with you* is a big fucking act, which nobody believes because look at him and look at *you*..."

My eyes find Sullivan across the room, still trapped by the drunkenly rambling Angus. He's watching me and Jessica, and he doesn't look angry anymore...only sad.

With his face still, his eyes dark and deep, I don't know if he's ever looked more beautiful. Jessica's words hiss in my ears...

"You're a loser, Theo. You were a loser in high school, and you're a weak, pathetic loser now. Because people don't change, not really. Especially not people like you. He didn't want you then, and he doesn't want you now. He's using you—and you're too stupid to see it."

It's like she's speaking the darkest thoughts from the ugliest, muddiest well in my brain. Everything I fear...everything I believe when I doubt myself. That I haven't gotten stronger or smarter or braver...that I've only deluded myself.

With each exhale, I sink lower.

Whatever hope and happiness were inside of me die in my chest and leach out in a kind of invisible black mist that Jessica sucks in with every breath.

She's never looked lovelier. And I've never hated her more.

"Just wait..." Her plastic lips curve in a hard, cruel smile. "Watch how quickly he dumps you when the deal is done."

She walks away without a backward glance, leaving me as flimsy and empty as a crumpled paper bag.

The pounding single drills through my brain, Jessica's robotic voice warbling,

The brightest stage where dreams are told,
Stars and planets, space unfolds,
Through a night gone dark and cold
Shines a sparkling gilded soul...

My soul is thick and black as pitch. I see, hear, feel nothing as I wander through the crowd until Sullivan's hands grip my arms.

He looks into my face, his eyes dark and unsmiling.

"Did you tell Martinique?"

My stomach does another sickening roll.

"Yes," I whisper. "But I—"

"You promised me you wouldn't."

The look on Sully's face is devastating because it's deva*stated.* I broke his trust. I hurt him.

I'm stuttering and stammering, trying to explain that I didn't actually tell Martinique until this morning, that Jessica guessed the truth all on her own...

But then I realize it doesn't matter. Jessica got her information out of Martinique either way, and I still broke my promise.

I stop and hang my head. "I'm sorry."

Sully's face is pale, his jaw iron tight. "What were you talking to Davis about?"

I don't want to tell him but I don't dare lie again. "We were talking about prom night. Why you...fought him."

Sully's dark eyes flash. "What did he say?"

"He said you attacked him for no reason."

"And you believe him?"

"No! I—" But Sully's already turning away, furious.

I grab him by the arm, pulling him back. He wheels on me, face storming with fury.

"You still think that's who I am! A psychopath who'd beat the shit out of a friend. You don't trust me when *you're* the one who broke your promise. I haven't lied to you since we started this. I kept my word, I haven't let you down. But you still don't believe in me."

Tears streak down my cheeks, hot, flooding. "That's not true! I—"

We're interrupted by Angus, who flings a heavy arm around Sullivan's shoulders, as much for support as for camaraderie. He's falling-down drunk.

He blows boozy breath into Sully's face. "I hope this place you're showing me tomorrow's better than the last one—"

Then he blinks his bloodshot eyes, noticing the state of his blubbering assistant.

"What's wrong with Theo? Lovers' quarrel?"

"Too much salsa on her taco," Sullivan says coldly. "We've never had a lovers' quarrel."

"Consuela's a sadist," Angus agrees, mopping my cheeks with a sticky drink napkin.

By the time he stops, Sullivan has slipped away through the crowd.

35

SULLY

I wait up all night for Theo, but she doesn't come home. I'm praying she stayed with Martinique.

I tried to call her ten times and texted her, alternating between fear, fury, and cold, sinking misery.

By morning, I'm sure I lost her.

It's all my fault. I lost my temper. I saw the look on her face, the way she was reeling from whatever poison dagger Jessica deposited, but instead of asking her what was going on, I erupted, boiling over with the hot, molten rage that bubbled up in my guts when I laid eyes on Davis-fucking-Verger.

It was a shock, all our old classmates, all those same staring eyes, the ones that followed me everywhere I went in a wind of whispers, *There he is, I heard his mom was cheating, I heard his dad went crazy, I heard he shot her himself...*

And then that smug fucking bastard whispering in Theo's ear, telling her all the old lies, all the old rumors...

I should have punched him just for taking her to prom. That little worm never deserved her.

And now, neither do I.

What the fuck do I care if she told Martinique? That was always going to happen; they're best friends. It wasn't fair from the beginning, and she told me that—I had Reese and my dad, while she had nobody else to talk to.

I should punch *myself* in the face for how I spoke to Theo, after everything she's done for me. Right now, at this very moment, my dad's sitting at the kitchen table drinking a latte with me. He hasn't come inside the house in years—not before Theo came.

The sun shines on his clear blue eyes, on his bright and open face. Bernie Sanders rolls around our feet, nipping at our ankles. Dad's telling me how Reese got him a bodyguard gig next week.

"It's just a couple of days, but it pays a hell of a lot better than roofing—"

"That's incredible, Dad. Good for you."

He puts his hand over mine on the table. Our hands are almost exactly the same size, but his is battered and weather-beaten, with tattoos on the knuckles. Mine is the same smooth olive tone as Reese's and our mom's.

"You're not gonna need to cover the bills anymore, Sully. I'm sorry you ever did."

"What are you talking about, I live here, too—"

"And you're welcome to live here as long as you like. But I'm not gonna drag you down anymore."

I turn my hand over to grip his. "You never dragged me down, Dad. Everything good in me comes from you."

He squeezes my hand tightly, eyes bright and blinking. "And everything great comes from your mom." He lets go of my hand to ruffle my hair instead. "Where's Theo?"

The smile slips off my face. "She went home."

I can't stand the pity in my dad's eyes, so I stare at the table instead. It doesn't help much—those baby blue lasers will burn right down to your soul.

"How'd you fuck that up?" he says.

I sigh, slumping down in my chair. "The usual way. Bad ideas, worse priorities, shit behavior."

"Ah." He nods, taking in all of me, the whole, familiar, frightful mess. My dad knows me inside and out, for better and for worse. Mostly worse. "How are you going to fix it?"

"I don't know if I can."

His snort startles me. My head jerks up, and I see my dad shaking his head at me.

"Sully, there's not a damn thing you can't do if you put your mind to it. You're trying to tell me you can't win back this girl who's head over heels for you?"

"I don't think she is, Dad. I fucked up. I've been fucking up this whole time—"

"And she liked you this whole time."

"You know we were just—"

"Oh, shut up about your stupid plan!" my dad roars, startling Bernie so he yelps and dives under my chair. "The only thing stupider than pretending to be in love is pretending *not* to be. You don't play with love, you don't treat it like a game—because it's the most important thing on this whole fucking planet. It's what we live for, what we work for, what lights up everything else...It's the realest power there is, and if you tasted it with Theo, you should *never* it go."

That might be the most words I've heard my dad say in a row.

I stare at him, chest full to bursting.

"Thanks, Dad. That's good advice."

He sinks back in his chair, flushed and breathing deeply. "I don't give advice. That's just the truth."

I lean over to hug him and kiss the top of his head. "See you tonight."

As I hurry out to the car to meet Angus, I text Theo one last time:

I'm sorry. Please call me.

My heart leaps when I see the three dots that mean she's finally answering.

But when the message comes, I sink back down again, heavy as lead.

It doesn't matter, Sully. I don't want to pretend anymore. Finish this thing with Angus and let's be done with it.

36

SULLY

Angus and I spent the last two hours walking my property. It's fucking beautiful, eighty acres of lush, unspoiled land with access to utilities and even a distant, glittering view of the ocean.

It truly would be the perfect location for Angus' campus. But deals aren't made off their merits. Contracts are signed by the emotions of whoever wields the pen.

That's why my original plan was to pretend I was going to keep this land for myself. I was going to dangle the lure for Angus—show him the land as if I were building my own house here. And the wickedest hook of all, I'd tell Angus that it was all going to be for Theo, that I was about to propose to her...I bought a ring and everything.

The point of making Angus jealous was to capture his attention, inflame his interest, and create a burning desire to take what I have.

It worked better than I ever could have hoped—he's certainly jealous, and I see the lust in his eyes as he surveys all these green, rolling acres.

I found Angus' weak spot. It's not Theo, not exactly—it's what she represents: actual, real love from another person.

It's the one thing Angus doesn't have. The thing he's never had.

He's been sued by his own parents. Divorced three times. And he's built this whole, shining empire for himself, surrounded by people who see him as nothing but a checkbook.

I saw his face at dinner. I saw how he looked at Theo and the way she was looking at *me*.

He wants what I have—badly. And that makes him easy to manipulate.

But I can't seem to bring myself to pull out the ring in my pocket. I can't make myself tell any more lies—not about Theo.

My heart feels swollen and bruised in my chest. Theo won't even talk to me. The idea of telling Angus we're about to be engaged, using her as bait once more, makes me sick to my stomach.

So I don't tell him any of that. In fact, I barely speak at all as he surveys this beautiful plot that once seemed so promising but has almost become the death of me.

I understood all too well when Theo told me she only lied to Angus about her diploma out of desperation.

When my ex-partner stabbed me in the back, I was weeks away from bankruptcy. I've only held onto this property by the skin of my teeth, working nights and weekends for months to pay the back-breaking interest payments.

If I sell it to Angus, all my problems will be solved.

Except the one I care about most.

My phone lies heavy and silent in my pocket. There have been no more texts from Theo, and no calls.

Her absence is a void all around me, dampening the sights and smells. The blue sky looks dull, and the birdsong is shrill. I just want this to be over.

"You're quiet," Angus observes. "I know what that means."

"That makes one of us."

Angus laughs. "You can't fool me, Sullivan, no matter how cool you play it—this is the one you want me to take."

I sigh, and it feels like I sink down into the dirt another inch. "You got me."

He turns in a circle, arms outstretched. "And I have to admit, it's got most of what I need..."

Today Angus is wearing an outfit that makes him look a big game hunter, only his cargo shorts are lime green and his hiking boots are bright orange. Neither one is helping my nausea.

"It has everything you need." I didn't mean the words to come out so clipped, but that's the best I've got today. I'm brittle, hollow, rigid.

Angus stops spinning and gives me sharp look. "True. It's almost uncanny...like you had it waiting for me all along."

The mood has shifted. It's as subtle as the breeze blowing across the treetops, but we both feel it.

Angus faces me squarely, all his joviality and idiocy fallen away. Now I'm looking at the man who beat, clawed, and barreled his way to billionaire status.

Quietly, I say, "Maybe I did."

The twitch of his lips betrays his satisfaction. "That's what I thought."

We face off like gunslingers, the woods seeming to whirl around us. I should be nervous, but my heart is still an aching lump in my chest. It hardly seems to beat at all.

In a deceptively casual tone, Angus says, "Jessica seems to have some idea that you're scamming me."

The dullness I feel helps me not to react. "Jessica has a lot of interesting opinions."

"That's what I thought, too. But she made some good points." Angus' eyes flick across my face, hunting for evidence.

I feel a hundred years old and weary. It's hard to even muster the energy for this conversation.

"Let me guess...she thinks I'm using Theo to get to you."

Angus looks surprised that I'd even say it out loud. "Well...are you?"

The sigh I let out comes from the bottom of my toes. When it's over, I feel empty inside, completely cleaned out. No space for lies, only the truth.

"I'm crazy about Theo. In fact, I fucking love her."

I should feel worse than ever, but somehow saying those words gives me my first bright bolt of hope. My heart wakes in my chest, sudden as a bird fluttering against my ribs.

I love Theo.

I love her.

It's real and it's true.

Even Angus can see it. His eyebrows knit together, and he shifts uneasily. "I don't believe you."

I shrug, defeated and depressed. "It doesn't really matter what you believe."

He's not getting the reaction he expected. Angus brought me here to confront me, expose me. Maybe some other day we could have had an epic battle of wits and deceit. But I don't want to lie anymore.

Angry and confused, he sputters, "I don't believe you! But I'll still give you what you want as long as I get what *I* want, too."

"What's that?"

"I want Theo back." He glares at me, chin lowered. "I want her back in the office, working like she used to. I'll buy your property —I'll sign the deed right now. But I want you to break up with her."

There it is.

The solution, offered to me on a platter like a golden apple.

It would be so easy to say yes. For all I know, Theo and I are already broken up. Hell, we never actually "dated" in the first place. It would be the simplest thing in the world to say, *Sure, no problem, let me call her right now...*

A five second phone call, and I could have everything I dreamed of.

The only problem is...that's not what I dream about anymore.

Now when I fall asleep, I sink into eyes the color of an indigo sky, pearlescent skin pale as moonlight, and a river of jet-black hair. I see a dimple that flickers like starlight, and I hear a voice softer and sweeter than any music...

I dream of Theo.

And that dream is more precious to me than anything I own, including every inch of this land surrounding us.

I won't betray that dream, not for Angus, not for anything.

I won't betray *her*.

"I'm not going to break up with Theo. I'm not even going to pretend to do it."

Angus blinks, his head tilted like a robot that can't compute. "Excuse me?"

"You heard me."

He really can't believe it. The kind of money we're talking about is the kind of money Angus could use to buy anything...

Except this.

"I love her," I say. "And I'm not going to break up with her, not now, not ever. If she wants to keep working for you, that's her choice. But I'm going to tell her she should quit because you never appreciated her one minute that you had her. I'm not going to make the same mistake."

Angus stares at me blankly. He still doesn't get it.

I turn my back on him and leave him there, on the land that would have been perfect for Angus' dream, if he could only see it.

37

THEO

I spend all night crying on Martinique's shoulder. In the morning, I know what I have to do.

First, I write out my resignation letter to Angus. I'll give Sully one more day to close his deal, but after that, I'm quitting. I don't care if I'm broke and homeless, I'm not working for Angus anymore.

Then, I go for a very long walk. I walk all the way down to the Santa Monica Pier, right to the end, and sit with my toes dangling over the ocean, watching the waves break against the pilings.

I sit there until the sun toasts my shoulders and my feet are freezing. All the while, I'm composing what to say to Sullivan.

When I pull out my phone to text him, it vibrates in my hand, startling me so badly I almost drop it in the ocean. My fingers shake as I answer.

"Sully?"

"Where are you?" he says.

I tell him. He says, "I'm on my way," and hangs up the phone.

I stand and slowly walk back down the pier, heart racing. This is my chance, probably my only chance, to tell Sullivan the truth.

I see him, a dark figure stepping out of a sun-dazzled car, and I start running. He turns. The look that lights up his face is all I need to throw myself into his arms.

He hugs me until I'm breathless, finally setting me down.

I burst out with everything I've been planning to say to him tumbling out of my mouth at a hundred miles a minute.

"Sully, I'm so fucking sorry, can you ever forgive me? I promised you not to tell Martinique, and I swear I tried so hard not to, but Sunday morning I finally did, and I know what a mistake it was. I broke your trust, but I swear to you, I'll never do that again. I'm so, so sorry! You kept all your promises to me; you didn't deserve that. And I didn't believe Davis for one second! I know you didn't hit him for no reason; you always have a reason, and whatever it was, I bet he deserved it. And if he didn't, it doesn't matter 'cause you were a kid and you just lost your mom, and fuck him anyway for bringing it up again!"

I search his face, expecting to see pain and anger, but he just laughs.

"There was a reason," he says. "But probably not a good one —Davis sold pics of my dad passed out in a pile of bottles to the tabloids. The prosecutor used it against him in the trial."

I think of the betrayal, a picture stolen in Sully's own home, in his family's most vulnerable, most devastated moment. And I kind of want to punch Davis myself.

"*Fuck* him," I say fervently.

"I'd rather not," Sully says. "And anyway, it was punishment enough that I stopped him getting in your pants on prom night. Looking back on it, I might have had ulterior motives..."

I don't know if that's true, but it gives an extra thrill to the memory of Sullivan dragging away my prom date.

"Is that everything?" he says, smiling.

"No," I pant. "There's one more thing—I love you, Sully. I know I'm not supposed to, you're not even my boyfriend, but I did it anyway; I fell in love with you. And I wondered if maybe...we could try going on a date for real?"

Sully lets out a laugh like a sob and swoops me off my feet. He kisses all over my face, hands cupped around my jaw so he can kiss my forehead, my cheeks, my lips...

"I love you, Theo. I love you," he says with each kiss. "You're going to take me on a thousand dates, and I'm going to take you on a thousand more. But none of them will be our first date because every one of our dates was real. The way I felt about you was real from the moment I asked you to dance."

My face is wet with kisses and tears. The happiness I feel is as blinding as a bomb. It levels everything I knew before.

"You love me?" I squeak.

Sully laughs and hugs me like he'll never let me go. "More than I could ever tell you."

I can't believe it. I'm so light I could float away if I weren't anchored in his arms.

"That's great," I say. "Because I'd really like to keep staying at your house...I think I need to quit my job."

Sully's face darkens. "That's probably a good idea."

Nerves swirl back in, and I cling to his chest. "What happened with Angus?"

"He's not taking the property."

The words hit like a hammer. I take a step back, hand rising to my mouth.

"I'm sorry, Sully—"

"It doesn't matter," he assures me. "I sold it anyway."

"What?"

"Not for very much—I had to take what I could get. But I made two hundred K in profit."

"That's incredible!" I let out my breath. "Is that enough to pay off your dad's house?"

"Actually," Sully says, "I bought something else."

His expression is secretive, but I can tell he's pleased. I slip back into his arms, tilting up my lips for a kiss. "Tell me everything..."

He grins down at me. "Better yet...how about I show you?"

HE DRIVES me to a little hole-in-the-wall in West Hollywood. I think we're there for lunch, but the dark windows and cracked front door make me concerned that they might not be open at all.

"Have you eaten here before?" I say a little nervously. I'm not against diners and dive bars, but this place looks like it's never had even a passing acquaintance with food safety standards.

"Not yet," Sully says.

He pulls out a key and unlocks the front door.

That's when I finally get it.

"Oh my god. Did you—"

"Yup," he grins, throwing the doors wide open. "Come see your new restaurant."

We walk into a dark, dingy space cluttered with mismatched tables and chairs. There's an inch of dust on the windows and two inches on the countertops, not to mention several shattered bottles scattered across the floor. A dead plant rots in the pass-through window, and three of the four mousetraps I can see are already full.

"Sully..." I whisper, hands clutched to my chest. "It's perfect!"

He laughs. "It is now that you're standing in it. Hold on—" He runs into the kitchen, returning a moment later with two brand-new, matching frilly pink aprons. "One for me and one for you."

I never thought an apron could make me cry. But I can't pretend it's just the dust—pretending is over.

"Sully," I sob. "I can't believe you did this..."

"Tell me the truth if you don't like it—because I can still back out of the deal. We can find something else if this isn't what you pictured—"

"No, no," I shake my head. "I told you, it's perfect."

Sully holds my hands in both of his. "It *will* be perfect—we'll make it perfect together."

"You're going to help me?"

"God, I hope so. I'm so fucking sick of real estate. Will you take me as your partner, Theo? I want to work at something I believe in—and there's not a thing on this planet I believe in more than you."

I'm already saying yes, tearfully, joyfully, when I realize Sullivan has dropped to one knee on the filthy floor. He's holding up a box in which something glimmers brighter than a star.

"Will you take me as your business partner and your real, actual fiancé? Will you move into my house and stay there forever? Will you let me love you, Theo? Now and forever?"

"Yes, yes, yes," I sob.

He stands and slips the ring on my finger. It shines brightly in the dingy space, like all our future hopes concentrated in one sparkling point balanced on my finger.

Sullivan wraps me in his arms. He holds me tightly with his lips pressed against my ear.

"Love's the only thing that matters, Theo. The only thing that can be counted on. Tragedy comes to all of us, pain and unfairness. You can only avoid it for so long. When it hits, the only thing that helps is not to be alone. The next shitty thing that happens—I want you with me when it comes."

He holds me in our new restaurant that's filthy and full of junk. But those things are only temporary and easily fixed.

What's real is his arms around me and the warmth in my chest.

Already I can see how bright and lovely this place will be

when we've emptied it out and scrubbed it clean and filled it with new tables, new recipes, new friends...

This place will grow and bloom like everything does when you pour love all over it, investing your time and your work.

I see our future, and it's bright and beautiful, just as real as the present.

EPILOGUE

SULLY

September 25, Theo's birthday, is the grand opening of the Vinyl Cafe. Theo and Martinique outdid themselves on the decor, reupholstering the booths in burgundy and papering the walls with old album covers. The de-jacketed LPs dangle from the ceiling, strung with lights in makeshift chandeliers.

During those three months of preparation, Martinique and Reese dated and broke up three separate times. They both give completely different reasons for why they finally split for good, while agreeing it's for the best.

"I've got to focus on my career," Reese says. "It's not the right time for a relationship."

"He's so fucking messy," Martinique complains. "He makes *me* look tidy. Also, he wore a T-shirt to dinner with my mother that had a picture of a naked duck on it that said, *Don't Look At My Butt-Quack.*"

"Aren't all ducks naked?" Theo says, snorting into her hands.

"Don't make excuses for him." Martinique shakes her head.

My brother's relationship isn't the only casualty of that

summer—Angus and Jessica Kate also broke up. Theo learns about it when she sees a picture of Jessica and her new boyfriend on TMZ.

"Angus is going to be mad that she's dating a football player," she observes. "But if she really wanted to annoy him, she'd go out with Jeff Bezos."

"I'm sure he's next on the list." I consider playing "Gilded Soul" on the jukebox for old times' sake, but I don't want to scare away our customers.

The cafe is packed, every booth full and diners lined up along the bar. Martinique posted a photo of Theo's "exploding shakes" that went semi-viral, bringing in all the local foodies.

Each shake is a work of art, the garnishes seeming to burst out of the glass in gravity-defying directions. Theo's currently serving up "Breakfast in Bed" to a delighted customer, skewered pancakes and bacon topping a maple-flavored shake, the rim rolled in Cheerios.

She's wearing the apron I bought her, her hair twisted up in a messy bun on her head. Her cheeks are flushed with happiness, and her pockets are stuffed with tips.

It's not as much as Angus offered her to come back to work, but Theo turned him down flat.

"No raise is as good as working for yourself."

"Are you sure?" I teased her. "Because if you ever miss Angus, I've got some dreams I need documented..."

"For you I'll make an exception," Theo said, tilting up her lips for a kiss. "But otherwise, the only dreams I'm writing down are mine."

Dreams are funny things...sometimes the ones we picture aren't as good as the ones we get.

I wanted to pay off my dad's mortgage, but it's a hell of a lot better watching him pay it off himself. He's back at work full-time and three months sober.

Reese has been attending most of his AA meetings with him though he's no longer mining tragic stories for useful anecdotes. Instead, he signed up for a script-writing course at the local college.

The one who's probably changed the most is Bernie Sanders. He's not even a year old yet, and he's already 160 pounds of hair and drool. My dad's been teaching him tricks and manners, but the only thing he's mastered so far is suckering them both into unexpected naps.

If my dad didn't already love Theo with all his heart, Bernie would have sealed the deal. He's got a soft spot for that galloping furball that's got him hauling home hundred-pound bags of dog food and building Bernie his very own poolside cabana for when he wants to sleep in the shade.

I've had my own projects keeping me busy, including building cabinets for Theo's new kitchen and a double set of bookshelves for our room. Theo didn't have much in the way of clothes or furniture to move in, but she had about a hundred paperbacks moldering away in old milk crates. Now they're on display where she can color coordinate to her heart's content, spending entire Saturdays rearranging her shelves.

I never knew I could love coming home so much. The best part of my day is when I call out for Theo and she comes running into my arms.

We still eat outdoors on the picnic table most nights, but my dad will come inside to eat with us if it's raining.

Well, maybe that's not the best part of my day...

Maybe the best part is when Theo and I roll into bed at night, exhausted from hours of work but in the best sort of way. Because working for yourself really is different—it's building something instead of earning a paycheck.

I fucking love what I'm building with Theo. I've never been prouder of anything than I am of our cafe. We cleaned and decorated every inch of this place. We designed it together, from the marketing materials to the menus.

Martinique and Theo are already talking about expanding next door—there's an old printing shop that Martinique wants to turn into a bakery.

She only lasted a week with Angus after Theo quit. Theo's been subcontracting her to make the morning pastries, but Martinique has grand plans for wedding cakes, which will need a lot more space.

The way things are going, it shouldn't be long before we can afford to expand. The bell over the door jingles, and another pack of excited influencers streams inside, already snapping pictures of the vintage jukebox and the pretty painted chairs.

LATER, when everyone is gone and Theo and I have wiped the last table and tucked in the last chair, I join her in the kitchen.

She looks exhausted, adorable, and extremely happy. She also has a dusting of icing sugar on her nose.

"You've got sugar on you..."

"So do you," she says, flicking some at me.

We haven't finished cleaning the kitchen yet, so I have no problem grabbing a handful of sugar and chucking it at her. Theo shrieks with laughter, pelting me with raspberries. I catch one in my mouth, but the rest go bouncing off my face and shoulders, rolling everywhere.

"You're making a mess," I growl, scooping her up, lifting her onto the counter.

"How about now?" she says, smearing chocolate sauce on my face.

"You little devil..." I give her the messiest of kisses, tasting chocolate and powdered sugar and the honey-sweet lips of my beloved.

The kiss deepens. Theo's legs wrap around my waist. She looks into my eyes, and I know she's remembering that we haven't christened this space yet.

"I'm so fucking proud of you," I say, my lips on her mouth, the edge of her jaw, the side of her neck...

"I can't believe we did it." Theo's hands twine in my hair. "You made my dream come true, Sully."

"*You* made your dream come true. I just helped."

I kiss her again, unbuttoning her top, untying her apron, unwrapping her like a gift.

She *is* a gift, a miracle, a treasure...

I think of the day I first started researching Angus and I saw a picture of Theo standing next to him.

I recognized her immediately, some strange, electric current zipping through my blood. It was the same feeling I used to get when I'd see her at school.

I don't know if I believe in fate. But what I know for certain is that I wouldn't be where I am today, and neither would Theo, if we weren't drawn together.

She's what was missing in my life. And I know exactly what *she* needs to be happy.

Life can be brutal and unfair. But it does bring us these gifts, the people we need and the ones who need us...

I open her shirt, revealing the beautiful breasts I waited so long to see. As usual, I lacked imagination. The reality is so much better...

"What are you smiling about?" Theo says.

"You." I touch her breasts, I kiss them, caress them... "I'm smiling because of you. I'm happy because of you."

Theo's nipples stiffen and her skin flushes. Every part of her blushes in its own way, even her breasts. The scent rising off her skin is still sweet but edged with something naughtier...

My cock rises in response. I pull down her underwear beneath her skirt, sliding it down her legs, tucking it in my pocket. Then I unzip and bury myself inside her.

Theo gasps, head tilting back, thighs tight around my waist. I grab a handful of her hair and pull her head back even farther, licking and sucking on the side of her neck.

She picks up a raspberry, placing it between her lips. I take it from her mouth with mine, crushing it with my tongue, kissing her in the bright burst of tangy sweetness.

She wraps her arms around my neck and pulls her body tight against mine, squeezing inside like a hand gripped around my cock. I groan and kiss her deeper, hands slipping under her ass to lift her up.

We fuck standing up, pants puddled around my ankles. Theo clings to my body, wrapped around me with her calves tucked behind my thighs. I thrust into her in short, sharp bursts of pleasure and sweetness. Her breath is raspberry scented, her skin is soft and creamy everywhere we touch.

Theo starts to come, sliding up and down against me, making friction in her favorite place. As often happens, her climax triggers mine. I don't know if it's the feeling of her squeezing around me, or the high, soft sounds she makes, or the scent that rises from her skin...

All I know is that when Theo comes, I helplessly follow, chasing after her into the oblivion of orgasm like I do everywhere else. Wherever she goes, that's where I want to be. And I never want to be without her.

We clean up the sugar-dusted kitchen together, and when we get home, I run Theo a bath.

"You were working all day, too!" she protests.

"Not as hard as you."

It's true—I've never seen anyone whirl around faster than Theo as she manned the grill, assembled sandwiches, and blended up shakes.

Besides, I need her distracted so I can clean up the rest of the house. Reese made an unholy mess, and I don't want Theo to see it or she'll feel like she has to help.

I follow the trail of shoes, shirts, and empty plates back to his room, where I dump all the shit on his bed. I'll tidy up for Theo, but I'm not going to be Reese's maid. Not when he still owes me fifty bucks.

As I'm tidying up the kitchen, I find the contract I signed with Theo stuffed in a drawer.

It feels like a document from another time. Another person, really.

I look at what I wrote down, what I thought was important, and I have to laugh at myself, at what a fool I was.

All my grand plans were nonsense. What I thought was important didn't matter at all.

There's one thing and one thing only I should have put in that contract:

Let me love you.

Love *is* the dream, it is the goal, it's what we're here for. It's what heals, what motivates, what satisfies...

We'll do for others what we'd never do for ourselves, and that's how it should be. Because we grow our souls when we join them.

A selfish person is a starving thing. It's love that feeds us.

SOPHIE LARK
powerful romance

LOVE CONTRACT TRILOGY

Book One

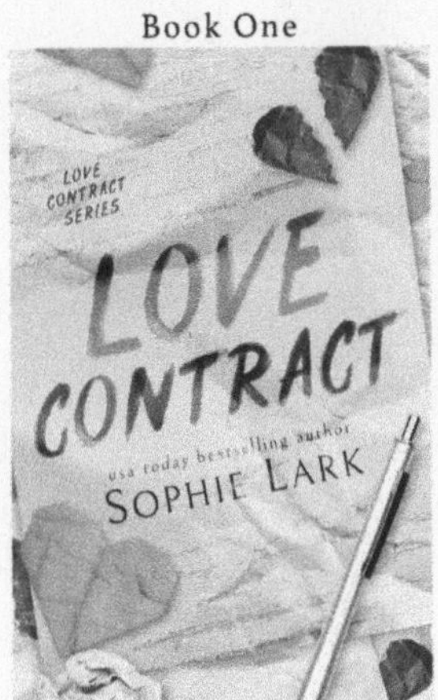

Fake dating via blackmail
Enemies-to-lovers

Book Two

Fake dating
Reverse grumpy/sunshine

Book Three

Hot dad bodyguard
Forced proximity

Sophie Lark
powerful romance

MAFIA/ROMANTIC SUSPENSE

Brutal Birthright
complete 6 book series

Enemies-to-lovers

Beauty & the Beast vibes

→ 2nd gen

Kingmakers
complete 5 book series

Draco Malfoy-inspired antihero

DARK ROMANCE

Complete duet

Standalone

FANTASY ROMANCE

Historical reimagining

CONTEMPORARY

Pet play meow

ACKNOWLEDGMENTS

Thank you always to Rhino first, a partner I'm truly blessed to have in all aspects of our lives 💪

Thank you also to the other full-time members of the Sophie team, Maya, our mistress of media, and Brittany, master of operations, and also to Emily Wittig, who designed this fantastically adorable trio of covers—no matter what I throw at you, you always make it sing!

Thank you to Kerry, who helps us with our little ones, especially our baby Lark who needs extra special care 💕

And finally, thank you to everyone who sent me kind notes and messages over the past two years. I was in a difficult period, and I can never tell you how much every single touch meant to me.

The most beautiful thing in this world is people doing good for each other. I'm so lucky to have felt the love I have from all of you 🙏

Sophie lives in Southern California with her husband and three children. Her favorite authors are Emily Henry and Freida McFadden. She's an Aquarius who loves fitness and looks forward to Halloween every year.

SPECIAL EDITIONS | ART PRINTS | MERCH → SOPHIELARK.COM

Instagram | TikTok

@SOPHIE_LARK_AUTHOR | @SOPHIELARKAUTHOR

MY WEBSITE AMAZON PATREON

Milton Keynes UK
Ingram Content Group UK Ltd.
UKHW041005190224
438093UK00004B/70